DRAGON LORDS: BOOK THREE

# THE DARK PRINCE

## Michelle M. Pillow

Futuristic Romance

New Concepts

Georgia

Be sure to check out our website for the very best in fiction at fantastic prices!

When you visit our webpage, you can:
* Read excerpts of currently available books
* View cover art of upcoming books and current releases
* Find out more about the talented artists who capture the magic of the writer's imagination on the covers
* Order books from our backlist
* Find out the latest NCP and author news--including any upcoming book signings by your favorite NCP author
* Read author bios and reviews of our books
* Get NCP submission guidelines
* And so much more!

We offer a 20% discount on all new Trade Paperback releases ordered from our website!

Be sure to visit our webpage to find the best deals in e-books and paperbacks! To find out about our new releases as soon as they are available, please be sure to sign up for our newsletter (http://www.newconceptspublishing.com/newsletter.htm) or join our reader group (http://groups.yahoo.com/group/new_concepts_pub/join)!

The newsletter is available by double opt in only and our customer information is *never* shared!

Visit our webpage at:
www.newconceptspublishing.com

The Dark Prince is an original publication of NCP. This work has never before appeared in book form. This work is a novel. Any similarity to actual persons or events is purely coincidental.

New Concepts Publishing, Inc.
5202 Humphreys Rd.
Lake Park, GA 31636

ISBN 1-58608-731-2
2004 © Michelle M. Pillow
Cover art (c) copyright 2004 Eliza Black

NCP books are available at special quantity discounts for bulk purchases for sales promotions, premiums, fund raising, or educational use. For details, write, email, or phone New Concepts Publishing, Inc., 5202 Humphreys Rd., Lake Park, GA 31636; Ph. 229-257-0367, Fax 229-219-1097; orders@newconceptspublishing.com.

First NCP Trade Paperback Printing: February 2006

Other titles from NCP by Michelle M. Pillow:

Tribes of the Vampire 1: Redeemer of Shadows (In Trade
Paperback)
Tribes of the Vampire 2: The Jaded Hunter (In Trade
Paperback)
Tribes of the Vampire 3: Eternally Bound
Portrait of His Obsession
M&M Presents: All Hallows' Eve
M&M Presents: Christmas
Dragon Lords 4: The Warrior Prince
Naughty Cupid 1: Cupid's Enchantment
Naughty Cupid 2: Cupid's Revenge
Dragon Lords 1: The Barbarian Prince (In Trade
Paperback)
Dragon Lords 2: The Perfect Prince (In Trade Paperback)
Dragon Lords 3: The Dark Prince (In Trade Paperback)
Dragon Lords 4: The Warrior Prince
Lords of the Var 1: The Savage King
Lords of the Var 2: The Playful Prince
Lords of the Var 3: The Bound Prince
Lords of the Var 4: The Rogue Prince
Galaxy Playmates 1: Sapphire
Galaxy Playmates 2: Quartz
Galaxy Playmates 3: Diamond
Silk (In Trade Paperback--Ultimate Warriors Anthology)
The Mists of Midnight
Animal Instinct (In Trade Paperback--Ghost Cats
Anthology)
Mountain's Captive (In Trade Paperback--Caught
Anthology)
Théâtre de Passion 1: Phantom of the Night
Emerald Knight
Ghost Cats II

Dedication:

To Tracy Sutherland
For something you once said

## Chapter One

Olena Leyton's calculating eyes shot hot sparks of angry fire, as she met her reflection in a broken piece of glass on the ground. She swallowed, scowling in annoyance at the seeping wound in her arm. Moving to press her fingers to the ripped black spandex of her top, she cursed, feeling a chunk of metal embedded deep within her skin. She gritted her teeth, digging her fingers into the wound to pry out a jagged strip. Dispassionately, she eyed the metal before dropping it to the ground.

Her arm continued to ooze, but she ignored it. Now was no time for weakness. She was in the crate storage of some metal space dock. The large open door let in a cooling breeze from outside, making her shiver as it hit the layer of sweat on her skin. Leaning forward, she squinted, trying to read the address label on one of the crates. *X Quadrant, Earthbase 5792461.*

*X Quadrant!* She let loose a long breath. Her ship really had gone off course. Glancing out over the lush alien countryside that she had just run three miles through, she took a calming breath. Her heart hammered in her chest, more from the sprint than the pain in her arm. Her escape had been too close of a call.

Damned bounty hunters, trying to get back what she rightfully stole! They shot up her ship, scattered her crew, and now she was stranded in the X Quadrant. Things couldn't get much worse.

With a frown, Olena watched as an orange ball of fire lit up the distance. Clearly, she was wrong. They could get worse.

She cursed and closed her eyes as she saluted the fiery last breath of her ship. With that kind of beacon, the bounty hunters would be all over this planet like flies on manure, not to mention the local law enforcement. Wouldn't they love to get their hands on this little pirate?

"Not going to happen," Olena grumbled, darkly. She looked around, knowing she'd been in tougher spots than this. Granted, she usually had her crew with her.

Seeing a row of small luxury crafts and personal transport ships lined up for pre-flight maintenance, she grinned. Oh, this was almost too easy. Standing, she was instantly sorry. Her head became light and she swayed on her feet. Blinking to keep from blacking out, she glanced at her arm. Her blood had spilled onto the floor, staining the black spandex of her pants and dripping onto her leather boot. She needed a medic and fast. But, worst of all, she was in no condition to fly. She could very well pass out during the gravity shift of take off.

Creeping stealthily forward, she looked into the windows of the personal transports for a first aide kit to tide her over. The rich people who owned these crafts were always good for a supply of painkillers. Right now she needed both.

Seeing a kit, Olena glanced around. The place was empty. With a swift kick, she smashed in the window and unlocked the transport. Within moments, she had her arm bandaged and a couple pills stuck and dissolving in her dry throat. She gagged, trying to work them down.

"Who's there?"

Olena froze in her search for a bottle of liquor, cursing silently. Blasted dock security guards! Why didn't they find themselves a real job?

Olena edged to peek over the side of the transport. The security guard came into view. She cursed again. Her arm was in no shape for self defense. Looking down at her waist, she saw that her gun was registering empty. She had used all her ammunition to fire her way out of the ship's metal side. The hatch had been jammed by the ground.

Hearing a rush of feet coming from the other direction, she stiffened. A woman hurried near them, covered with a rich fur cloak from head to foot and laden down with numerous suitcases. As Olena watched, she shifted her bags and pulled the cloak tightly around her, jerking it over her head, as if frightened of the dark and lonely docks at night. Olena smiled. She might not be able to drive, but this rich woman would definitely have her own vehicle.

Olena heard the guard move. He stopped to smile at the rich lady. The woman jolted in mild surprise to see him, but managed a weak nod of acknowledgement back. The guard appeared to know her, because he waved at her and pointed down the docks. Olena looked in the transport. Seeing a coat, she slid it over her shoulders and buttoned the front to hide her pirating attire. Then, grabbing a hat, she sat it atop her flaming red hair, tucking ponytailed locks up beneath it.

Some floral bags were sitting in the back seat and she took all four of them. She loaded them on her shoulders, trying not to flinch at the pain, as she walked after the cloaked lady. Smiling innocently at the security guard, she was glad to see that he had forgotten his investigation and was going back to the monitor room. He waved at her, pointing the same direction down the docks he had for the other woman. Olena smiled brightly like she knew what he was signaling about.

She took the plank reserved for first class, again seeing the rich woman. She was next to a uniformed man with a clipboard. Her hood was down, her brown hair looking very respectable pulled back into a bun. Olena squinted, seeing the glittering of diamond earrings on the woman's ears. Instantly, her mind calculated the worth of them. Oh, she'd love to get her hands on those! It might make this little detour worth it.

Olena pasted a cunning smile on her face as she saw a bunch of women loading into the spacecraft, beneath a banner that read, *Galaxy Brides,* in curving script. Carting her new bags, she came forward.

"Perfect, Miss … ah … Aleksander," the uniformed man was saying to the rich woman. "Welcome aboard the flight to your future!"

Olena didn't pay the woman's answer any attention as she set her bags down. She turned to dig through her gun belt.

"No, Miss. Galaxy Brides Corporation owes you." The man answered whatever Miss Aleksander had said.

Pulling out the first ID she came across, Olena quickly pushed the coat to cover her weapon. She pushed her luggage closer, kicking it lightly across the floor with her foot. Glancing over her shoulder, she thought she heard air sirens outside the dock. They would be going to investigate the explosion. She could only hope the blast had made her ship unrecognizable.

"I wish to evoke the right of privacy law. If anyone asks, I'm not here," the rich lady said.

"Police?" the man questioned in surprise, though the idea

did not seem to concern him. He obviously had a quota to fill and Olena knew that these corporations were notorious for looking the other way.

Olena didn't hear the woman's answer, but saw the man nod in understanding. She tried to edge closer, taking another peek at the earrings.

"I'll make a note, Miss. That won't be a problem." The man began writing on Miss Aleksander's file.

"And, by the way, where are we going?" the woman asked, her voice again mild and unwavering.

Olena stepped closer. She knew what Galaxy Brides was. They were a corporation who peddled marriage to barbarian planets in need of women. Once she had been asked to shanghai a load of brides by a lower breed of humanoids. It was one of the few jobs she had turned down. Not even she could take profit from delivering hapless women to men who squirted slime from their … well …

The man chuckled. "Most women ask before they come down here. It must be some maniac you are trying to get away from."

The woman gulped but said nothing.

The man reigned in his humor, and answered, "You're heading to Qurilixen, Miss."

The woman nodded before she walked away, following a droid who carried her bags. Instantly, Olena turned her sweetest smile on the uniformed worker. He nearly flushed in response.

"Hi," she murmured in a sultry vixen's tone that she knew drove men to instant distraction. Pouting out her lips, she said, "Oh, these bags are so heavy. I never thought I would get them all the way up the dock by myself."

"Are you here for a last minute replacement?" the man inquired, his breath beginning to pant at the look she gave him. Coming forward, he took her bags for her and moved them forward.

"Oh, thank you," she gushed. Olena blinked, innocently. "I'm so glad I made it on time. Rick at the office told me it would be all right if I tagged along. This is the flight to Qurilixen, isn't it?"

"Yes, Miss. I know Rick," the worker lied. "Fine man."

"Why yes, he is," Olena giggled with a toss of her hand

and a playful bat of her eyes.

"Sign here," he said, handing over the clipboard. "We are several girls short so they'll be more than happy to have you. Your health screenings will be done in flight. You'll have room 209 on platform two. It's the room all the way to the back, left side. Ship orientation is tomorrow at 9:00 AM."

"That is perfect," she whispered, as she set her ID on top of the clipboard. To her surprise, it was her real name. It was too late to grab an alias, so she signed her name with flourish. The man looked at the ID and handed it back.

"Oh," Olena said. She looked down at the man's name tag. "Rick said it would be all right if I evoked the right of privacy law. He said just to tell Bernie and you would personally see to it my privacy isn't violated."

"Stalker?" the man asked.

"Oh, is it that obvious?" Olena pouted, trying her best not to laugh at the all protective man look the guy gave her. She dabbed fake tears from her wide eyes and sniffed.

"No, Miss," Bernie answered in a self-important tone. He motioned to a droid to pick up her bags for her. "There just seems to be a lot of that going around lately."

* * * *

*One month later...*

Olena sighed, resting back in her seat in obvious comfort. A droid massaged her feet in the pedicure basin and another rubbed her neck with two hands as the other four of its hands did her hair. Looking around the beauty parlor, she had memorized almost every one of the bride's names. It was an old habit, one that had saved her hide more than once.

Besides, what else was she going to do during the last month of space travel? Plan her future with a barbarian husband? Knit him and their future children a sweater?

No thanks. Not likely. Never going to happen.

The brides were being prepared for the Breeding Festival that night on Qurilixen. It was the one night of darkness on the otherwise light planet and considered the only night the men could choose a bride. Olena had every intention of finding a poor sucker to marry her. What easier way to lay low for a few months as she plotted her escape? Besides, free room and board? Who could resist.

Smirking, Olena inwardly laughed at the other women aboard the Galaxy Bride ship. They were all such dopes, with their high hopes of royal marriage. Yeah, like anyone ever found true love at the end of a glowing crystal. Olena knew what these foolish women would find, and it had nothing to do with love. When it came to men, they didn't know the meaning of the word.

Olena chuckled, a grin forming on her lips. Why else would the Qurilixian men call their wedding ceremony a *Breeding Festival*? It was so laughably obvious. It had nothing to do with love and everything to do with a planet full of horny males, with no females of their own, who needed to find release. Hell, it was easy to say 'I love you' to one of the only women on the entire planet. How else were the poor bastards going to get laid?

Olena took her feet out of the water at the droid's gentle push. Setting her feet on the edge of the basin, she watched the droid staining her toenails with permanent polish. She couldn't help thinking of what the Qurilixian males must be like--a whole planet of Medieval Earth warrior types. Qurilixian women were rare, being as the planet suffered from blue radiation. Over the generations, it had altered the men's genetics to produce almost nothing but strong male heirs.

*Maybe, I'll find a Prince and make them all worship at my feet,* Olena mused with a whimsical smile.

The fact that they had no women of their own was why the services of corporations like Galaxy Brides were so invaluable to them. They could use portals to steal brides, but nowadays the intergalactic commission frowned on such practices. In return, the Qurilixian would mine ore that was only found in their caves. The ore was a great power source for long-voyaging starships, all but useless to the Qurilixian as they were not known as explorers.

Backwards as they sounded, she hoped they at least had a space port so she could hitch a ride off the planet. If her situation wasn't so dire, it would have been hilarious.

The planet of Qurilixen was on the outer edge of the Y Quadrant. Olena was familiar with the territory. She had once escaped a renegade hunter a few years back by flying into an asteroid belt that ran through its outer edge. She had seen the red-brown planet briefly and she almost stopped there for repairs. Even though they didn't land, a pirate always remembered a planet. You never knew when it would come in handy.

She closed her eyes briefly as the droid at her feet finished.

The Qurilixen men worshipped many Gods, favored natural comforts to modern technical conveniences, and actually preferred to cook their own food without the aide of a simulator. With the right crew, she was sure she could have scammed the superstitious kingdom for all their valuables in a month's time.

The trip hadn't been so bad. She'd traveled in far worse accommodations. The spacecraft was a nice one, but the only company she had been allowed in the last month of travel had been the other women. They were quarantined, to ensure nothing unseemly happened, which caused some of the women to jokingly refer to their quarters as the harem.

The pampered brides were valuable cargo. But, after a month of traveling with the giggling twits, Olena was sure not taking that shanghai gig had been one of her best calls. She would have dumped the brides out of her smaller rust bucket of a ship in a lunar second.

Personal droids were assigned to each passenger and she had used hers to no end, spending hours making a mess just to watch the thing pick up. It never complained. As soon as she heisted a new ship, Olena was going to make sure she got a dozen of those little numbers with it.

There were cooking units in each of their quarters that could materialize almost any culinary delight. Olena, having known firsthand the pangs of starvation, gladly feasted more than her share. Plus, the ship had a medic unit. She'd found it that first night, typed in her room number, and seconds later her arm was fixed without even a scar to show for it.

Yep, her accommodations could have been much, much worse. She could have been tied up in a prison hold at the mercy of some half-wit bounty hunter who'd more than likely try to take an advance on his wages out of her unwilling body. Then, she'd have to kill him, she'd be left helpless, the ship would crash ... disastrous.

Hearing Gena make reference--*again*--to her own

genetically enhanced breasts, Olena forced a false smile and giggled with the rest of them. Oh, yeah. This was getting old. Good thing they were docking in a few hours.

"Those Princes won't be able to resist me. Maybe I'll marry all four of them just for fun," Gena said. The woman tossed her auburn hair and dropped the examination of her new body. She'd been flat when she arrived and now she lugged around two gigantic luxury crafts.

Olena looked down. She had taken advantage of the services, having the hair on her legs and armpits permanently removed. She didn't care much for the body altering, though she did get one annoyingly puckered brand removed from her backside.

"How will you know who the Princes are?" came the cynical reasoning of Pia Korbin. Olena looked to her right. Out of all the women, she liked sarcastic Pia the best. "I've heard that all the men wear disguises. You could end up with a royal guard."

"Or a gardener," a brunette offered with a laugh.

"I hear they wear practically nothing at all," Olena said, just to get a rise out of the women. "Except the mask and some fur."

She wasn't disappointed. They nearly tittered over in excitement.

"You can't miss royalty," the self-important Gena announced, tossing her hair. "You'll see it in the way they move."

Olena rolled her eyes. She caught her reflection in a mirror. Weakly, she waved back the hands of the beauty droid who finished curling her locks. For a moment, she froze, not recognizing the woman in the plush white cotton robe staring back at her. Turning her head to one side and then the other, she frowned as she studied her upswept. The sides pulled up into a center knot only to cascade down her back in curls. She looked like a spoiled rich girl and it made her uncomfortable.

"Come on, Olena," a woman laughed, stopping to lean on her shoulder. "Let's go get ready."

"You go ahead," Olena said, unable to take her eyes away. "I'll be there in a minute."

Swallowing, she shook herself from the trance and stood to follow the others out to the hall leading to their suites.

She took a deep breath, telling herself it didn't matter. What was a little marriage if it would help her recover her freedom? It wasn't as if she had any plans of marrying for love or happiness. Like everything else in her life, this adventure was just a means to an end.

Then, forcing herself to look on the bright side, she looked down at her painted toenails and thought, *Won't the crew get a kick out of this!*

\* \* \* \*

Olena shivered, uncomfortably standing in her traditional Qurilixen gown of silk and gauze. At least it was black, a perfect color for her black mood. She felt like one of the female slaves being readied for the auction block of *Phatar*.

The revealing outfit hung low over her cleavage to give the men ample view of her pale white chest. The non-existent skirt hugged tight to her waist and hips, only to flare out around her legs in thin strips. A belt of sorts went across her back. But, instead of looping in the front, it continued to the sides, holding her wrists low like silken chains before winding half way up the arm to lock over the elbows. It greatly added to the whole slave auction affect the men seemed to be going for.

*What was marriage anyway, if not voluntary slavery?* she thought. She almost felt sorry for the guy who picked her. He would really have no idea what he was getting himself into.

The breeze blew over the line of waiting brides, who stood single file in the corridor leading out of the ship's port. Olena was the first slave on the auction block and was provided with an ample view of what was going on below. Instantly, she took stock of her primitive surroundings.

Below her, men hollered in delight as her dress blew up around her thighs. Olena was too proud to push the skirt down. She let the wind blow it where it would, as her chin lifted into the air and she refused to smile.

Standing before her, shoulder to shoulder in two long lines, were the more silent bachelors. Their bodies formed an aisle of naked flesh. Olena had already been instructed that she was to walk through it so the men could get a look at her. As her skirt blew around her again, revealing her athletic thighs, she mused, *There, let them have a good ole peek.*

The reddish-brown planet was surrounded by a blue-green dusk. Stars were beginning to show overhead, winking down from above as they framed a large spotlight moon. Alien trees grew high with colossal leaves. They towered over the planet's surface with trunks nearly a fourth of the size of the Galaxy Bride's spacecraft. The forest stretched out around them on one side, reaching into the distance where a mountain grew high before them.

Olena could see the soft glow of firelight, crackling from a giant bonfire pit as the flames lapped at the starry night, sending sparks of ash into the cool air. Behind the rowdy men, near the back, the married men sat in throne-like chairs with their wives firmly upon their laps. The married women could be heard laughing as they watched the barbarians too young to participate in this year's festival shout and pose for the prospective brides. The smell of burning wood mingled with the exotic perfume of nature. The couples kissed and petted each other freely and no one but the brides noticed.

Music and laughter resounded over the campgrounds. The grounds were set up with large pyramid tents. Torches lit dim earthen pathways. Ribbons and banners floated on the breeze in many brilliant colors. Olena was unimpressed.

The silent barbarian-grooms were larger than she first anticipated, though Olena was hardly a woman to back down from such a thing. They were every inch the proud warrior class they were rumored to be, some even appeared to tower nearly seven feet tall in height. Their pride would equal arrogance and she knew just how to play to arrogance.

The bachelors were completely naked except for three things--a fur loincloth that wrapped their thick waists to leave bare their muscular legs and chests, jewelry consisting of a bracelet of intricate gold around their sinewy biceps and a crystal necklace about their throats, and a black leather mask that hid their faces from view from upper lip to forehead.

Firelight illuminated their oil-glistened flesh. From solid neck to muscular legs, they were perfection. Their bronzed bodies were like statues, with only their lungs expanding and contracting to show they moved. They were waiting patiently for the brides to walk through so they could choose their mate.

Instantly, Olena saw their lust. It shone bright and feverish from the eye slits of their masks. Their heated gazes were like liquid metal--possessive, dominate, sure.

*Yep,* Olena mused, no longer feeling any guilt for what she was about to do. *Slave auction.*

* * * *

Yusef of Draig stared at the red-headed vixen at the front of the bridal line. He did not need to confirm his instant attraction to her by checking to see if the crystal was beginning to glow about his neck. He knew the moment she stepped out onto the deck that she was going to be his, even if he had to buck tradition and the magic he believed in to claim her.

Glancing down, he saw that such drastic measures wouldn't be necessary. A sultry smile curved up the corner of his mouth. The magic of the Gods agreed with him. The fiery woman was destined to be his wife.

The black of her dress whipped boldly around her athletic body and she did not even try to hold it at bay. He saw the pride in her bright emerald eyes as she stood very still. Her lips curled with what could have been mocking disdain for the whole affair. He smiled. Yes, this one definitely had fire and Yusef always did love to play with torches.

* * * *

Olena sighed. Following the pilot's signal to step down, she led the procession to the long aisle. The soft slippers on her feet were uncomfortable and she longed for her boots. Boredom was starting to set in when … *bam.* She was breathless, captured by a spell.

Eyes of a dark and dangerous gray rose to challenge her, glowing from the face of an ungodly dark creature of a man. This man was so unlike the lighter companions at his side. His possessive gaze sent chills over her skin in a way so unfamiliar to her that she had to shake herself to be sure she was still breathing.

The man smiled a dark, sultry smile she had seen so many times before. She wasn't fooled. This man wanted her. He was staking claim to her with his animal magnetism. Even as she resented his confident smirk, she was stirred by it.

*I'm surprised he doesn't pee on my leg to mark his territory,* she mused.

As she passed him, he had the audacity to bow to her. Olena snarled viciously at him, snapping her teeth in a saucy wench sort of way, which greatly upset the plans of his male vanity. Nevertheless, soon he was recovered and she saw the unmistakable light of daring in his gaze. His mask shifted as his brows rose in acceptance of her challenge. Again he bowed, blowing her a kiss just to watch her face flame.

## Chapter Two

Olena was too angry to eat the great feast laid out before her. The presumption of that man! Thinking she would come to him willingly, just because he wished it. Oh, she knew what he wanted from her. It was clear in his very lecherous gaze.

Wearily, she admitted to herself, *His very handsome, lecherous gaze.*

Shivering as she thought about his dark, come-hither smile, Olena sighed.

A large buffet had been prepared, spread over the long wood table that the brides were directed to. It was a veritable feast of roasted two horned pigs, blocks of Qurilixen blue bread with whipped cheese, strange fruit, and crusted pastries. Olena grabbed a slice from the pig, taking a bite out of spite, just to prove to herself that she wasn't distressed over this latest turn of events.

Glancing over, she saw the married couples feeding each other by the firelight. None of them bothered the brides who ate in isolation. The style was obviously long hair for both sexes. The women wore dresses of flowing material. The men wore simple tunic shirts and breeches, definitely appearing of a Medieval Earth influence.

Servants carried pitchers full of a strange berry wine and Olena eagerly waved one of them over. The man's light blond hair fell over his shoulders as he bowed. The servants were more fully clothed than the bachelors had been. She held up her goblet, barely giving him a second glance.

"He makes for a peculiar servant," a thoughtful Pia pondered at her side.

Olena glanced over, drinking as she did so. The woman's gaze was suspicious as she watched the blond man walking away.

Olena glanced at the blond giant. He looked like a servant to her, not a very good one by the way he spilled some of the wine on the ground as he walked away, but a servant nonetheless.

"They make for a peculiar race," Olena mumbled, secretly searching for the dark stranger. She absently ran her fingers through her hair, touching the firefly hairpin she had put in her locks. Its cold, black stones brought her a little comfort. After having been quarantined with a bunch of gossipy women, she was ready for a good challenge.

She smiled, knowing that the men were forbidden to have sex this night. That just might work to her advantage. She'd have the dark barbarian turned around in circles before he ever knew what hit him.

Pia laughed softly and nodded in agreement. "Do you believe this whole deal?"

"What are you doing here anyway?" Olena asked curiously. "You hardly seem like the type to get trapped into coming."

"Free benefits," came Pia's enigmatic answer. Her eyes shadowed for a moment and Olena wondered at the look. This woman was definitely hiding something. Before she could comment, Pia said, "I think I am going to follow that servant. He's up to something."

Pia stood, when suddenly the grooms were before them, walking up to the platform table. They hadn't changed as they came to claim their brides. Not all brides had been chosen and Olena grinned to see Gena still sitting alone, a look of horror on her stunned face.

"I am Yusef."

Olena glanced up. She had been pretending not to notice the dark warrior coming for her. She purposefully yawned, looking up at him. She felt Pia stand by her side and go around the table.

"Come," Yusef said, his accent as thrillingly dark as his gaze. He lifted his hand to take hers. It was a strong hand, with long tapered fingers. She saw calluses along the palm and shivered. Such a hand would feel so delectable against her skin.

Olena glanced over his bronzed skin as if he was a piece of meat and she the health inspector. His chest was cut and chiseled, an effort of much hard work and training. Seeing his large arms, she knew she would never be able to take this man in a fair fight. He would crush her if she even dared. There was pride in him, an arrogance that came with such handsomeness. But the confidence didn't deter her.

She liked a man who knew his own worth. Being trapped with him for a few months might not be so bad. It might even be downright enjoyable.

Finishing her bold examination, she shrugged as if it were no big deal and said, "Sure, babe, why not?"

A quizzical smile came to his mouth at her words. Olena took another leisurely drink of the wine. His expression wasn't what she expected.

Without taking his offered hand, Olena pushed up from her chair and strode around the table by herself. Her hair blew lightly in the wind, whipping in seductive red contrast to the black of her gown. She let her hips sway slightly, knowing from years of experience that he would be looking at them. Even though she appeared calm, her heart was beating erratically fast. His voice sent chills over her flesh and turned her nervous system to water.

When Yusef merely watched her step down the platform to the ground in amazement, her emerald eyes sparkled in mischief, as she said lightly, "Well, come on, won't you? Let's go get this over with."

Yusef came slowly down the steps, stopping to eye her as she had him. It was a bold stare, one that left no doubt he was undressing her with his mind. Olena's confidence wavered slightly. He licked his lips.

"Are you done?" she demanded, her voice coming out a little harsh. Olena covered up her emotions with ease, slipping from one role to another despite what she felt on the inside. It was the only way a pirate of the high skies could survive.

"No," he answered obstinately, continuing to look his fill. Olena's arms crossed over her chest. He looked at her creamy breasts, pushed up and together by her defiant motion.

The crystal about his neck pulsed and Olena discovered that her body was trying to pulse along with it. Narrowing her eyes, she stared at the stone. Something wasn't quite right. Her head was beginning to fog over with pleasure. What exactly were these barbarians up to? She glanced back at the table, seeing that more brides were being led off, their eyes glassy as they followed listlessly.

Olena grinned, remembering all she had learned of the Qurilixen customs. Stepping boldly forward, she reached to grab his fur covered manhood. To her surprise, it was already at half arousal. Squeezing it, she asked, "You want it here, barbarian?" Yusef stiffened. His breath caught in amazement that she had actually grabbed him in public viewing. Her boldness excited him, but he also knew this was not the place. He wouldn't dishonor his family or his name by acting like an uncouth peasant. Reading the mischief in her eyes, he knew she was teasing him.

Olena waited, her brow poised dangerously on her forehead, as she slowly licked her lips. The arousal beneath her fingers lurched slightly. She grinned.

Before she knew what was happening, Yusef leaned over and lifted her over his shoulder. Olena gulped. He tossed her as if she were nothing more than a feather. Her stomach lurched causing her to lose her breath. Yusef's hand curled over her thighs, digging under the thin strips of material to fasten boldly on her naked skin. His other arm wrapped around her dangling legs, trapping her to him.

Yusef strode away with his battle prize, smiling like a fool. Seeing his friend Agro nearby pointing at him and laughing, he waved jauntily. A cry of amusement went over the married couples.

Olena, not to be outdone, ran her fingernails over the muscular curves of his back, scratching lightly as she drew over the trails of his firm back. He shivered beneath her arms and she smiled wickedly. His heart beat steadily in his chest, thumping wonderfully erotic beside her leg.

Without losing breath, he carted her through the entire encampment to the far end of the field. Keeping her on his shoulder, he pushed open a gray tent flap and carried her inside. He did not let her go, choosing to hold onto her, liking the solid feel of her body.

Olena pushed up on his shoulder to look around. His arms wound around her, holding her up from beneath her back side, hugging her tightly to his chest. His face pressed near her stomach, as he breathed in the womanly scent of her.

A bed covered in fur was in the middle of the tent, with chains strapped to the four posts. Those might come in handy, she mused. Then, looking at the three pyramid corners, she saw a bath in one, steaming and hot and very inviting. Olena shivered. It had been a long time since she had a water bath. The Galaxy Bride ship had a decontamination unit, which basically sucked the germs and oil off your skin in a swift puff of air.

The tent had torches lit up in sconces. It gave the gray walls an eerie light and glowed off the bronzed giant, who held her with glistening abandonment. Tapping her nails lightly on his shoulders, she turned to look the other way.

In the second corner, to her left, she saw a table laden with food and drink. If she remembered correctly, they were gifts to her from the man's family. If he had no family, then he had made the chocolate candies himself.

*How very industrious of them,* she mused wryly.

Slowly, Yusef turned with her in his arms. Olena grew nervous, but did not let it show. He pulled his grip back slightly so she leisurely slid down his chest. He hugged his massive arms around her narrow waist. Her breast came before his face and he smiled impishly up at her.

Yusef held the woman in his arms, enjoying the contact. Her soft body easily molded to his. Her exotic cinnamon scent carried over into his senses, propelling his blood in tumultuous desire and lust. His body ached to taste the sweetness of her flesh. She wanted him too. He smelled it on her, wafting up from her hips like a perfume to tempt him into beastly madness.

Suddenly, her legs wrapped around his waist and she lowered herself letting her breasts brush by his lips. With one swift move, he could've taken her right then.

Olena grew nervous, wondering if she was pushing things too far. He was a man after all and she didn't have a weapon to defend herself. But, seeing the restraint on his face and knowing the penalty for him would be great if he coupled with her, she relaxed. It was just a game, a game the Pirate Olena was determined to win.

Wiggling her hips, she said throatily, a pout forming on her lips, "Aren't you supposed to ask me something, Yusef?"

Yusef smiled, simply stating, "Choose."

Olena grinned at him, but it was an emotion she couldn't feel in her trembling heart. The heat of his body was starting to spread into her limbs and his skin was driving her mad with his erotic scent and power. But once Olena chose a course of action she did not back down. That was what made her so good at her trade. That was what made her one of the most sought after thieves in galactic history.

"Well, if you insist," she purred. Threading her fingers into his soft black hair, she wound the locks around her fingers. His dark skin clashed with the white of her hands. She took much more time than necessary to work the mask off his face without untying the straps.

When Olena saw his face for the first time, all well thought plans momentarily left her. He was handsome, breathtaking. He was staring at her with the most gorgeously shaped eyes she had ever seen --and she had seen a lot. His dark gray gaze shifted before her, flashing with yellow.

Now, that was something she hadn't seen for awhile. This man was a shifter.

The thought brought her up short and she knew she had to be very careful. Shifters could be exceedingly dangerous, depending on what they shifted into. It was a genetic defense, so it wasn't like he'd turn into a cute and fuzzy bunny. No, they usually shifted into strong, warrior beasts.

"Why don't you put me down," she murmured, impishly throwing the mask behind her head, "so I can unwrap my prize?"

Yusef held back, wondering what she was thinking as she studied him with her serious eyes. Olena's face gave nothing away. He felt her heart beating fast, almost as if she was afraid, but he couldn't smell fear on her. Her eyes were in a constant state of mischief, though he guessed the look was meant to hide her other emotions. His little bride was a great mystery. He knew she was up to something, he just couldn't tell what. He would have to be careful until he figured her out. But, in the meantime, he'd just wait and enjoy whatever wild ride she had in store for him.

Yusef lowered her to the ground, letting her feel the entire length of his heated body, including his scaldingly hot desire. To his amusement, she trembled a little at the intimate press of him and lost a bit of her composure.

Olena swallowed, her eyes trying not to widen as she felt the hard length of him hitting dangerously close to her stomach. Her nipples ached, reaching for him like little traitors. She was not supposed to desire him. The idea was to get him to desire her. Once she had him so frustrated with need, he would be putty in her hands and give her anything she wanted for just a chance of fulfillment--a fulfillment that would never come.

To her horror, as he let her go, her knees weakened and she stumbled. Yusef grinned arrogantly at her. Her fist tightened, automatically wanting to wipe the insolence off his features. When she saw his eyes narrow in warning, she held back and smiled instead.

"Well?" she questioned, waving at him. "Let's see."

"I thought you wished to unwrap your prize," Yusef expressed. His voice again ran over her body like warm syrup. His Qurilixen accent burred soft and rolling from his firm lips. Olena swallowed. Those lips moved in such a way that she knew he would be able to shower her with toe-curling kisses--just looking at them made her skin tingle and her heart race.

Olena took a step forward, forcing her legs to be still. Cocking her head, she licked her lips and looked him over. She lifted her hands to his chest to drift down the hard length of him to the fur waistband of his loincloth. When her tapered fingers reached his stomach, the muscles tightened and he grabbed her wrists trapping her in his palms.

"What?" Olena pouted prettily, before teasing, "Embarrassed are we? I'm sure it's fine."

"Use your mouth," he commanded, not taking the bait.

Olena was stunned, but she never showed it. Swallowing, she let him urge her down towards his waist. Bending over, she thrust out her backside.

Yusef knew he was pushing her, waiting for the eruption that appeared to be simmering under her fiery surface. Maybe it was her flaming red hair, or perhaps it was the way she seemed so sure that she was in control of the situation. Whatever the reason, he wanted to push her, and keep pushing her until she ignited into a passionate explosion. If he boiled this little vixen's blood, he knew the rewards would be great.

Yusef groaned, seeing the lush curve wiggling beneath silk, just beyond his reach. He held her hands out to the side, so she couldn't cheat. Lightly, he felt a kiss on his abdomen and then the dragging of her tongue. His stomach stiffened. It was glorious torture.

Olena worked her mouth to the fur. Getting hold, she

jerked her head back in a shower of red waves. When she stood before him, fur in mouth, hair wildly tousled about her back and shoulders, she impishly winked at him.

Unable to stem her curiosity, she looked down. Her eyes widened before she could hide her amazement. Now that was something she hadn't seen before. It would seem this dark barbarian toted a large warrior all his own.

Yusef stepped to her, spreading her arms wide as his hands remained shackled around her wrists. The material straps at her waist ripped free with the bold movement. Olena shivered at the sheer power of him. With a quick strike, he grabbed the end of the fur with his own lips and took it from her mouth like a wild dog, tossing it to the side.

Before she knew what was happening, he kissed her. It was a blistering kiss that stole her breath and stopped her heart in her chest. It was a kiss full of passion and unleashed desire. Here was a man who knew what he wanted and went for it without thought. Before she knew what she was doing, Olena was kissing him back.

Olena moaned. She had been kissed before, but never like this--never like she was the last and only woman in the galaxy. With her arms out to the side, she couldn't fight him off. To her shame she realized, if not for his hold on her arms, she wouldn't have been fighting him, but encouraging him.

Angry more at her loss of control than at him, she bit him--hard. Yusef jerked back, his lip bleeding. He blinked, stunned. Looking at her swollen lips, he saw the matching trail of his blood staining them. She licked her mouth, daring him to punish her for it.

To his bewilderment, she said, "You didn't say please."

"Please," he growled under his breath, his gaze dancing with heat. Stepping forward again, he resumed his kiss where he had left off. Only this time he bit back. Olena gasped, her leg lifting to kick him in reflex. He dropped her arms, only to wrap her in his forced embrace. Her leg missed its target, moving instead to intimately rub down the side of his naked hip.

"Let me go," Olena demanded hotly, struggling against him as she tasted their intermingled blood on her lips, not knowing how much of it was hers and how much was his.

"Please," he whispered, leaning over to lick her wound. Nudging her lightly with his jaw, he said again, "Please."

Olena couldn't refuse the rolling sound of his seductive words. The crystal pulsed between them, but this time she ignored her suspicions as he once more claimed her. His kiss was gentle, probing and soothing. She melted into his arms, forgetting the battle as he called her unwillingly to a truce. She couldn't think against his onslaught of tenderness. She wanted him, like she had never wanted anything.

Yusef felt her weakening in his arms. Pulling back from the kiss, he looked into her passion-hazed eyes. He knew she wanted him, nearly as bad as he wanted to posses her. Questions swam in his head. He wanted to know who she was, why she came to his planet. He knew it was partly their combined fate that brought her to Qurilixen, but he wanted to know her other reasons. Was she hiding from something? Was she looking for something? He knew there was more to her, just as he instinctively knew he wouldn't get the answers easily.

"Now," he breathed hotly against her lips. "Let me see what I have won."

Olena shivered, too stunned by the feel of his lips to move. He caressed her skin. The fog that tried to invade her all night, had crept into her brain during that last kiss and now held her in its mist--unwilling to let her think, only feel what its master wanted her to.

He trailed his hands over her gown, burning through the silk as if it didn't exist. He flexed his fingers, letting his palms do most of the touching. They moved down her hips, over her waist to come up, cupping naturally around her smaller breasts. The soft globes fit beautifully into his hands and he touched them as if they already belonged to him.

Olena gasped, too stunned to move. He kept his eyes locked to hers. He ran his finger up her delicate neck, so strong that they could have strangled the life from her. They did not cause her pain, except the bittersweet agony beneath their gentle gliding. Her blood simmered, pooling between her hips to create a feeling of desperation and longing.

Taking the dress in his firm grasp, Yusef tore it. The

material ripped loudly, causing her to jump in surprise. The warm air of the tent hit her naked flesh as the gown was tossed to the side. Her nipple puckered, beckoning him, tempting him.

Yusef stepped back, boldly taking her in. Her skin was white and flawless. It had looked so pure against his tanned flesh. Panties hugged her hips, taunting him with their lacy barrier. Oh, how he'd like to bite through them. Freckles dotted her shoulders, like light and airy kisses. He promised his mouth he would kiss each and every one of them in time.

Her body was well-built, muscled and strong, but still gentle and soft--just like her playful eyes. There was a quiet innocence to her gaze, but Yusef could feel deeper inside her than mere appearances allowed and knew it wasn't all true, and yet it wasn't all an act.

He could tell she worked hard by the calluses on her hands, though they did not look rough. Already he concluded that this woman knew how to use a gun. He felt the intent in her trigger finger as if she had fired one often.

Olena held still, watching him devour her with his eyes. It made her hot to see his desire for her, unfiltered in its brazen heat. A wave of guilt overcame her for she knew she would never succumb to him. She knew she would be using him and then leaving him behind as soon as she got a chance. He was just a means to an end--and her end was escape from this exile of a planet.

Thinking of that end, she blinked away the fog, fighting it. She knew her feelings had something to do with the crystal around his neck as well as the wine they had given her to drink. She had tasted that unique blend of herbs before. Psychiatrists liked to use them because they opened the mind and loosened the tongue, though they were illegal in many quadrants. Narrowing her eyes, she stiffened her resolve. This man had tried to drug her, tried to take away her will.

Her eyes shone brightly with an innocence she did not feel. "Like what you see?"

His response was a bestial growl. He didn't look away.

Taking a finger to her lips, she felt the drying blood on them. The straps still wound up her arms and she left them. She kicked off her shoes. Sucking her finger, her eyes growing wide, she turned to pose shyly for him.

Yusef swallowed, already tortured by what was to come. Still, he couldn't think to stop it.

Olena blinked and murmured in her most sultry of tones, "I think I got myself dirty, Yusef. Maybe you should come give me a bath."

## Chapter Three

Yusef couldn't help the fever that ignited in his body at the request. He knew he was going to regret it. His warrior instincts told him to be careful, that this woman was cunning, that she was going to be trouble. Not heeding his own instincts, he let his lust do the thinking and walked over to the naked vixen staring at him.

The firefly pin atop her locks glistened as she moved. The little black gemstones sparkled like stars, winking mischievously at him. Reaching, he glided a hand down her cheek, cupping her jaw, his fingers coming over her sensitive ear.

Olena froze, not allowing her body to shiver at the gentle caress. Slowly, he drew his hand over her shoulder and down her arm. Taking up the tattered end of her belt that hung from the winding straps on her wrists, he backed up, leading her by the straps to the steaming tub.

Olena let him look at her, unashamed of her body. She wasn't a fool. She knew in the end, he would want the same thing all men did. He would want her complete submission. She would never do it. She'd been a man's slave once. Once was enough.

Yusef was unaware of her turmoil. When he looked at her, she smiled a beautifully dazzling smile. Bringing her forward, he tried to kiss her. Her lush, full lips called to him. They pursed when she talked, begging to be touched. He saw the swollen cut where his teeth had bitten her and he felt the matching sore on his own lip.

Olena moved past him, mischievously passing up his offered mouth. She shrugged out of her panties and got into the bath. Standing naked before him, she waited.

Yusef did not have to be commanded. He stepped into the large basin joining her. Slowly they sank into the warm water. Their backs to opposite sides, they faced each other. Her legs lying to his side. Olena closed her eyes, momentarily content to enjoy the water.

Soon, his fingers were on her feet, lifting them to his

chest so he could lather them with soap. His soft touch took
her in for a moment, entranced her mind with the pleasure
of it. He let his hands roamed, gliding up her calf. When he
touched the intimate curve of her knee, she stiffened,
ticklish. Opening her eyes, she bathed him, as he did her.

However, as she lathered his feet, she too found herself
working up to his hair-roughened thighs. The soap slid
delightfully erotic on their skin. Their touches stayed on
task, heating and building fires wherever they journeyed.
From the thighs they discovered hips, from the delectable
hips they discovered stomachs, and from flat stomachs they
found chests.

Yusef took his time, teasing her breasts, learning their
feel, testing their response. He was not disappointed. As he
ran his thumb over a sensitive nub, her body jerked in
pleasure.

To Olena's surprise, she found they were kneeling in the
warm water, her hands moving in circles over Yusef's
shoulders. His mouth was inches away from hers, parted,
ready to kiss her but holding back. He worked his large
hands over her back, massaging her closer to his chest.

The raven strands of his hair were on his shoulders. The
dark tips were wet where she had brushed against them.
The texture of him mesmerized her. It was hypnotic to her
fingers. She couldn't seem to find the will to stop touching
him. The smell of him, of the soap, it drove into her senses.

It was insanity. She knew it. Being with him would go
against every code that she lived by. It would ruin the
balance of her life. But she could no more stop herself than
she could stop the march of time or change the will of the
seasons. He was desert heat to her arctic cold. They would
never survive together, yet here they were--touching,
feeling, stroking, burning.

His tenderness cracked the ice block that had settled over
her heart years ago. She couldn't fight this kind of passion.
He didn't demand anything from her, only gave. How
could she refuse such a gift? No one had ever treated her
like she was delicate, like she was a real woman.

Desire overwhelmed her, scaring her.

Yusef watched her. The mischief faded from her emerald
eyes and he saw the raw agony of pain staring at him. In
that moment, a veil was lifted, baring her soul to him. He

smelled her longing for him, but also the deeply buried fear. Her eyes moistened with tears as she looked deep into his gray eyes. Whatever it was that she had planned by luring him to the bath, she was not following through.

Olena didn't know if it was the man, the wine in her veins, or the crystal glowing brighter with each passing moment, that was driving her onward. All she knew was that her body would never be the same. As her desire had begun to respond naturally to his, she forgot her plans, forgot that they shouldn't be doing this. She forgot to hate him.

Slowly, Olena leaned forward, her arms winding slowly around him as she kissed him. Yusef held her, enjoying himself as he let her make the first move. Her lips were open and sweet, pouring a tender vulnerability over him. Her body pressed more firmly against him as he leaned back in the tub to support her weight. Her legs adjusted over his waist, careful to keep him from touching her with his arousal.

Yusef growled into her opened mouth. Her lips quickened to a fevered pace as she moaned into him. He found her hips, naturally urging her body closer, seeking to tame the ache she had created. He paused in their kiss, opening his mouth as he slid her next to his arousal. The water caressed her, burning hotter near his erection.

Yusef suddenly pulled back. If they finished this mad tirade, the council would sense it on them. If he broke the law, his marriage would be disapproved and he would be forced to live the rest of his very long life alone. Not until she publicly declared she wanted him by breaking his crystal, could he claim her.

Olena, too impassioned with the new feelings to stop, went forward to nuzzle his neck. His pulse jumped beneath her kisses.

"No," he commanded. "Stop."

*Stop!* Her brain screamed in disbelief. *Did he just tell me to stop? Nobody tells me to stop!*

"We can't do this," he said, feeling like a fool as the words came out. He wanted to caress, but he took them away from her skin in denial. Her lips slid along his jaw to his mouth. Her wide emerald eyes stared into his gray ones.

"Why not?" she asked, persistent. "Who would ever

know?"

"I would know," he answered with pride. "The council will know."

Olena shrugged, moving to kiss him again. Her body was at such a pitch that she didn't care about the council or this man's sudden discovery of honor. Just a moment ago, when he was trying to nestle his erection closer to her inner thighs, where had his sense of honor and his fear of the council been?

"Kiss me," she demanded, her eyes alighting with the mischievous shield to block him out. "Now."

"Say please," he teased.

Her eyes hardened. All vulnerability was gone when she looked at him. Her smile cocked dangerously to the side. A wave of bitterness and despair crashed inside her, caving in her heart. She was a fool. This man was good, she'd give him that. He'd turned her own con back on her and like a dupe she'd fallen for it. He'd made her admit to wanting him only to deny her. A lovely pout on her features, Olena leaned forward.

Yusef watched her, thinking she was perhaps one of the most beautiful creatures in the world. Soapsuds clung to her breasts, drawing his eyes. He would never know how he got the willpower to stop her advances. Her naked arms stretched above her head. Sometime during their play the wristbands had fallen off into the water. Yusef swallowed as her cream colored breasts shifted with the movement of her arms.

Olena took her fingers to her hair and pulled the firefly pin from her locks. With a shake, her hair spread over her skin like trails of fire. Her wide, sultry gaze looked deep into his. His breath caught. She saw the look and knew the battle was now hers. He wouldn't be refusing her again. Leaning forward, she brushed a kiss to his lips.

"Please…?" She pulled back with a pout. Her eyes hardened and she jabbed the tip of the firefly hairpin into Yusef's neck. Pushing the firefly's wings down, she injected a sleeping agent, so strong that it could easily put an elephant out, into his bloodstream.

Yusef stiffened, feeling the poke. His arms lifted to grab her. Instantly, his vision blurred and his hands dropped into the water with a big splash. He couldn't move. Even as he was passing out he managed a light curse, his dark eyes glaring hotly. As his vision faded around the treacherously lovely being watching over him, he saw her smile waver into a hard look. She waved at him, insolently wiggling her fingers, as she said darkly, "I just don't say please, husband."

Olena pulled the pin from his neck. The wound dotted with blood but did not drip. He would be out for the rest of the night. Standing, she did not smile as she slipped the pin back into her hair.

When she finished pinning up her locks, she looked down at Yusef, staring at his naked body for a long time. He was incredible. His touch was fire and her body sung with what he did to her. She would have to be careful. This barbarian had almost tricked her into forgetting herself.

Not bothering to dress and knowing he would be out until morning, she leaned over to haul his arms over the side of the bath, making sure he wouldn't drown. It wouldn't do to add his murder to her long list of crimes. He was too heavy to move much further than the edge of the tub, so she just left him there.

Striding across the fur-covered ground, Olena didn't bother to dry her wet body. She dripped a long trail, as she went to the table laden with food. She grabbed the earthen jug in the middle and took a long pull off of it to try and calm her nerves. Emptying half the jug, she set it down with a gasp. Then, seeing a knife left on a tray of sliced fruit, she picked it up.

She glanced at Yusef. Crossing over to him, her face hard, her heart harder, she clutched the knife in her steady hand. As she reached the bathtub, she stopped directly above him. Her fist turned white around the blade as she studied his chest lifting with shallow breaths of sleep.

"You almost bested me," she said softly, pointing the knife at him, ire pouring from her expression as she glared at him. Her eyes narrowed, as she swore vehemently, "Never again."

Olena turned the knife in her hand and held it steady. She took a deep breath, gritted her teeth, and drew the blade through her upper arm with a stiff jerk. A whimper left her lips at the pain and she instantly dropped the blade to the ground. Blood ran crimson trails down her arm. She fell to the floor, clutching the injured appendage and refusing to cry out.

For a moment she just rocked, naked and frozen on the ground, waiting for the worst of the initial pain to pass. As the agony of her self-infliction started to dull, she grabbed a nearby bath linen and wound it around the cut to stop the bleeding.

Staring at Yusef, she nodded her head at the prone man and professed, "To the Pirate's Code, Yusef. You won't best me again."

\* \* \* \*

After cleaning up her mess and washing the knife, Olena spent the entire night dozing on the bed. Occasionally a loud, passionate cry from a nearby tent would jolt her awake. Sleep never claimed her completely as she watched Yusef's chest rising and falling in the torchlight. The ache he stirred in her gave way after about an hour to leave a pain much worse than the one in her injured arm.

Yusef didn't move. Olena knew he was going to be sore when he woke up from being in the same awkward position all night--not to mention livid. She couldn't really blame him. She'd be livid too if he had done it to her.

As dawn crept into the tent, the torches had all but burnt out. Olena had memorized every line of his face and shoulders. The more she looked, the more handsome she thought him. It didn't matter. The throbbing in her arm served to remind her that she couldn't let him affect her.

Hearing a shuffle outside the tent flap, Olena yawned, pushing her tired body out of bed. Taking the fur coverlet, she pulled it around her shoulders and stumbled to see who was there. As she pulled the flap aside, the waiting manservant seemed surprised to see a half-naked woman answering him. Blinking, he tried to see over her shoulder.

"He's taking a bath." Olena smiled naturally for the man, letting a blush she didn't feel fall over her features. The lie came a little too easily to her, as she continued, "He should be along in a moment."

"Very good, my lady," the servant mumbled. His kind brown eyes drew down, politely refusing to stare at the beautiful but married woman. He was dressed in a simple tunic and brown breeches, his hair pulled back from his face in a queue. Lifting his hands laden with garments, he said, "Your clothes, my lady. The council bid me to tell you they are ready to see you as soon as you are dressed."

"Me?" Olena squeaked, mistaking his meaning. How could they have known what she did? Were these shifters telepathic too? That hadn't occurred to her.

"Yes, my lady," the servant said. "You and his lordship."

"Lordship?" Olena asked, looking over her shoulder. She took the black cloth from him the best she could save her coverlet attire. A quizzical smile came to her face. *A lord, eh?* "Yes, yes, I'll be sure to tell his ... ah ... lordship to hurry."

"Very good, my lady," the servant answered. The gray tent flap fell in his face before he even finished.

Olena turned, looking at her husband with renewed eyes. What exactly had she stumbled into? So Yusef was a lord, was he? That meant he would have money and men with money usually had things--things like spacecrafts and jewels and other valuables that could fetch a good price on the black market.

If her crew still looked for her, as she knew they did, then they would be much happier to greet her if she were laden with gifts. It would be a nice gesture to them as a thank you for their loyalty. Maybe she could afford to take them to Quazer for a well-deserved vacation. Maybe she could even get the slave brands removed from their backsides as well. She tried not to grin.

Setting the clothes on the bed, she dug through the pile with one hand. Her injured arm still pained her when she moved it. On top was a black tunic jacket, too big for her to wear. It was made from a soft cotton-like material, woven fine with simple edging. A silver dragon clasp held the jacket together in the front. The jacket went over an undertunic and a pair of tighter pants that were also severely black in color. On the jacket's chest was the emblem of a dragon embroidered in silver.

Olena grimaced, as she came to her clothing. "Ugh, another dress."

Her gown was of a matching shade. Before putting it on, she carefully peeled the bandage from her wound. The cut was angry and red but, for the sake of her honor, she wasn't allowed to do anything about it for three days. Only then could she disinfect it and help it to heal. Ripping her wedding dress on the floor, she tore the black silk into strips and tied up her arm.

The tunic gown hugged tightly to her waist, dipping low at the chest in a very elegant way. Silver overlay fit at the shoulders and bodice, moving to trail over the back portion of the flared skirt. She too had the dragon on her chest, a smaller version than on Yusef's tunic. The sleeves swung wide from her elbows to the floor, leaving her forearms exposed. She was glad her cut was high enough to be hidden from view by the sleeves.

Slipping into the boots that had been delivered with them, she sighed in comfort. If she never saw a pair of slippers again, it would be too soon. Everything fit perfectly, but she took little time to wonder about it.

She combed her fingers through her hair, pinning the bulk of it into a serviceable knot at the back of her head. It was slow going with one arm injured, but she did manage to get it back. Then, as she was placing the firefly into the top of the coiffure, she heard a low growl.

Olena froze, gulping in sudden fear. She dropped her hand to her side. Slowly, she turned. That was not the sound of a man.

## Chapter Four

Spinning just in time to see a flash of brown skin, Olena gasped in fright. Yusef had awakened in a dragon-like mood. Well, dragon-like wasn't necessarily true. He was literally a human dragon. She had suspected he was a shifter, but she hadn't been ready to see it firsthand.

Golden eyes of fire stared at her as Yusef's talon like fingers gripped her arms. She cried out in pain as he pressed into her cut. His beautiful black hair was the same, but his forehead had stiffened and pulled forward, bringing a low ridge down from his hairline to his nose. His breath came out in ragged draws of breath, rumbling with a growl in the back of his throat. All his flesh had turned as hard as armor and would be near impossible to pierce with a knife blade. Still, she wished she had a knife. She would have liked to give it a try.

"Ah," Olena gasped as he squeezed harder.

Olena clenched her eyes, trying not to cry out as he hurt her. Moisture pooled her vision and she squeezed it back, refusing to show weakness. His breath hit against her skin, skin that was too easily becoming excited by his show of power.

Yusef's nostrils flared. Glancing over Olena's pale face, he smelled her fear. It didn't stop him. He tried his best not to rip her treacherous head off, as he crushed her arm in his palms, bruising her flesh. Then, catching the scent of blood, he stopped. He leaned forward, sniffing at her neck.

He continued to follow the scent of blood, moving down her arm. Discovering that the source was beneath his hands, he stopped. He fought for control, thinking he might have gouged her with his talon.

The grip became less rigid on her arm and Olena could again breathe. When she opened her eyes, he was back as she knew him. She had seen shifters before, but never like him. He was so powerful, so strong. It did something wicked inside her to see it. Her heart was racing and not all in fear. She had the strangest urge to jump on him and kiss him.

Yusef was staring at her arm. His face contorted with anger, he demanded hotly, "Why?"

Olena didn't waver in light of his voiced outrage. She could handle this better than his tenderness. The throbbing in her arm brought her comfort and normalcy.

"You drug me, I drug you," she declared. "We're even. Fair is fair."

"What?" he demanded in outrage.

Yusef let her go before he shifted again and ripped the delicate throat from her neck. His arms ached from his awkward night in the bath, but he wouldn't give her the pleasure of seeing him stretch the muscles. "I never--"

"Don't lie," Olena said in warning. "I know exactly what was in that drink. A little Maiden's Breath mixed with just a dash of Last Ember's root. It makes the victim nice and malleable. Too bad for you, I know what it does and can fight it."

"It's a traditional drink," Yusef defended, "not a drug."

"Nice tradition, dragon. Why don't you just skip the drugging and get straight to the rape?"

She didn't think it was possible, but his look blackened.

"Listen, we're even," she growled. Her arm throbbed and she wanted nothing more than to grab it. She refrained. "You don't try to drug me and I won't drug you, deal?"

"We do not rape," Yusef growled forebodingly, deeply insulted by the insinuation. His hair fell forward over his shoulders as his naked chest heaved. "The crystal chooses the pairing. With the crystal, the wine makes the mind open. That is why it's against the law to come together this night. The woman's will must be left free, so that she may choose freely. The wine helps to connect, to start the foundation of a good life. It helps to…"

Yusef stopped. He didn't want to tell her it opened the ports between their minds so that someday they would be able to read each other's thoughts and feelings. Already he could feel the beginning stirs of her emotions, though they were too tumultuous to get a good reading on them.

Olena raised a brow. "Pray, please continue with this lovely lesson on male dominated logic."

Yusef frowned. Instead, he stated, "I smell blood."

Olena paled. She tried to hide the look but he caught it.

"You are injured?" Yusef asked, afraid he had done it to her in his anger.

Olena looked towards her sleeve. A trickle of blood made the slow journey down the back of her arm. She gradually turned her hand so he couldn't see it.

"No," Olena lied. "I'm fine."

"Let me see."

"I'm fine," she said, growing uncomfortable. "Listen, it looks as if we are going to be spending countless hours together, so do you mind if we cut this pleasant little scenario until later? I didn't sleep too well and I have a wicked migraine. Besides, a servant came by and said to tell you that the council is ready to see us as soon as we are dressed."

Olena motioned to his clothes on the bed. Yusef realized he stood before her completely naked. He was beginning to feel a chill. She kept her gaze averted while he donned his clothing. Yusef would have laughed by the show of modesty after having witnessed her little performance last night, but he felt too drained at the moment.

Looking down, Yusef saw his crystal still glowed. She shouldn't be able to feel such pain this morning, unless it was like she said and she was immune to the drink. Come to think of it, it might be her headache he was starting to detect inside his brain. It would make sense if he could feel inside her.

*This damned thing might be broken,* he mused, again eyeing the crystal.

But when he looked at the red-haired vixen keeping her back to him, he saw her tremble. He felt their connection as strongly as the first moment he'd seen her. She was his life mate. She was his perfect match.

*Damn perfection anyway,* Yusef thought.

"You are not frightened?" Yusef asked, noticing how she said nothing about his dragon form.

"Of what?" she returned absently. She had been flicking absently at the dragon on her chest and stopped to inquire, "Of you?"

Sure she was scared of him. She was scared of what he'd made her feel the previous night in his arms. She was scared that even the wound she'd given herself wouldn't be enough of a reminder for her to fight him--to not fall for his handsome face and fierce dragon eyes.

"Of me, yes," he said quietly. He came up behind her, placing a tentative hand on her shoulder. There were many stories of brides going insane with the realization and leaving their mates to hundreds of years of lonely torment.

Olena flinched but did not back away. Glancing over her shoulder, she saw his eyes were serious. He drew his over her back, resting on the opposite shoulder as she turned to look fully at him.

"You mean because you're a shifter?" she asked, with a light, unconcerned shrug.

"Yes, because of that." Yusef was awed by her easy acceptance.

Olena wanted to laugh but didn't. Lufa, a member of her crew, was a walking amphibian and left a slime trail whenever he was near her. MoPa was a hairy yeti from the Bogylands. Hedge had prickles on his head instead of hair. In a pinch, he made for a damned fine needle. No, she wasn't scared of a little shifting.

"No," she said truthfully. The ache in her heart replaced the ache in her arm. She really did miss her crew. They were the only family she'd ever really known. Olena pulled away from him when he would have pulled her into his arms. Turning to study him, she said truthfully "I have no fear of different creatures. So what if you are a shifter?"

"But, the other brides..." Yusef tensed. Her sadness washed over him and he wondered about it. She was so lonely. For a moment, he forgot about her drugging him.

"I won't say anything. Besides, I don't want to be the one to catch them when they faint," Olena said, forcing up the smiling mask. "Let their husbands deal with them."

"But they are your friends."

*Friends?* Olena thought in surprise. She'd never had a female friend before. No, a friend was someone who had your back. Those girls on the ship would turn their backs as soon as they found out what she was.

"No," she said, with a calmness that made him pause. She closed herself off to him, not letting him feel anything within her. "I just traveled with them. I didn't have any friends on that ship."

Sighing, Yusef pulled on his boots and held out his elbow for her to take. "Shall we?"

"Sure, why not?" she mumbled, not really thinking about where they were going or what they were going to do. None of it mattered anyway and her mind was elsewhere.

It was not the enthusiastic response a husband expected, but then again, this woman was not the bride Yusef expected.

"By the way," he said as he led her out of the tent. "Do I have your promise that you will never drug me again?"

"Sure, why not?" Olena repeated. But, this time, she flashed him a bright, impish smile. Her eyes shone with disobedience. "So long as you don't deserve it."

\* \* \* \*

Olena stood before the council leaders, bowing her head regally to the King and Queen in the center. They nodded back, their crowned heads tilted pleasantly as they smiled at Yusef and his bride. The royal couple was dressed in matching purple tunics. Looking over at Yusef's black outfit and then hers, she frowned. They weren't going to have to dress alike every day, were they?

Councilmen stood to the side of the royalty. The bonfire in the main yard had burned low sometime during the night. Looking around, Olena noticed no one looked the worse for wear, expect for one beefy warrior on the sideline with two black eyes. Seeing he had her attention, he smiled jovially and nodded his head. Olena insolently winked back.

Rubbing absently at her arm, she flinched as the wound stung beneath her hand. She was glad Yusef had stopped asking about it. It was not something she could explain without first telling him she was a pirate.

"Queen Mede, King Llyr, may I present Lady…." Yusef's voice trailed off. With a sheepish grin, he turned to his wife. Her hand was on his arm. Leaning to whisper, he put his hand over hers and said, "You know I never got your name."

Unable to stop herself, she smirked, "I know."

"What is your name?" Yusef asked softly, the words coming in a rush.

The King and Queen shared a look. The bride smiled prettily at them and the Queen hesitantly smiled back.

"You should have thought about that earlier, dragon," Olena said mischievously

Standing straight, Yusef heard someone from the gathered crowd behind him beginning to chuckle. Loudly, he announced with a handsome grin, "My lady wife."

The Queen hid her amusement behind her hand. The King bit his lips and nodded his head at the dark man before him. Olena's body quivered with laughter beneath his hand as she tried not to burst out in her own merriment.

"Beware, wife, you've had your fun, but I'll discover your name," he said quietly, his voice held much promise in it. "Now crush my crystal and be done with it."

Olena's suppressed laughter died at his words. Her smile wavered slightly. Lifting one hand, she took the crystal from his neck and dropped it on the ground. With a hard whack, she crushed it beneath her boot. The gathered crowd cheered.

Through a haze, she heard the Queen speak, as if in slow motion, "Welcome to the family of Draig, my lady. I hope you will enjoy your new home."

The gentle fog that Olena didn't realize remained over her, lifted. Her eyes became suddenly clear and the pain in her arm intensified tenfold. She blinked, her face becoming pale. It was as if some protective shield had broken and she was again human.

"Yusef." The Queen rose to her feet. She pointed at Olena. The proud smile faded from his features at his mother's pale look. "Grab her, she's bleeding."

A commotion started as the word spread. A councilman called for a medic.

Olena blinked, not understanding what was going on, not understanding the queen's frantic words as she pointed in her direction. Numbly she looked down at her arm. Her hand was covered in blood. Her ears rung, deafening her with the rush in her brain. She saw Yusef reaching for her as she fell. It was like watching a dream. Her eyes rolled back in her head. She was out.

Yusef gathered his wife into his arms, catching her against his chest as he lowered Olena to the platform. Her blood pooled by her side. He ripped her sleeve open, revealing the blood-soaked bandage wrapped around her upper arm.

The King ordered the onlookers back and the crowd parted to let a medic through. Yusef unwound the bandage as the medic ran up the stairs. The man dropped his kit beside her and pushed the Prince back.

"Yusef," his mother asked in shock. "You … you… Never mind, I know you couldn't have, but how could you not see this?"

"What happened?" the medic asked.

"I'm not sure," Yusef answered quietly, so that the curious crowd couldn't hear. "I did not see."

The King looked at him, revealing with his eyes that he expected a full report later. Yusef nodded. He had nothing to hide from his parents.

The medic grabbed a hand laser and began searing the wound shut, burning the flesh together in a thin thread. Olena's eyes popped open. Yusef grabbed her hand. She squeezed him tightly.

"Stop," she demanded.

"No, it's all right. He's fixing it for you," Yusef said softly.

"No," she said, growing more insistent. The medic was almost done. Turning her emerald eyes to the man searing the wound, she startled him by mumbling, "Don't take the scar."

Yusef shared a look with the medic. Slowly, he nodded, assenting to his wife's request. The medic pulled back. The wound looked angry but it no longer bled.

Quietly, the medic took a reading of her blood before giving Yusef instructions and some medicine from his kit. There was nothing else he could do, except remove the scar later if she changed her mind. The medic then announced that she was going to be fine. The crowd cheered happily with the news

Yusef picked his new wife up in his arms. Then, bowing his head to his parents and to the council, he carried her off to his home.

The Queen watched her son leave. Turning to her husband, she whispered, "What is going on? That is two of our sons with troubled marriages."

"I'll speak to Yusef and Olek. They are dependable men and will have it all in hand," King Llyr answered, moving to take his chair.

"Let us hope our other two have an easier time." Queen Mede joined him as they awaited the next newlyweds' arrival.

* * * *

Olena curled into a little ball. She felt like she was five years old again. Her skin burned as if she were on fire. The man in the dirty black coat was coming for her. His old, leathery hand shook as he wielded an injection needle. She was like an animal, so small, so scared, kept in a cage she couldn't stand in as they drugged her to sleep … to sleep….

Olena's eyes popped open in horror, wild and dazed as she thrashed around on a bed. She saw a hand coming for her and screamed. But the past was not through with her as she drifted back into her black torment of dreams.

She was in a ship, her spaceship. Her crew was gone and she was crashing onto an unknown planet. Her heart pounded in fear, fear she never admitted to herself. She was alone. She was sure she was going to die alone, but she didn't die. She crawled out of the wreckage, shooting her way as the path was blocked, and then she was running and she wasn't going to stop.

"Hey, wake up."

Olena blinked. Her eyes looked wild and confused as she stared at him. Hoarsely, she said, "My ship."

"Shh." Yusef studied her face carefully. He'd gone back to the tent, sniffing out her blood by the tub. It hadn't been hard to conclude she'd inflicted the injury on herself with the knife from the fruit tray. He could also smell traces of her blood on the blade, though she had washed it. The only question was why? Pushing back her hair, he murmured, "The medic says he found tantren fruit in your blood stream. The knife was used to cut it before you…. You're allergic to it and that's why you feel so ill."

Olena's arm was an angry red and her pale skin was even whiter. Her hair spilled out over the pillow in flaming waves. He'd dressed her in one of the nightgowns from her formal bags. It looked frumpy on her with wide ruffles and lace on flannel. She nearly swam in it, but it was the only nightgown he could find.

Frowning, he glanced at her bags. He'd also found a gun, an expensive one that could be slipped past most security points. Next to the weapon, he'd discovered a wad of intergalactic cash and a packet full of different ID's--all with her picture and all from different planets and sectors.

Who exactly had he married? Margaret Meriwether? Torch Fontaine? Olena Leyton? Sage Miller? There were about twenty different names to choose from.

As her eyes looked at him, she rose up on the bed. Painfully, she clutched his arm, and said, "My ship has crashed. I need a new one fast. They're coming."

Yusef frowned. It was clear she hadn't heard him and was still in the throws of her nightmare. The medic had warned him that she might have an adverse reaction. Thankfully they'd crushed the crystal when they did. It had been numbing her to the worst of the pain and if she'd stayed under its spell she'd have died before any of them realized what had happened.

"Here, take some medicine," he offered, getting up from his bed to get her some water. "It will help you to sleep."

"Don't," Olena growled. "No painkillers, it's against the code. No killing the pain for three days. Let it bleed."

Yusef frowned. What code? What was she talking about?

He went to her, lifting up her head to force the medicine back. Her round emerald eyes looked at him and she stubbornly pressed her lips together and shook her head in denial.

"You won't best me. Let it bleed," she said, growling with the insistence of her words.

"It will help," Yusef murmured soothingly. He kept the frown from his voice. Never in a hundred years would he have imagined his first day of marriage like this. He tried to force the pills into her mouth, but she stubbornly refused, biting at his finger when he would pry her teeth apart.

Standing, he went to the wall and talked quietly into the intercom. Within minutes the medic was there. Yusef ordered him to inject her with the medicine.

The medic obeyed. Olena saw the needle and freaked, trying to scurry across the bed. Yusef caught her and held her down. Soon it was over and she was limp in his arms.

"Don't look so worried," the medic said, standing. He moved to help adjust her on the bed. "She'll heal up just fine. Once this medicine kicks in, she'll be good as new. It will kill that bacterium in her blood stream. Just make sure she never eats a tantren. It could kill her if she doesn't get help immediately."

"Thank you," Yusef said, leading the man out. When he

came back carrying a bowl of hot water, she hadn't moved. Yusef sat on a chair next to her and cleaned the dried blood from her arm.

"Torch?" he asked, thinking that her hair indeed deserve such a fiery name.

She didn't move.

He tried a few more before saying, "Olena? Margaret?"

She answered to none of them.

"Sage, can you hear me?"

Olena mumbled in her sleep, but didn't speak. Yusef looked at her ravishing face, thinking how beautiful she was and how fragile she seemed at the moment.

*Sage,* he thought. *Her name just might be Sage.*

## Chapter Five

It was a long first day of marriage for Yusef, watching over his delirious wife. He sent word to the King and Queen through the medic that she would recover. As he watched her sweating body toss and turn for several hours, he wasn't so sure. Due to her allergy, her reaction was much worse than it would have been if she'd merely been cut.

Questions swam in his head, but he did not reveal to anyone what he had found in her luggage. Watching her toss and mumble once again, Yusef knew he would have to wait for his answers.

After careful examination, he would almost venture a guess that the luggage wasn't hers at all. All of the clothing, but for the tight black number with the torn sleeve, wouldn't come close to fitting her. The name written on the luggage tag read, *Doris O'Rourke*, a name that didn't match any of her numerous ID's.

That first day of marital bliss came and went with her moaning gasps of pain and insane ramblings of crashed spaceships, slavery, and pieces of adventures Yusef couldn't begin to decipher. It would appear his little mystery wife had led a very exciting life. He wondered what would bring her to Qurilixen as a bride.

Letting her have his bed, he chose to spend the night on the couch. It was a long time before he finally slept. And when dreams finally came, they were troubled and full of unanswerable questions.

\* \* \* \*

Olena cracked open her eyes. Aside from needing a drink of water, she felt wonderful. Her dreams had been dark, nightmarish horrors of the mind, but she was used to that. Nightmares had plagued her ever since she could remember. Not once could she recall having a good dream.

Looking around, she frowned. It took a moment for her to remember where she was--Qurilixen. The word was like a slap of cold water in the face. Blinking, she looked at the disgustingly proper nightgown she wore. It was as if she'd been attacked by ruffles in her sleep. She practically gagged in disgust of it. Olena never slept in a nightgown, preferring to sleep with her gun and nothing else.

Yawning, she scratched her backside out of habit, where her slave brand used to be. The bedroom was wide, with low ceilings. A fine breeze drifted through a crack in the picturesque window that made up the far side of the wall. A dark curtain was pulled over it and Olena could see just a sliver of trees outside.

The bed she laid on was stuffed with feathers, light and downy and the thickest she had ever felt. A black coverlet draped over her legs, the emblem of a large silver dragon's head across the top. Wearily, she kicked it off, realizing she was naked beneath the gown. She took mental note of her body, checking it for injury. Aside from the slight ache in her bandaged arm, she appeared unharmed. For that she was relieved.

Seeing the floral bags she had stolen, she froze. The ugly nightgown had come from them. Olena rushed to the bags and began digging through them. The ID's were right where she'd left them but the gun was missing. Olena scowled. That weapon was rare and had cost her a very extraordinary pearl the size of her fist and nearly two years of negotiating with the Boiler Sect to acquire.

Having spent the better part of the last month in a robe being pampered, mainly because she didn't have anything else to wear, Olena dug through a large carved dresser of dark wood. She didn't find anything worth putting on. All the clothes belonged to her 'husband' and would undoubtedly swim on her.

Again, she scratched her backside. Olena smirked, thinking it very hilarious. *She* was married. Poor sod who'd taken her on. She felt only a little sorry for him. As soon as she got her gun back, she was out of there.

"Swim," she said softly, crossing to the window and looking out into the bright forest. She yawned, stretching her arms. She could use a little exercise. Smelling under her arms she flinched--ugh, and a bath.

Padding barefoot to the bedroom door, she cracked it open. The house was large and open and very much like a lodge. Wood made up the walls in giant, round logs. She recognized the wood as coming from the forest outside. A fireplace of natural stone was set into the wall, with a chimney working up from it to the roof. Little wooden figures were on the mantle. Fur rugs were everywhere. A small skylight dome in the ceiling was covered with curtains, matching the dark curtains hanging on one of the walls. Olena could detect another large window beneath the curtains and smaller ones on the opposite side of the home.

The house was split into two levels. Where she stood on the top level was the bedroom. A large bathroom was across from the bedroom and a sliding door led out to a back patio of broken limestone. The top floor curved around the center lower section to the kitchen area. Taking two steps down would get you to the living room and fireplace.

By the small windows was a wooden dining table set into the wall with rounded cushioned booth seats. An open kitchen with wooden cabinets, glossy countertops, and a food bar with stools was next to it. Everything was dark wood accented with black. A carved dragon's head was above the food bar, embedded into the wall where the ceiling rose higher. It matched the design on the coverlet.

Before the fireplace was a wood couch with plush black cushions, a matching wide-based chair, and a rocking chair--now that was something she'd heard of but had never seen. Draped over the end of the couch, she saw a tanned masculine hand. It wasn't moving. She guessed Yusef was asleep, as she could hear a soft snoring coming from his general area.

Seeing her husband took her a little by surprise. It shouldn't have, as she expected to see him eventually. But remembering his hands, so strong and sure as they touched her, sent a shiver over her spine. Instantly, she grabbed her sore arm and frowned. She wondered what the Pirate Code said about someone else healing you against your will. Honestly, it had never once come up until now. Most pirates were a callous lot and did not take well to nurturing each other.

Ignoring Yusef, she stealthily moved across the wood floors. The boards did not creak as she walked over them. Going to the sliding glass door, she unlatched it and snuck outside without making a sound.

The air was surprisingly cool for such a bright day. Birds sang beautifully in the distance. Little noises of insects came from the large forest. The air was fresh and the sky a clear greenish-blue. Olena saw that there were three suns shining in the cloudless sky--two yellow, one blue.

Seeing a path leading into the forest, her curiosity got the better of her and she wandered off. The new, longer length of her hair was heavy on her back but she ignored it. She was sure she looked horrible. If anyone came across her, they would probably scream like they were under attack. Olena smiled. It wouldn't be the first time she was mistaken for a witch. She just hoped the Qurilixen didn't burn anyone at the stake. She didn't want to go through that one again.

To her pleasure, she saw a small pond just off the side of the path. Picking her way through the yellow ferns she came to the edge and smiled. The water looked clear. Dipping her toe in, she smiled. It was warm.

Olena glanced around and listened. The insects buzzed, but aside from that the forest was quiet. Without further contemplation, she pulled the nightgown over her head and dove naked into the pond.

\* \* \* \*

Yusef yawned, rubbing his tired eyes. He had been up most of the night looking after his wife. Her fits had stopped during the late hours and he could finally relax enough to sleep.

After going to the bathroom, he went to check on his patient. Cracking open the door, he frowned. She was gone.

Yusef pushed back his hair and made a quick survey of his home. Seeing the latch to the sliding glass door was unhooked, he went outside, not bothering with boots. It wasn't hard for him to pick up her scent and he followed the trail to the east pond. Hearing splashing, he slowed. Seeing the discarded nightgown, he grinned.

Coming up through the trees, he quietly pulled back a branch. The surface of the water rippled where she had gone under. He made his way to the shoreline, crossing his arms over his chest as he waited for her to emerge.

Olena came up with a graceful flow of the arms, leaning forward to float naked on the water before diving back under the surface. Yusef wanted to growl at the little wood sprite scene. His eyes blazed with fire.

Beneath the water, Olena chuckled to herself. She had seen Yusef on the shore, but chose to ignore him until she could compose herself to properly handle him. He was a handsome man, standing so tall against the forest background. No longer able to hold her breath, she broke through the surface and treaded water. Slowly swimming her arms, she brought herself around to face him.

"You really shouldn't be swimming in there," Yusef called lightly when she looked at him. A stunning smile formed on his handsome, dark face, making her skin tingle with a little shiver of feminine longing.

"Why? Afraid I'll drown?" she called back, leaning back to get her hair off her face. The red flames pooled in darkened glory around her on the surface.

"No," he mused, "*givre*."

"Giv--what?" she asked, her tone playful as she again dove under the surface, giving him a quick view of her very muscular derrière. When she resurfaced, she had swum closer to better hear him.

"Ah, snake, I believe is your word," he answered with a serious nod. "They love to swim these waters."

Olena, seeing the look, laughed and swam back out to the middle where the sunlight was brighter. The warm light struck upon her body, as she turned in the water to let it hit her pale flesh. The water was just too good to leave quite yet.

"Nice try, knight," she chuckled.

"I am Yusef," he frowned. Did she not remember him?

"Whatever you say, knight." Olena spit a mouthful of water in his direction. It fell very short of him, but she grinned impishly nonetheless.

"Come," he motioned his hand, not sure he liked the way she said the word 'knight'. It didn't exactly sound like a compliment. "It's time to get out."

"No," she sighed, again rinsing her mouth and spitting. "I'm not finished."

"Come on," Yusef said. "Seriously."

"Oh, seriously?" Olena giggled, shaking her head. "Well, seriously then, you'd better tell those boys over there that the show is over. I wouldn't want to come racing out and startle them into manhood too quickly."

Olena jerked her finger to the far tree line and twirled herself in little, playful circles. Yusef frowned, instantly seeing what she meant. He saw a head pop back behind a large trunk. Giving a gruff wave of his hand, he shooed them away. A pack of obnoxious boys ran off into the forest, laughing.

"See," Olena piped up with an impish grin. "They've had me trapped for sometime."

Yusef looked at her. She didn't seem all that concerned by it.

"The medic warned that you shouldn't spend too much time in the sun today. The injection he gave you can make you sensitive," Yusef said, delightfully eyeing her pale flesh and eager to see it more fully.

"Nice try, knight," she called, swimming forward. She came up closer than before. Droplets of water clung to her face and lips, as she said in low murmur, "You're just trying to get a show of your own."

"If I wanted a show, wife, I would go swimming with you," he answered without flinching.

That brought Olena up short. Merely looking at his bold figure was doing strange things to her insides. She wasn't sure what she would do if he were to touch her with it. It wasn't like he had festival rules to stop him. Remembering how he denied her, after she practically threw herself at him, helped to cool her ardor some--but not much.

Olena waited to see if he was going to turn around. When he didn't, she shrugged, and stood in the shallow water.

Yusef shivered, his eyes devouring her naked, wet flesh before he could stop them. A smile came to his dark features. Olena rang out her hair, twisting the locks before throwing them impishly over her shoulder. In the sunlight, he noticed that her nether hair was a darker shade of her fiery locks. If he was a weak man, he would have swooned right there or in the very least fell to his knees to worship at her feet.

"Finished?" she asked, her hands moving to her hips as she didn't even try to cover herself from his view.

"No," Yusef answered sheepishly, pleased that she was not shy before him. "You're shivering. Come here. Let me warm you."

"No thanks, knight," she tossed glibly. "I'm warm

enough."

"Then come cool me for I am hot," he murmured, a devilishly wicked grin coming to his features. Olena stepped forward, her mouth opening to return a quick jibe. Instead she gasped, flinching as a sharp pain shot up her leg from her ankle.

"Ah, great," Olena said with a hiss of irritation, looking more annoyed than hurt as blood trailed over her anklebone. She blinked heavily, her eyes rolling in her head as she fell forward into Yusef's arms.

Yusef caught her naked body against his chest. His wife was unconscious. The telltale red and black tail of a *givre* was trailing off into the water. Cursing, he easily lifted her up into his arms and carried her quickly back to his home. Laying her naked body on the bed, he immediately called for a medic on the intercom. His home was directly linked to the mountain palace.

Olena's body was limp as he dried her off and she didn't make a sound. He noticed that her skin was turning a subtle pink. Yusef continued his tender administration even as he cursed at her unmoving body for being too stubborn to listen to him. His stomach still tight with worry, he gruffly called for the medic to enter when he heard his respectful knock

"*Draea Anwealda*," the same medic who had taken care of Olena the day before said. Seeing his wet patient wearing one of Yusef's large cotton shirts, he frowned. Her skin was slowly becoming redder, burning angry and bright.

"Tal," Yusef acknowledged with a curt nod. He stepped back to let the man work.

"This is a stubborn one you have," Tal answered, shaking his head. He sighed heavily, setting down his bag and delving through it with precise hands. Instantly finding the instruments he needed, he asked, "She went out in the sun, didn't she?"

Yusef nodded. "She did."

"And swimming, I see," Tal said, taking a reading from her arm. He shook his head slightly. "I take it she met up with a *givre*?"

"Yes," Yusef said, his brow furrowing. "She just fainted from the bite."

"It probably wasn't the bite that did it. It was more than likely the shock of the *givre's* mild venom combined with the medication I gave her for her allergy," Tal said, injecting his patient with a new medicine. Olena jumped in surprise, instantly opening her eyes.

She glanced first at Yusef and then at Tal. Seeing his needle, she jerked away and swung her arm in defense. Tal easily avoided being struck as he pulled away with a frown.

"Ow," Olena gaped at the pain the movement caused her. She flinched to feel her hot back. Accusingly, she glared at Yusef. "Ugh, what'd you do to me, knight?"

"You did it to yourself," Tal answered with the authoritative tone of a doctor scolding a wayward patient. He took another reading from her arm and nodded to himself in satisfaction. Almost distracted, he ordered her, "This time, try to stay out of the sun for the rest of today. You should be fine by tomorrow."

"What about those burns?" Yusef asked, nodding at her face. The flesh had turned to a bright, angry red and even her eyes had a pink tint to them.

Tal frowned at her. Lecturing, he said, "I should let you wait it out to make sure you've learned your lesson … but, I'll give you a lotion to put on it. It too should be fine by tomorrow. Take it easy, drink plenty of water and you should be just fine."

Olena would've talked back, but her eyes burned from sun exposure and her skin felt as if she was indeed being burned at the stake. Wearily, she nodded to get the man to stop reprimanding her. If he hadn't just helped her for the second time, she would have beaten him senseless for his tone despite her sore body.

The medic turned to Yusef, handing him the cream and some eye drops. "Give her those pain pills if she will take them. I can't give her any more injections just now until the other medicine filters out of her system."

"Thank you," Yusef said. When Tal had gone, he turned to Olena and shook his head. "You really should listen to me when I tell you things."

"Could you save the lecture until a little later, knight?" She closed her eyes. "I'm kind of hurting right now and that doc just made my head swim with his yammering."

"You going to take the medicine this time or should I just

leave you?" he asked. He tried not to smile at her fighting spirit. Was this woman just bent on doing herself harm? He had half a mind to tie her to the bed and keep her prisoner, just to save her from herself.

"I'll take it," Olena murmured sheepishly.

"All right, that's more like it," Yusef said, glad to see he wasn't going to have to pin her down like the night before. Wearily, he went to get a glass of water and the pills. When he came back, she hadn't moved.

After she dutifully took her medicine, Yusef touched her back to help her lift up. She was hot. "Let's get this tunic off and I'll get some of that cream on you."

"You'd like that, wouldn't you, knight," she mumbled. But she did not fight him when he lifted the shirt off her skin so she could lie against the cold sheets. A weak moan left her lips as she shut her eyes and concentrated on being very still.

He slowly rubbed the cream over her burning body, careful to keep his touch light. Almost instantly the worst of the burn faded and she felt better. She moaned again, but this time it was in pleasure. His light touch was creating a burn all its own and if she wasn't so sore, she was sure she'd have jumped on top of him.

Yusef's body lurched in answering response to the soft, feminine sound. He quickly held his passions at bay. Now was definitely not the time.

Peeking at him through red eyelids, she said, "You're quite the nursemaid."

Her tone was soft and he could tell by the look on her face that those simple words were the closest she had ever come to saying thank you. He smiled at her, running his hands over her face. His palm whispered over her lips and she shivered uncontrollably.

He wished to have his fingers linger on her skin, but he forced them to make quick work of his task. She was in no condition to receive his attentions. When her body was soothed and healing, he placed eye drops into her eyes, and covered her with the sheet.

Olena smiled wryly at him even as the pain pills kicked in, forcing her to fall into a drug induced sleep.

Yusef stood, looking down at his wife. Her face was rosy, but not as bad as a moment ago. Her hair was tousled around her head in damp tangles. Slowly, he shook his head and picked up his discarded tunic.

Retrieving a brush from the bathroom, he brushed her hair out for her in quick strokes, doing what he could to keep the locks from drying into knots. Then, going to the kitchen, he made himself breakfast and ate alone at his dining table.

The second day of his marriage was spent as the first, tending to an unconscious, sick wife.

\* \* \* \*

That evening when Olena awoke, it was to find Yusef at the end of the bed. His feet were resting on the edge, the legs of his chair pushed back to tilting. He was studying her intently.

Olena flushed. She was lying on her side. Her arm was beneath her head, the other bent seductively over her waist, and the top sheet was pulled down around her hips to reveal her breasts and stomach.

"Don't move," Yusef ordered quietly. He worked his hands, but she couldn't see what he was doing in the dim light. His voice was low and hoarse as he spoke. Something in his tone kept her from sitting up.

"What are you doing?" Olena asked. Suddenly scowling, she asked, "You're not … ah, playing with yourself, are you, knight?"

Yusef chuckled, before saying honestly, "No, wife, I would rather have you play with me."

Olena blushed. Yusef couldn't see it in her rosy features.

"So what are you doing then?" she asked. Her lids dipped slightly over her vivid green eyes.

"I'm carving you," he answered. Suddenly, he dropped his feet. The chair righted itself with a thud. Yusef set a small knife on his dresser. "You can move now."

Olena sat up, pulling the sheet to hide her breasts.

"How do you feel?" he asked, standing.

"Ah, fine. I've been through worse. But I tell you if that Tal comes at me with another shot, I might lay him out good."

Yusef chuckled. "I would be nice to him if I were you. He's saved your life twice."

"Oh." Her frown deepened, and she grumbled, "I'll send him a card or something."

"That won't be necessary," Yusef laughed. "Tal sent the bill around this afternoon."

"You're a nobleman," she said, defensive. "I am sure you can afford it."

Yusef's smile faded and he watched her carefully. "What makes you think I am a nobleman?"

"The servant at the festival called you lordship and this house," she answered smoothly. Olena waved her hand absently around them.

"Ah," Yusef mumbled.

"You're not, are you?" Olena grinned. She gave a delicate shrug, causing the sheet to dip low. "Oh, well, a girl can't have everything."

Yusef chuckled at her teasing tone. She didn't seem too terribly disappointed by the idea of being married to a common man. That pleased him. His dark eyes lit slightly to see the curve of her breast. He'd been staring at her body for about an hour without being overrun with passion. But, now that she was awake and moving, his body wasn't so easily tempered back.

"I much prefer not to be nobility," she mused honestly, confirming his assumption. It would be harder to sneak around the galaxy if her picture was published everywhere as a missing ladyship.

"What's your name?" Yusef's tone was light, though the question had been driving him mad.

Olena just smiled widely. Yusef knew she wasn't going to tell him. She was enjoying teasing him too much.

"Well, knight, are you going to let me see me or what?" Olena demanded, holding her hand out and wiggling her fingers.

Yusef tossed the carving at her. Olena caught it with both hands. To his delight, she dropped the sheet to do it. Quickly, she righted it, pulling back to lean against the dragon headboard. She held the sheet down with her arms.

Olena was amazed. The carving looked exactly like her, though the edges were a little rough and unfinished, down to the way her hair curled by her temples when she let it dry naturally. It was perhaps one of the most beautiful things she had ever had done for her. Hiding her emotions, she forced a sardonic tenor to her words, as she expressed, "Typical."

Yusef raised a brow. Olena tossed it back at him.

"You made my breasts bigger," she explained, acting as if she didn't care. Inside, she shook violently. This game was getting too close.

*Remember your scar,* she thought, trying to remind herself to be strong. As he watched her, she saw hurt flicker in his eyes before he hid it. Or did she see it at all? Did she just feel it as if it was her pain, too?

*Great,* she thought, growing bitter. *I must have hit my head when I fainted. Fine pirate I'm turning out to be.*

Olena had a feeling her whole body would be marked with cuts before this ordeal was over--especially if he kept looking at her with those liquid, shifting eyes of molten gray.

Yusef pulled open a dresser drawer and dropped the sculpture unceremoniously inside. Olena's eyes nonchalantly followed the movement. She itched to get a hold of the sculpture. She wanted to keep it.

"Are you hungry?" he asked.

"Mm, starving," Olena admitted. Without thinking, she added, "You wouldn't happen to have any clothes I could borrow, would you?"

Yusef glanced at her bags on the floor.

"Oh, yeah, that," Olena forced a giggle, lying easily. "The guys grabbed the wrong luggage and I've been stuck with those things the entire trip."

Yusef detected the falsehood and said nothing, merely nodded.

Olena cleared her throat, not sure how much this dark warrior suspected. She didn't dare mention the gun. "So, you got a shirt or something I can use?"

"Sure," he said, opening another drawer and tossing her a light cotton shirt. Olena slipped it over her head. Then, crossing to her bags, she pulled the first one open and looked inside. Digging, she found her bra and underwear and slipped them on under the shirt.

Yusef watched quietly. When she turned back to him, she inquired, "Pants?"

"Sure," he said again and, leaning over, he opened a bottom drawer.

Olena's head angled slightly to the side, admiring his firm backside. She straightened and affected a look of perfect innocence before he turned around. Yusef tossed her a pair of light cotton pants and she slipped them over her hips.

"If you stay out of trouble," he said. "I'll take you to the dressmaker and pick up some things that fit."

"Dressmaker?" Olena wrinkled her nose in instant distaste. "No thanks, knight. I'll stick with these. I don't care if I never see another dress again."

"That might not be possible. Dresses are required formal attire at the palace. If we ever go there, you'll have to have a gown."

Olena shuddered dramatically.

"Come on, wife, you must be hungry," he urged.

"I don't care if we never go to the palace," Olena mumbled under her breath.

Yusef led the way to the kitchen, hiding his grin at her distasteful look.

## Chapter Six

Yusef and Olena spent the evening chatting about non-important things until it got late. She still refused to tell him her name, though he had tried several times to trick her into revealing it. Seeing her yawn, Yusef urged her to bed to get her strength. Yusef again spent the night alone on the couch.

Yusef found, to his pleasure, that his wife had a quick wit, an open laugh, and a smile that curled easily to her beautiful lips. Her bold emerald eyes shone in constant mischief, even when she did nothing. It made him curious to discover everything about her and at the same time perfectly content to know nothing.

To Olena's horror, she kind of liked him too. His dark eyes penetrated as if they saw everything and would reveal nothing. His smile was slow to come, but it was genuine. He was laid back, easily taking her jokes in stride, never taking offense at her impishness. He was polite and mannered. He treated her like a lady.

Since she had recovered almost completely by the next morning, aside from a slight glow to her skin that wasn't at all unappealing, he took her to the village like promised. Yusef wore one of his casual black tunics with the dragon emblem and Olena wore his baggy clothing over her thin frame. Several people stopped to stare at them. Olena grinned widely at the attention, not discouraged one bit. Yusef watched her reactions from the corner of his eyes.

Olena thought the Qurilixen village very nice--for a barbaric race in the middle of nowhere. Her *husband*--she giggled silently at the thought – appeared to have the biggest house on the edge of town. It was a short walk from the village, but a pleasant one through a wide open road of forest. Yusef didn't touch her as they strolled, but there was an easy companionship between them carried over from the night before.

The village was spread out over a valley, close to where the marriage festival had taken place. Olena noticed that all the tents had been taken down. The field looked barren without them.

"That is the royal palace," Yusef said pointing to a giant mountain at the edge of the village.

"Where?" she asked, craning her neck to see up the spiraling of cliffs to the top.

Yusef laughed, his accent becoming thick, as he said, "The mountain."

"I don't see a palace," Olena answered skeptically. Again she moved her head around to eye the mountain.

"It's hidden inside the mountain," Yusef replied. "There, see where that man just came out of the side?"

"Yes," she drawled. It almost looked as if he came straight out of the rock.

"That's the front gate. The four Princes designed it to be an impenetrable fortress," he continued. "This village is under the protection of the House of Draig."

"Smart," Olena mused wryly, not noticing Yusef's frown at her sarcasm. "That way, their noble backsides are protected while all these villagers take the brunt of the enemy's wrath." She shook her head in distaste. "No matter where I go, royalty is all the same."

A courtyard surrounded the palace fortress, close to the surrounding valley. Olena detected men on a long practice field to the side, training for battle.

"Why do they train in human form?" she wondered aloud, nodding her head. "Wouldn't it make sense to shift for battle?"

"It would," Yusef answered, still stunned by her easy acceptance of his Draig form. "But not all the wives know of the shifting and --"

"You don't want to scare them by a show of battling dragons," she broke in with a nod. "Too bad. I would really like to see that. Though, judging from some of the women on the journey over, it's a very wise idea you don't do it."

Yusef chuckled quietly to himself.

"So what do you call yourself anyway, dragon?" she asked, continuing on up the path.

"Do you so easily forget, wife? I am Yusef," he answered.

Olena chuckled and rolled her eyes.

"What is your shifted form called?"

He smiled. "We are Draig."

"Named after?" she prompted, unable to help her curiosity. She glanced at him from the corner of her eyes, getting a chill. She wondered if he could change for her on command. She'd really like to get another *closer* look at him in Draig.

"It means dragon," he admitted. Her chuckle joined his. "Draig is what our race is called, the name of our royalty, what we become when we shift."

"Ah, inventive," she teased.

"Easy to remember," he teased back.

The villager's homes they passed were constructed of rock and wood, so that even the poorest of families looked to be prosperous. The village roads were of the rocky earth, smoothed flat and even. They were built with almost a military perfection of angles. The village itself was kept immaculately clean.

The Draig wore light linen tunics during the day much like the royal family, but minus the dragon crest and finer embroidery. They were a happy people, hard working and honest. Some smiled and waved at Yusef, looking up from what they were doing as he walked by. Olena noted that he appeared to be well liked.

To the dressmaker's dismay and Yusef's amusement, his wife refused to be measured for a dress. Olena picked out several cotton pants and tighter feminine shirts with built in bras. She piled them haphazardly in her arms before changing behind a screen. When she finished, she tossed the borrowed clothes back at Yusef and smiled brightly.

"Now this is more like it," she beamed, stretching her arms around. Seeing a pair of black leather boots in her size, she grinned. "I'll take these too."

Before Yusef could protest, not that he would have, she was pulling them on her feet. The dressmaker gathered the impudent woman's discarded pile of clothes and clucked in dismay as she folded them and placed them carefully into a bag.

Olena frowned at the dressmaker in turn and grabbed up the remaining pile and dumped them on top without folding. The dressmaker's old face contorted with irritation and she began scolding Olena with a pointed, wrinkly finger. Olena, who couldn't understand one word of it, smiled back and nodded with eyes wide with mischief.

The woman tossed up her hands and waved Olena away. To Yusef's surprise, Olena leaned over and kissed the old woman's cheek. The dressmaker's face rounded in shock and she shook her head, continuing to shoo Olena from her store. Though, this time, she was smiling as she did so.

Yusef waved a boy over and pressed a coin into his hand along with the bags. After asking him to deliver the purchases to his house, he continued to give a tour of the village, stopping to speak to a few people in his language. Bright blue birds flew overhead, singing in a strange low shrill. An animal Yusef called a *ceffyl* grazed in a fenced yard. It had a fat elephant body and a single horn mounted on his head. As she watched, it hissed at her.

The villagers eyed her curiously, but did not speak directly to her. Olena didn't take notice. Seeing a boy laughing and pointing at her to his friends, she wondered if he was maybe one of her peeping toms. She blew him a kiss and he nearly fell off his perch in shock. The boys ran away from her laughing, calling out words she didn't understand.

"Ach, Yusef!" came a loud cry. "I was just on my way to see you."

Olena jolted in surprise to see a giant of a man with two blackened eyes lumbering towards them. She remembered him vaguely from the morning after the Breeding Festival. The man had an easy smile, full of a mischief that Olena could readily relate to. Instantly, she liked him.

"Agro," Yusef mused so Olena could understand. "Meet my wife."

"Hello, wife of Yusef," Agro said. He audaciously winked, showing that he too remembered her. "Have you a name of your own?"

"She's not saying," Yusef said, with a carefree shrug. "Maybe you can get it out of her."

"I wouldn't dare," Agro said gallantly, grinning at her like a fool. "A little mystery never hurt a woman none. Don't you dare tell him, lass, at least not for the first fifty years or so."

"I wouldn't dream of it," she grinned, liking this beast of a man's easygoing nature.

Yusef groaned. It was quite possible she wouldn't.

"In fact, I don't want to know it either," Agro declared

amiably. "I'll lie awake at night thinking about it. It will be good for me."

"Don't let your wife hear you say that," Yusef said, unconcerned. Everyone in the village knew that Agro was more than taken with his bride. He was a doting fool and didn't care who saw it. But, try to tease him about the obviousness of his undying affections for her and he'd knock your skull in.

"I didn't say I'd be lying awake alone," he grinned with a meaningful raise of his brow.

"Why were you looking for me?" Yusef asked, turning slightly serious. "Has anything happened?"

"No, nothing like that." Agro's natural grin widened. He latched his hands to his waist and rolled back on his feet. Eyes narrowing, he stated seriously, "Word is you just got back from a hunting trip to the north last week."

Yusef laughed, already knowing where this was going. Agro had a terrible fondness for roasted *baudrons*. They could only be found in the north hunting grounds.

"That I did," Yusef said, nodding.

"Catch anything?" the big man asked, throwing out an overconfident smirk.

"Maybe," Yusef said, drawing out the suspense. He had already planned on asking the man over, as he did after each hunting trip.

"Could be you want some company over at that house of yours to help you cook it?" Agro asked.

Olena watched the friendly ritual in vast amusement.

Yusef scratched his chin. "I don't know. I might have to clear it with the wife first."

Agro turned his wide green eyes to Olena. Gazing through his bruises, he said, "My most gracious lady, would you do me the honor of telling your husband to take his--"

"Hey." Yusef growled in mock battle.

"What?" Agro asked with an innocent shrug.

"I already have several times," Olena said. "The stubborn man won't listen to me."

Yusef threw his hands in the air, not able to fight an attack on both fronts. Agro's hearty laugh bellowed over the village, drawing smiles from around them.

"You don't need an invitation from him, Agro," Olena said. "You just come on over and we'll help ourselves to whatever is in the fridge."

"Now, you've done it," said Yusef with a mock frown of horror. "This giant will eat us out of house and home."

"Ach, off with you," he said to Yusef, before bowing over Olena's hand. "Tonight I'm a guest of the lady."

"You'd better bring the wife," Yusef said. He casually draped his arm over Olena's shoulders and steered her away. "I might need help keeping you at bay."

"She'd love it," Agro announced, grinning like a fool. "She's pregnant again, by the way."

"Congratulations, friend," Yusef called, beginning to walk away. "Why don't you bring the boys with you?"

"Will do," Agro called, saluting gallantly as he trotted off to the practice field.

"I like him," Olena said. She liked the feel of Yusef's hand on her shoulders, but artfully got out of his embrace with the pretence of picking a yellow flower from the ground. When she stood, she moved out of his reach.

"I could tell," Yusef mused, disappointed by her withdrawal. He had felt her stiffen under his arm. When he looked at her, the easy companionship of the morning was gone from her guarded features.

"How many sons does he have anyway?"

"I think, with Cordele pregnant again, this will be twelve," he answered, turning his steps back home. "Do you need anything else while we're here?"

"No, I'm fine," she answered in distraction, before continuing, "Is that normal? I mean having so many children in one family?"

Yusef grinned, seeing where she was going with this. "Agro has been, ah, blessed with good fortune. Although, anywhere from two to six sons is more normal a size for our families."

Olena was quiet.

Yusef bumped her playfully in the shoulder and asked, "Why? Do you want to try and beat him?"

Olena paled at the thought of one. Vehemently, she shook her head. "No. I don't want any."

His spirits were dampened a bit by her heated denial and they made the journey home.

\* \* \* \*

Later, Olena found herself covered in a dusting of flour

and elbow deep in Qurilixen blue bread dough. She scowled at Yusef as she kneaded and formed the blue dough into loaves.

"I didn't realize I would have to do all this," she grumbled, hating it. "Can't we get a servant or something?"

Yusef, who was helping her prepare for her guests, laughed. "You're the one who invited him."

"Yeah, one man," she said. "And he offered to help cook. You had to go and invite the entire brood."

"It's improper for a woman to extend an invitation to a man and not his wife and sons. I was saving you an embarrassment."

"Who says I would have been embarrassed? Anyway, how was I to know?" she mumbled. She finished forming the last loaf. They weren't perfect, but they would do. Yusef grabbed them and put them in the brick oven over the low fire.

Olena jumped up to sit onto the countertop. Brushing a sweaty strand of hair off her forehead with the back of her arm, she sighed. "I'm about ready to go get bit by another snake so I can lay down and let you do this. In fact, I think I'm coming down with something."

Yusef chuckled. "Come on, you're almost done."

"You need a better job," she continued to complain, though she smiled shyly at him. She pushed gracefully back on the counter, making her legs go straight. Her feet stretched over the edge, dancing absently in the air. She leaned forward towards her toes, folding over in half, to stretch out her back. Laying her head on her knee, she finished, "Then you could afford to pay someone to do this stuff."

"That's why I got married." Yusef eyed her flexibility with interest. Instantly, he though of different ways he could bend her body to accommodate him.

Olena gasped, scowling at his comment as she sat up, until she saw him wink playfully at her.

"Oh," she screeched, taking a handful of flour and flinging it at him. Yusef ducked, laughing.

Olena grabbed another handful, launching it at his dark head before he could stand. It hit him and showered over his shoulder to the floor. Flinging his hair up as he stood, he lurched for her. To Olena's surprise, his eyes flashed with gold and he hopped from the floor to the countertop in one swift motion, landing effortlessly on his feet. Bending at the knees, he crouched over her.

Olena's breast heaved in excitement of his power. A timid laugh left her lips to see his flour dusted tunic.

"You think you're smooth, don't you?" he chuckled wickedly.

Olena's heart skipped. Yusef leaned forward. Before she could react, he kissed her swiftly. Her chuckling died down against his lips. His eyes bore into hers with a fevered heat. He grabbed her forward and lightly kissed her, pulling back as her mouth opened, trying to follow his.

"I know I am," she murmured. Her voice came out husky and inviting, unintentionally changing the meaning of her words.

Yusef's gaze dipped down over her neck. Her flesh did indeed look as smooth as cream. Finding a little freckle all by itself on her collarbone, he grinned. Unable to resist, he dipped his head to flick his tongue over the dot. Olena shivered at the soft, wet caress.

"May I judge for myself?" Yusef's hand lifted to touch her flesh, teasing her neck. "Mmm, soft."

He leaned over and sniffed where his hand had been. Olena's breath caught. She was mesmerized.

"So sweet," he murmured in a tone that vibrated along the indent of her neck. He tasted her again, licking her racing pulse. "Delicious."

"Ah-haa."

"Will you let me taste more, I wonder," Yusef said, as if to himself. "Will you let me dine on your flesh?"

Olena felt the back of his hand brush along her inner thigh, lightly moving towards her heated center. It was clear what he wanted a taste of.

Yusef's eyes trailed down, devouring her with their liquid gold. Olena nearly swooned. Seeing his shifting eyes, she shivered. Part of her trembled, scared of what he sought of her. Her eyes dipped to his mouth, wanting him to continue with his wicked words and knowing she should make him stop. Her desire flooded out of every pore, calling to him. It was the one thing she allowed to flow freely between them.

Yusef suspected it was because it was the one thing she didn't know how to mask. He growled, giving her what her aching lips craved. His head dipped forward to sip from her parted offering, stealing her breath inside him, tasting of her passion. He held her head in his hands, dipping his fingers into the red silk locks to force the kiss deep.

Olena whimpered a soft sound that he captured within him. Her body was on fire and every thought left her but one--the thought of being possessed by him. Impatiently, her hands pulled at his tunic, trying to strip it from his shoulders.

Yusef broke his kiss long enough to toss the shirt aside. As he came to her again, her eyes were half closed in pleasure. His arm brushed the counter, sweeping the bowl to the floor. With one powerful movement, he spun her around to lay on the hard countertop, trapping her beneath his weight.

Olena gasped, liking how easily he could control her body. He tossed her around, as if she was a feather. His dark, glorious chest loomed before her, haloed in light from the ceiling dome. Raven locks reached down, tickling her cheek before his kiss could meet her lips once more. His tongue came to her mouth, dipping inside as his hardened body wished to.

Soon she was urging him on top of her, spreading her legs to fit her knees beside his firm waist. He pressed his hard arousal into her, his pelvic bone grinding through their clothes. They shared a groan of passion. Olena's eyes popped open only to lazily fall. Yusef refused to stop the onslaught to her senses. A torrent of pleasure ran rampant through her limbs, making her weak and strong at the same time.

His hands were on her shirt, pulling it up, revealing the lacy bra cupping around her. Without bothering to remove the lacy undergarment, he pulled it down beneath the soft globes. Yusef devoured a nipple with his mouth, biting and licking her with growling delight.

"Ahhh, yes!" Olena's back arched as gratification shot through her limbs. She couldn't stop. Her body melted beneath his strength, folded beneath the determination of his will. His hips were rubbing against hers, making her mad with anticipation. Her legs wrapped around his waist, gripping him tightly. She stretched her fingers into his hair, pulling him closer. Their bodies heated behind the layers of constricting material. Their breath came out in tortured gasps.

Yusef's hands went to his hips, intent on freeing himself and her. Her movements were as eager as his and he couldn't slow. Later, he promised himself to enjoy her more fully, but for now he needed to end the torturous aching in his loins. He needed to find his release.

Just as he was about to free his straining manhood, he stopped. Gulping, he lifted up. Leaping off the countertop, he pulled his stunned wife with him.

Olena blinked in surprise as she flew to the floor. Her legs almost fell out from beneath her, protesting their use and she had to grab the counter for support. Her breasts were bared, budded and reaching. She swallowed in confusion to see Yusef straightening his pants.

Yusef grabbed her by the shoulders and pulled her in front of him to adjust her shirt. He covered her breasts from view just in time to see the front door open.

Olena gasped, as she heard their company coming in. Before turning, she righted her bra beneath her shirt. Yusef's naked, panting chest rose and fell before her. His scent was still in her head, stinging her body. A loud laugh sounded behind her. Flushing with embarrassment, she turned to see Agro and his very slender wife.

Agro knowingly looked around at the mess the couple had made of the kitchen. His mouth opened to speak. Olena's eyes narrowed in warning and she held up her finger to him.

"One word from you and I'll do more than blacken your eyes," she threatened.

Yusef laughed, not embarrassed about being caught making love to his wife--even if it was on his kitchen counter.

Olena nodded to the amused woman at Agro's side, "Cordele, I presume?"

Cordele nodded, speechless. She was a slender, pretty woman and didn't look anything like Olena would have guessed. For someone who was pregnant with her twelfth child, she didn't look a bit overused.

"Nice to meet you," Olena answered Cordele's nod with dignity, pushing her tousled hair from her face. "Now, if you would excuse me."

Olena walked to the bedroom and shut the door.

"Handled like a true Princess," Agro murmured in serious approval when she couldn't hear. Yusef grinned charmingly. He leaned over to pick his shirt up from the floor.

"If you like we could leave," Cordele began.

"Ach, no!" Agro denied, reaching a hand around her to playfully cover his wife's mouth.

Cordele giggled as she freed herself from Agro's teasing embrace. Eyeing the countertop, she considered, "Maybe we should eat outside then."

Yusef laughed louder, nodding his head. He didn't bother to put his shirt on, instead balling it in his fist. "Where are the boys?"

"Ah, we left them at home to fend for themselves," she said with a dismissing wave.

"Good thing, too," Agro said. "I'm not sure I want them bearing witness to this little stunt of yours."

Cordele hit her husband on the arm. Tilting her head to Yusef, she suggested, "Why don't you go check to make sure she's all right? We women are not so used to your bold ways when we first arrive. I'll tend to the bread."

Yusef grinned, jogging across the house to the bedroom door. He didn't need to be told twice.

"Ach, now, make sure you don't take too long in there, or else we might eat without you," Agro yelled, earning him another solid punch from his loving wife. His brow lifted in innocence. "What did I say?"

\* \* \* \*

Olena gulped for breath once she was alone. Her whole body trembled, not only at being denied, but with mortification of what she had almost done. She was glad Agro and Cordele had stopped it, for she hadn't been going to. To her everlasting shame, she had been willing to let Yusef have her--completely. She had given no protest.

Taking the bandage off her arm, she studied the thin pink scar and shuddered. She would just have to be more careful in the future. Obviously, when Yusef kissed her with those expert lips of his she was a goner. Jack would be doing angry somersaults in his grave if he saw her now.

*Hell*, she thought. *It's possible he's done dug himself out and is coming to get me for betraying the code.*

"Wife?" Yusef asked softly, as he had taken to calling her. Olena jumped, not having heard him enter. Yusef shut the door behind him. He looked down to where she poked at her scar. Olena immediately dropped her hand. "Are you okay?"

"Fine," she said. Yusef's tanned muscular chest was not helping her inner struggle against him. Her nerves jumped, more than ready to resume where they had left off. She glanced at the bed, swallowing. Weakly, she lied, "I was just going to get cleaned up a little."

"They didn't mean anything," he said, thinking she maybe was embarrassed about being caught. Yusef went to the dresser, grabbed a clean shirt, and pulled it on.

"I know," she shrugged, unconcerned. She was angrier at herself for needing them to break it up. If she had to cut herself a hundred more times, she wouldn't be letting that happen again. Suddenly, the memory of Yusef's naked body in the tent came to mind and she had an unbidden fantasy of him leaning her into a wall and taking her standing up. Taking an unsteady breath that was abnormally loud, she asked, "Why don't you go start the fire pit? I'll be out in minute."

Yusef leaned over to kiss her but she turned her face away. Instead, he stroked back her hair, trying to hide his disappointment. His low accent washed over her, as he spoke softly, "I'll see you in a minute then."

\* \* \* \*

"What I'm wondering," Olena announced looking pointedly across the soft fire at Agro, who was cuddled next to his wife. The meal of roasted *baudrons* was long since finished. It was a fine, dark meat of whose origin Olena was too scared to inquire into, being as she had seen some strange creatures around the village.

They were enjoying the soft light of the evening dusk. The haze would last all night, not getting nearly as dark as the festival evening had been. The men and Olena drank a stout beer and Cordele had water.

Lifting her glass, Olena continued in a murmur, "Is who darkened those daylights of yours?"

Agro chuckled, looking meaningfully at Yusef. Yusef, who was slowly watching his wife get tipsy, smiled at her unique turn of phrase. It seemed the more she drank, the less refined her speech became. Stretching his legs before him, he leaned back.

"Ach, lass." Agro grinned at Yusef, unable to help getting a jibe in at him and his brothers, especially knowing Yusef wouldn't dare answer back and reveal who he truly was. "It was one of those boorish Princes, the oldest Ualan. He was a bit testy at the festival and needed to vent."

"Oh!" Olena said, sitting straight. "So he took his frustrations out on you, did he? Isn't that just like royalty?"

Yusef grimaced, his eyes pleading with Agro to let the matter drop. Agro, who had grown up with all four Princes and could rightly call them all friends, did not heed the Prince's plea. His eyes gleamed with mischief.

"Isn't it, though?" Agro shook his head sadly. "I should sic you on them, firebird. I bet you could teach them a thing of two."

"I bet without the title behind his name and in a fair fight, you could have taken him easily," she insisted. "I bet you'd lick all four of their royal ass--anyway."

Yusef flinched. Cordele hid her face in Agro's chest and giggled uncontrollably.

Agro lifted his glass to her and drank to her words. Yusef set his on the ground and shook his head, refusing to toast his insolent friend.

"So are you a dragon, too?" Olena hadn't seen any shifting tendencies in him. "Can I see?"

Agro choked on his drink in surprise. Blinking, he looked at Yusef who simply shrugged his shoulders and threaded his hands behind his head.

Olena glanced at her husband. Oh, but he was handsome. She had been trying to avoid looking at him all night. His long, thick legs stretched out towards the fire. His lap just begged for her to climb onto it. His mouth parted at her attention, his eyes flashing wickedly to yellow, noting her mild obsession with the shifting. Fire shot through her and she finished off her drink in several gulps.

"Ach, enough of that," Agro grouched.

"I could say the same to you." Yusef was annoyed by the interruption. The stream of fiery passion her face had unwittingly sent to him was almost more than his denied body could take. "What with number twelve --?"

"Music," Cordele broke in lightly, pushing up from her

husband's arms. "Yusef, would you mind playing for us? It has been awhile."

Yusef smiled at the request and nodded his head. Olena blinked in surprise, but said nothing.

"I'll go with you," Agro said, feeling his wife push at his back.

When the women were alone, Cordele said, "You know, the royalty around here aren't that bad."

Olena eyed the woman. Was she related to the royal family? "You're not … a Princess, are you?"

"No," Cordele laughed.

Olena relaxed and was again able to breath. For a moment, she'd been scared the royal family would get wind of her insults. That was definitely some attention she didn't need.

"I am a dance instructor," Cordele said. "In fact, I am teaching one of the new Princesses a traditional Qurilixen dance in a few days. Prince Ualan came by and asked me just this morning."

"He probably felt bad for doing that to your husband. You should have told him to stick it."

Cordele chuckled. "To tell the truth, my husband probably deserved it."

Olena conceded to the woman's insight with a nod. "I can see how you have your hands full with him."

Inside Yusef pulled his *gittern* from the back of his closet and strummed the instrument's four strings to make sure it was in tune.

Agro leaned on the frame of the door, watching quietly for a moment. When Yusef finished, he said, "She knows about the Draig, yet you say nothing about who you are. Why?"

Yusef wasn't surprised by the prying question. He let a sad line edge his mouth and said nothing.

"Ah, so you think she would reject you if you told her," Agro stated.

"You heard what she thinks about royalty. What do you think would happen if I told her she was a Princess?" They spoke in their native tongue so they couldn't be over heard by the women. "There is no rush. If she asks me directly, I'll answer honestly."

"Your wife has fire, friend, that's for sure," Agro said,

leading the way back to the patio. "I don't envy you that. My Cordele is as sweet and mild as any man could dream of wanting in a woman." Then wiggling his eyebrows wickedly, he added, "And, oh, can she dance. Drives me nearly insane each time I see her practicing. I swear that's why she's pregnant more often than not."

"I always did like fire." A soft smile grew on his features as he thought of the challenge his nameless wife presented him. "Now, if only I could figure out what to call her."

Agro laughed, "You know, the same thing has been bugging me."

## Chapter Seven

Soft music filled the evening as Yusef played a simple melody. Olena watched him, enthralled by the movements of his fingers as they plucked deftly at the strings of his *gittern*. He really a man of many talents.

Yusef felt Olena's eyes on him. He turned to her, not breaking the song as he winked in her direction. Her heart skipped. Olena flushed and looked away. Her glass was empty and so she couldn't hide her face in a drink, as she had done all night when Yusef's heated gaze found her. Her mouth went dry each and every time.

Olena unconsciously rubbed her arm. It didn't hurt anymore but she could feel the thin scar through the cotton shirt. Maybe if she had been left to suffer it out, her resolve against her dark, barbaric husband would have been stronger.

Cordele suddenly stretched, yawning as she blinked. Olena knew what was coming, they were going to leave. Almost in a panic, she wanted to stop them, but she couldn't think of a single excuse to make them stay.

"Firebird," Agro began. "Thank you for inviting us, but I think I should get my lovely wife home to bed."

Cordele yawned again, nodding in agreement. "It was a divine evening."

Yusef's song finished and he stood. He began kicking out the fire pit. Olena gulped, growing nervous. She had seen the look in Yusef's eyes all night. He was going to want to finish what they started in the kitchen. She couldn't let that happen.

Yusef said his polite goodbyes as the couple took their leave, arm in arm. Olena dutifully invited them back sometime. They waved, saying they would love it. Cordele's head leaned against Agro's shoulder and he swept her into his arms and carried her down the path with ease. Olena could hear the woman's soft laugh as she hugged to her husband's chest.

Olena watched them disappear until she was left alone

with Yusef. She swallowed nervously, forcing a yawn though she was hardly sleepy.

"Well," she lied. "I think I'm going to go get some sleep. I'm a little tired myself."

Yusef grinned as she walked into the house. He finished smothering the fire and, grabbing the *gittern*, he followed her inside. Latching the door behind him, he set the instrument on the couch and left it.

Olena blinked, turning to look at him when he moved to follow her. The oddly seducing call of his song stayed in her head. She was besieged by him, captured.

"What are you doing?" she questioned, though it wasn't necessary. She saw the intent clearly in his devilishly handsome eyes. When his eyes flashed with his power, her heart leapt to dangerous speeds.

Yusef smelled her desire building, knowing his beastly side excited her. He let his eyes shift again, changing to liquid gold. To his pleasure, she visibly shivered. Slowly, he took his tunic from his shoulders and tossed it aside as he stalked forward. "I'm going to pick up where we left off."

"I'm too tired," she lied, thrilled by the look of him. This was a man who wouldn't be dissuaded with words. Even the pulse in her neck jumped at the sight of him. Weakly, she protested, "Maybe we should hold off."

His nostrils flared. "Your body says otherwise."

Olena shivered. Now that wasn't fair. She backed up as he came for her, realizing too late that he was forcing her into the bedroom. She looked around in panic, angling her body away from the bed.

"You're nothing but a race of horny men," she cried in dismay, trying to stop him and getting ready to fight off his pounce. Her legs wobbled with the influence of her drinking. "Invest in a pleasure droid or something, would you?"

That brought a dangerous smirk to his face. "You didn't seem to mind my attentions at the festival or this afternoon in the kitchen. In fact, I think you actually begged me to --"

"I was drugged at the festival," she defended weakly. She swayed lightly on her feet, tipsy from drinking. "I didn't --"

"I thought you said you knew what we were doing and could fight the drug," he shot in return, enjoying the game she played with him. He had no problem playing the hunter. Her mouth tried to deny him, but her body ached for his with each and every fiber. It called to him, begging even when her lips would not. Every fiber in his body answered the call most willingly.

"I was faking it," she lied boldly. Yusef laughed. Olena's hand went automatically to her hair searching for the firefly pin. He laughed harder.

"You didn't think I would let you have that back after what you did, did you?" He shook his head, his hair spilling forth over his shoulders.

"It doesn't matter. You couldn't make me feel if you tried," she spat as a last resort, hoping he'd back down. She really should have known better. His eyes lit up in delight and it was too late to take the words back. The challenge had been issued and he took it gladly.

Olena pulled back in alarm as he sprang forward with a supernatural speed to lift her into his strong embrace. Her feet dangled off the floor. Her arms were pressed into her sides. She struggled to get free but he was too strong. He let her feel the power his body had over her. He let the press of his erection mold confidently into her soft thigh. Her nipples hardened against his heat.

*Don't let him kiss you. Don't let him kiss you,* her mind chanted. Her lashes dipped over her eyes. *Don't let him ki – oh.*

Yusef's lips took hers in rough possession, stealing her breath from her lungs. Her battle was lost the moment she tasted him. She returned his kiss full force, without hesitation, groaning her aching need into his mouth. She found hold in his hair, dipping her fingers into the softness of it. He smelled like wood smoke. He tasted like mint. And he felt every inch of hard man.

Yusef was amazed at how easily her defenses crumbled to him. As Olena melted into his arms, he set her down on the floor. Her mind might hate her for it, but her body was all his and he had every intention of staking full claim. She instantly ran her hands to explore his chest. She tweaked her fingers over his nipples, causing a spasm of intense longing to course through him. He growled a low, barbaric, animalistic sound of domination and appreciation.

"I need you now," he said into her flesh. Before she knew

what was happening, Yusef worked her clothes from her body, pooling her pants around her ankles. He moved his fingers to her moist center, spreading her open so he could test her. She was more than ready for him and the discovery made his body ferocious in its response.

Olena jerked. Her hips bucked against him. Her eyes grew wide in shock of the sensations he stirred with just his hand.

Emboldened as her fingers roamed over his neck for support, his lips let her mouth free so he could incinerate her breasts with his lapping kisses. Her head fell back, arching into his expertly sucking lips. He held her to him. He licked the sensitive tips hard, feeling her quiver beneath the stroking touch of his hand to her heat.

Olena let her hands experience every niche of his body, roaming his back and strong arms, claiming his chest, his neck, his stomach. Hitting the barrier of his pants, she searched eagerly for the drawstring ties to free him and worked the material from his hips.

Yusef growled in enthusiasm and did not slow his assault. As her hand grabbed hold of his arousal, he slipped a finger up inside her. She nearly screamed, squeezing him painfully tight in surprise. Yusef tried to pull back, wanting to study her face. Her body flexed unyieldingly against his finger. She didn't let him look up, letting go to grip his head to her chest.

"Yusef," Olena breathed, panting hard. The one word stopped his inquiry.

He took his fingers from her so that his hands could cup her backside, firmly squeezing the cheeks as he lifted her up. Olena felt herself land on the top of the dresser. Her eyes opened weakly.

Across the room she could see Yusef's strong backside and legs in the mirror. She saw the length of his black hair over his commanding shoulders as his face buried in her chest to feast on her breasts. Her eyes stared at every inch of him, liking the way his muscles flexed when he moved. His hips artfully slipped between her thighs, forcing them to spread for him.

"Ah," she said, a soft feminine cry of approval and submission. Her head tilted back on her shoulders, spilling her hair back over the dresser. She grabbed onto his arms.

He took up her hips with his hands, forcing her to come forward as he prepared to enter her.

"Tell me your name," Yusef demanded hoarsely, stopping his kisses to listen for her answer. "I must have it."

"Olena," she breathed, unable to stop the pant of honesty and too far gone with desire to care. His body was poised on the brink of conquering her. His manhood was readied, aimed for possession.

"Tell me you want me," he commanded, edging to the brink of her. "Admit that you want me."

Olena froze. A thin shred of sanity enveloped her. Her body fought the clarity of her mind, but Yusef was demanding an answer. It was an answer she couldn't give.

His erection pressed intimately to her opening. She grew scared, never having let things get this far before. She could feel his hard tip digging slowly, into her. It was too fast. What was she doing? She needed time to think, to reason. He was going to hurt her with his size. Horror stories, told to her by her pirate father, came to mind in a rush.

Just then, her hand fell on the dresser. She felt the bump of his carving knife. Her mind latched onto the most familiar--fighting. She gripped around the handle of the small blade. Her chest heaving, she lifted it to his manhood. She had to buy herself some time, time to think and reason these strange feelings out.

"No," she ground out. "I don't want you."

Yusef froze. Her chest heaved for air and her breasts dipped before his astonished eyes. The blade hand quivered. She accidentally nicked him on the side of his shaft. He pulled back defensively, getting his most sensitive area away from her attack. His body pulsed with the agony of denial. But, as he looked down, he saw the blood tricking where she had dared to cut him. Rage overtook the passion in him.

Olena stared at him wide-eyed from the dresser top. Her lips were stiff and her eyes burned with tears she couldn't shed. She was unable to move. Her legs were like jelly from his touch.

Shifting furiously, Yusef went straight for her. His body hardened. His face pulled forward as his eyes glinted with a dangerous golden fire of outrage.

Olena wielded the blade in automatic defense. It scraped

*Michelle M. Pillow*

against the thick armor of his dragon chest, but did little harm. Wrenching the blade forcibly from her hand, he tossed it aside. Then, taking her up, he threw her onto the bed.

Olena landed, knocking her head on the carved headboard. She blinked, blindly trying to scurry off the other side, away from him.

Yusef pounced on top of her. She screamed, wildly thrashing against his barbaric hold. It was no use, she couldn't get free. Tears came to her eyes, shaming her as they spread fearfully over her cheeks.

Yusef, who had no intention of taking an unwilling or treacherous woman to bed, growled at her. His talon like claws ripped the pillowcase near her head, spreading feathers over her sweating body. They stuck to her flesh. Grabbing the strips, he tied her hands to the bed.

Olena trembled. He was too powerful to fight.

"Please, Yusef," she cried, desperate and scared. "Please don't do this."

The whimpering words, so unlike her voice, brought him up short. His face shifted, but his human form was no less threatening than his Draig one had been. His hard face came into hers, as he spat, "I wouldn't take you now if you begged me, wife."

Olena gasped at what she read in his eyes as hatred. She felt his blood smearing her thigh. She shook. Her arms weakly worked to loosen her restraints. It was no use, they were too tight.

"What will you do?" Olena asked, past the point of terror. To her amazement, he stayed true to his word and got off her. She laid there stunned.

"I'll do what the law requires me to do," Yusef said, ignoring the cut on his bloody member. His tone was hard. "You are in chastisement, Olena, if that is even your real name."

Olena shivered but didn't dare to speak. Whatever this chastisement was, it didn't sound pleasant at all. At least not the way he spat it at her.

He snarled viciously.

"What will you do?" she asked, her tone wavering again when he continued to stare at her naked form. At that moment, her body didn't seem to be bringing him pleasure.

"Law requires that I punish you. If I don't, the royalty you love so much will have to decide a fitting punishment for you in my stead." Turning, Yusef grabbed his pants and jerked them on with angry, stiff movements. "They might have been more lenient on you, until it was reported what you say about them."

"What is this chastisement?" she mumbled faintly, still shaking.

"You will have to obey everything I say."

"And if I don't?" she asked, fearful. His jaw hardened at the question.

"You die." Yusef knew it was not likely his family would choose death for her, but she didn't need to know that. Let her fear for her life for now. The King and Queen would more than likely concede to anything he planned.

Yusef closed his eyes to her and turned his back. He couldn't face her right now, not in his turbulent mix of outrage and denied passion. He needed time to cool down and to think logically before he did something he regretted. He had to go tend to his wound.

"I'm a slave," she said in alarm, as he walked out the door. Her words were barely a whisper.

Yusef heard her whimper and glanced back as the door shut between them. In that moment he almost relented completely. He saw the scared eyes of a woman staring out at him from her emerald gaze--vulnerable, afraid.

Olena's eyes rolled wildly in her head as she was left alone. Her feet dug into the mattress to push up beneath her. Her limbs shook violently as she worked her mouth to gnaw at her wrists. It was high time she got off this forsaken planet.

* * * *

Yusef stormed up the path to the village, barefoot and bare-chested. It was dark and the village was quiet so none saw his ascent to the castle. He left Olena tied to the bed, not knowing what else he could do with her.

The wound to his pride was much larger than the wound to his manhood, but he thought it best to tend to the latter. He grimaced darkly. It wasn't exactly the area he wanted an infection setting in.

What the hell was wrong with his wife? She had wanted him. He was so sure of it. Her reaction to him had been real. Or had it? Her wetness against his hand had been real. The heat in her and the scent of her body's longing had been real enough, too. Women couldn't fake things like that. Was he so blinded by his own passion for her that he'd missed her deceit?

Slipping through the raised gate, he ignored the guard who stood to salute him. He strode down the passageway, stopping at the medical wing. Grabbing a laser off the shelf, he ignored the sleeping woman at the front desk. Quietly going to the back room, he lowered his pants and sealed his wound up. It stung horribly, but he didn't pay it any mind as he left the laser where he'd found it and went in search of his father.

He didn't have to look long. His father was in his royal office, looking over a stack of papers. Glancing up, he was surprised to see his son.

"Yusef," the King began, but the greeting died from his voice when he saw Yusef's dark look and half-naked state.

"I came to inform you that my wife, whose name may or may not be Olena, is sentenced to chastisement," Yusef stated, using the more comfortable feel of their native tongue.

"Chastisement?" the King gasped, answering in kind. He stood from his desk and came around it to study his son's dark face. "She attacked you? She tried to kill you, harm you?"

Yusef nodded wearily.

The King grew worried. His eyes turned very sad. "Have the Gods cursed you with … with a touched bride, my son?"

Yusef laughed bitterly. "No, she is very much sane, father."

"Well, that's something at least," the King said in gruff relief. "What happened?"

Yusef growled and took a seat. Resting his wrist lightly over his knee, he waited for his father to sit back down behind his desk.

"She turned my carving blade against me," he stated.

"And I assume she drew blood if she is in chastisement. Could it have been an accident?" the King inquired hopefully. "Maybe she did not know you were there."

Yusef's eyes only darkened. "She took it to my erection

while we…. It was no mistake."

The King cleared his throat, knowing how hard such an admission was for his son. It would be for any man.

"Was she, ah, perhaps playing a game? She seemed very spirited," King Llyr admitted. "Spirited women are known for their … *bedroom mischief.*"

"It was no game," Yusef said, frowning.

"Was she scared?" his father asked, trying to understand.

"I didn't smell fear on her," Yusef answered, rubbing the bridge of his nose. Although, that hadn't been the particular scent he was looking for at the time. "I did smell desire for me--potently. But she turned. I don't know what caused it. I doubt it was fear. That little firebird is afraid of nothing."

"By royal decree, it is decided," the King said as a mere formality. "I agree to leave her in chastisement as long as you see fit."

Yusef nodded. "It will be until she admits she wants me as I want her."

"A good plan," the King said, pressing his fingers to his lips. He suddenly smiled. "The sexual tension might be what she needs to bring her around."

Yusef's body lurched despite himself. Such a punishment would undoubtedly be worse for him than for her.

"I'll inform your brothers," Llyr said, "but it will go nowhere else."

Yusef nodded in appreciation, knowing law stated all the royal males of age had to know of such things. He was sure he was in for a few good-natured jibes at the hands of his brothers, but he didn't care at the moment.

"I was planning on having a celebration in about a week to coronate the Princesses. There have been rumors that our brides have not been seen within the castle and I fear the Var have spies within our walls. If anything, we need to keep up the appearances of being a united family."

"She is stubborn," Yusef said in dejection. "I do not know if a week is enough time to make her behave. You saw how defiant she can be and she hates royalty with a readily voiced passion. Bringing her out in public might do our reputation more harm than good."

"I understand," the King said thoughtfully. "As long as your other brothers can get their brides to come around, yours can be excused. All saw how she bled on the morning of your wedding. I'll have your mother make something up and spread it through the maids. At least those gossiping girls are good for something. Give me a manservant anytime over a bunch of chattering women. With all the headaches they cause, I can see why our genetics weeded them out."

Yusef chuckled. It was an old joke, but still extremely fitting.

"Are you staying in your wing tonight?" the King asked.

"No," Yusef felt somewhat better after speaking to his father. "I'll go back to the Outpost. I have Olena there tied to a bed. She may be a bit angry right now and I don't want her screaming awake the neighbors."

The King chuckled. "Fair enough. I know you'll deal with it fine. You always had a level head son. It works fairly well with your hot temper."

\* \* \* \*

Yusef was tired when he arrived home. His ears turned to listen at the bedroom. All was quiet. He hesitated, wondering if he should just leave it alone for the night. Then, unable to stop himself from checking on her to make sure she was unharmed, he went to the door.

Knocking lightly, he called, "Olena?"

He was answered by silence.

"Olena?" He pushed open the door and looked at the bed, expecting her to be there. She was gone. His heart skidded to a stop. Her restraints looked as if they had been chewed through.

Seeing dots of blood on the floor, he frowned. He instantly went forward and dipped his fingers into the drying spots. Ribbing his fingers, he sniffed. It was hers.

Fear gripped him and he shifted, running with a supernatural speed out the back patio. He picked her scent faintly on the wind. She had been gone for some time. Dashing into the forest, he ran down the red earthen path, flying past the east pond. His bare feet sped over the crushed leaves of the forest floor. His eyes, enhanced in the form of Draig, scanned through the trees, searching her out.

She was nowhere to be found.

\* \* \* \*

Olena crouched low against the tree branch, rubbing dirt on her skin to mask her scent. The dusky colored night wasn't that easy to see by in the dense forest and she wasn't sure how far she could get before Yusef got home. Already her lungs rapidly inhaled with a sharp pain and she knew her weakened body wouldn't be able to run much further before she collapsed. It didn't help that she'd stepped on the carving knife in her haste to get out of the bedroom, cutting her foot.

To her horror, she heard a dark growl that sounded suspiciously like her name coming up the path. Yusef hunted her. She looked around wildly, as she crawled to a nearby tree. Hoping to find shelter from the path, she gripped the rough bark, hiding from view. She held her breath, trying not to move lest he hear her. Closing her eyes tightly, she swore she'd never be a man's slave again.

## Chapter Eight

Olena waited a long time, pressed against the tree, too afraid to move. Only when her arms ached to the point that she couldn't any longer lift them did she fall to the ground. Her body was weary, but she couldn't stay this close to the path. She couldn't risk Yusef making another pass by her.

Desperately, she clutched handfuls of mud and rubbed it into her already covered skin. Hopefully that would mask her scent long enough until she could figure out what to do. She'd never expected Yusef to turn like he did--from caring husband to slave master. When he didn't get his way, his nature had shifted as easily as his body. But she should have known to expect it. Hadn't Jack always said men only wanted one thing from her--her complete and utter submission?

Seeing a low branch, she went for it and climbed, working her way higher into a tree. Then, finding a particularly large perch, she lay against the trunk, high off the ground. She closed her eyes, taking a little rest. She would just wait out the dusk. Then, when her body was stronger from sleep, she would move on.

\* \* \* \*

Yusef ran nearly five miles knowing there was no way she could have gotten any further than that with the time she had been afforded, especially since she was bleeding. To his relief, he didn't detect any Var within the trees as he had first suspected and feared.

It was nearly morning and he knew the village would be waking in a few hours. Turning back, he took his time backtracking. He sniffed the air, trying to get even the faintest hint of where she'd gone. He'd lost her scent completely about four miles back, only to pick it up and lose it once more.

Jogging, barely out of breath, he turned back to human form. His eyes looked through the darkness for her, scanning the endless trunks of trees. He hated to do it, but he needed to get help. There was too much forest for him to search alone. Picking up his pace, he made the trek home.

\* \* \* \*

Olena was trapped. It was dark, so dark in the tight cargo port. Suddenly, little fingers came through her cage's grating. They were so tiny, those hands, just like hers. Her body was cramped and hurt so badly. They only let them out once a day to relieve themselves or else the cargo would smell too bad. It was impossible to stand in the little cage. They had been there for months, crunched in those little containers, stacked on top of each other.

Twisting around, she heard crying. The tears were nothing new in this hellish place. They always heard crying. There were so many children trapped in the crates. Soon the man with the needle would come to poke them with it, shutting them up when he could take their tears no more.

"Olena," came a faint call, followed by a sniff and a trembling whimper. "Olena?"

Olena continued to twist, trying to touch the little hand. When she managed to get around, she felt for the fingers. They were as cold as ice.

"Sage?" Olena squinted into the darkness to find her sister. A face pressed into the grate. It was an exact replica of her face staring back at her as if from a mirror.

"Olena," Sage whimpered. "I'm scared."

Olena nodded, too afraid to speak. She couldn't remember very well what happened next, not even in her dreams. She had only been five. Sage must have started to cry because the man came with his needle.

"Quiet!" he'd yelled in his stiff voice, slamming her sister's cage.

Sage cried louder, screeching in exhaustion and fear.

"I said quiet!" the man bellowed.

He must have been drinking, because Olena remember the smell of him. It was the smell of ale coming from an unclean body, stale liquor curling from his pores. When he moved to hit the cage, he missed and tripped over his feet.

Sage screamed louder in fright. Suddenly, all the children started screaming at the top of their lungs. Sage's cold fingers dug desperately at the grate, trying to get to her sister through the unforgiving metal.

Olena held quiet, clutching desperately to her sister's hand, whispering to her to be quiet, not to yell. The man in the black coat hollered for silence but the other children wouldn't stop. Their voices rose like a chorus of horror-- echoing for an eternity in the memory.

"Olena," Sage whined fearfully.

Sage's cage was open and she was being torn from Olena's five year old hands. There was a loud crash and then deadly silence. The children stopped screaming. All she heard was her heart beating in her ears.

The man stumbled off. Someone sniffed to her right. Slowly, Olena edged around.

"Sage," she had called weakly when the man was gone. Her sister never answered, would never answer her call again. When Olena finally got to the front of the gate, she saw Sage's lifeless eyes staring back at her. She'd been thrown into the sharp hook on the metal wall, dying instantly.

Olena's eyes jerked open with a cry. Her body flailed, forgetting where she was. The nightmares hadn't been that real for a long time. Suddenly, she blinked. Screaming, she realized she was falling from the tree limb. Her arms and legs flailed in the air. It did no good. She landed on the ground with a heavy thud.

* * * *

Yusef heard the bloodcurdling scream and his heart nearly stopped. Turning, he shifted once more and ran full tilt into forest, following the direction of the sound. It didn't take him long to discover Olena on the ground. Her eyes were rolling in her head but she did look at him.

He was surprised when she recognized him in his Draig form, as she said softly, "Knight."

She was covered in dried mud from head to toe. That was why he could only get faint traces of her scent. She had masked herself with the forest. Even as he cursed her, he bowed to her cunning mind. Stepping over crushed leaves and yellow ferns, he knelt by her side. Her arm was broken, the bone jutting out from her skin.

She stiffened when he pushed her hair from her face. The red flames were muted by the red mud of the earth. Yusef shifted to human form and lifted her up.

"You foolish woman." He swore he heard her chuckle.

"You won this round, dragon, but I'll escape you," she said on a faint breath. Her voice was strained. She fought

against the pain in her arm as he slowed to step over a
fallen log in his way. Gritting her teeth, she said, "I'll be no
man's slave."

"No, Olena," he swore, as he carried her to the path. She
grunted in pain, blacking out. "You will never be my slave,
but you will never escape me. You are mine."

* * * *

Tal placed his hands on his hips, eyeing the mud caked
woman wearily. He'd given her something to help her sleep
while he set her bone. Her arm was fixed and the bleeding
stopped. With little else to do, he put it into a sling and said
she would recover.

Setting his medic kit on the dresser, he turned to Yusef
and said, "I'm leaving this here for emergencies. I've got a
spare kit at the office. With as many accidents as your wife
is prone to have, I suspect you'll need it."

Yusef nodded his weary thanks.

"As you to, Prince Yusef, you must get some rest," Tal
said. "This exhaustion won't do you any good."

Yusef glanced at Olena to see if she heard the title. Then,
seeing she was out and realizing she couldn't speak their
language anyway, he relaxed.

"I will," he said, "just as soon as I get her cleaned up."

"Fine," the medic said. "I, myself, am going back to bed.
Do you want me to report this for you?"

"No," Yusef said. "My parents have enough to do right
now. I'll tell them of it later and I would appreciate it if you
didn't say anything to anyone else."

"Can't," he said, "It's the doctor-patient privilege.
Besides, I am loyal to your family, *Draea Anwealda*."

"*Draea Anw...?*" Olena murmured, blinking her tired
eyes. For a moment, caught in the haze of pill induced
sleep, she smiled to see Yusef's face. "What is that?"

"Dragon Lord," Tal answered, matter-of-factly. "It's what
we call him and his brothers."

Olena blinked, looking at Tal and then to Yusef. She
yawned, her eyes drifting, "I didn't know you had
brothers."

She was again out.

Tal frowned at Yusef.

"She must be out of it," he lied, urging the man politely to
the door.

"That's understandable," Tal said. "With as much as she's been through lately, a bit of bed rest won't hurt her one bit."

Yusef let Tal out of the house, thanking him for his loyalty and for the medic kit. It would undoubtedly come in handy.

When he went back to the bedroom, Olena was asleep. He was too tired from his night of searching and worrying to bathe her. So, instead, he crawled into the bed next to her. He pulled the covers over their bodies and held her in his arms. Holding her to his chest was the only way he could guarantee she wouldn't try to leave him again.

Closing his eyes, he kissed her dirty temple. She jerked and mumbled incoherently. Yusef sighed, not opening his eyes, as he murmured into her soiled hair, "Whatever am I going to do with you, firebird?"

\* \* \* \*

When Yusef awoke that late afternoon, Olena was still sleeping in his arms. He crawled wearily out of bed. Finding a blood gauge in the medic bag, he checked her. Her levels were fine considering her state. He sighed in relief.

She had awakened him a few times during the day as she tossed in her nightmares. He frowned, thinking of it. Calling up to the castle on the intercom, he asked his mother to send a maid down to clean the house and cook dinner. Mede inquired after his marriage. By her tone, Yusef guessed his father had told her what had happened. He lied and said everything was going well. She seemed relieved to hear it.

Then, crossing the hall to his bathroom, he ignored the waterfall style shower in the corner as he began filling the porcelain bath with warm water. It was a large tub, not as pleasant as a natural hot spring, but it had jets in it and was big enough to fit both him and Olena.

Once it was filling, he crossed back over to the bedroom. Olena hadn't moved. Gently, he lifted her up and stripped her of her dirty clothes. Then, as she lay there naked, he gathered the clothing up and put them in a pile by the door. Next, he striped his own clothing and set them atop her dirty ones. He grabbed a fresh change for both of them and put them in the bathroom, shut off the water, and went back to gather his wife.

As he carried her in his arms, she stirred. Blinking in confusion, she tried to look around. Her movements were still weak.

"Shhh," he whispered when she would speak. "We're just going to take a bath, nothing else."

She must have believed him because she settled into his arms and closed her eyes. Yusef carried her to the tub, shaking her gently so she'd wake up.

"Try to stand for a moment," he urged, setting her on her feet in the water. Steadying her, he was careful of her arm, which he had taken out of the sling. He stepped in behind her and slowly lowered her into the water.

Dazed, she looked at him, her eyes rolling slightly in her head. Her mind was numbed by the medicine the medic had given her. She didn't fight him, as he settled back and pulled her to sit between his legs. Though she was beautiful, there was nothing passionate about the way he held her. Even he wasn't such a monster as to think about sex at such a time. Marriage wasn't only about slaking desires. Although, that was a benefit he would like to someday have.

"Olena, can you wake up?" he asked. She murmured contentedly and opened her tired eyes. "I'm just going to help you wash your hair. I'm not going to hurt you."

"I know," she murmured. Her eyes closed once more.

Yusef's heart sang at the gentle admission. It was something at least.

He gently washed the dirt from her hair and then his. Rinsing was awkward, but he managed. Next he rubbed her skin clean and leaned to pull the plug with his toe.

Through the haze of her fogged mind, Olena had been enjoying the attention of his gentle hands. She blinked feeling the water drain and a chill set in. Looking at him, with big emerald eyes, she said, "Not yet. Can't we sit in here awhile longer?"

How could he not comply with such a simple request? He drained the dirty water and slowly refilled the bath with fresh, adding bubbles to it in an attempt to please her. She smiled, not opening her eyes. When he leaned to turn off the water, he felt her snuggle into him.

"Olena," he whispered against her wet hair.

"Mm?"

"Who's Sage?" he asked. She'd been saying the name over and over in her sleep.

"My twin," Olena answered without thought. Her legs absently stirred against his as she burrowed deeper into his protective embrace. He was so comfortable. She could think of nothing else. The texture of his moist skin was enfolding her. His gentle, yet overpoweringly strong, hands were stroking her side. "She's dead."

He stiffened. He couldn't imagine losing one of his brothers. He stroked her temple and she seemed to enjoy it because she nestled and turned into his chest to lay her cheek by his heart. She held onto his neck, absently twining the raven locks with her fingers. Her other hand skimmed close to his waist. His body stirred at the caress, but he forced his passion to behave.

"What happened to her?" he asked softly, desperate to know anything about her. He rubbed his hand over her back, stroking her wet skin beneath his palm as he tried to relax her tired muscles. She moaned in contentment as he glided his fingers over a hip.

"My father traded us for a cheap drug and to pay off a gambling debt about a month after our fifth birthday. We were sold into slavery." She stirred, laughing bitterly. Smacking her lips, she said, "Damned drug couldn't have gotten him very high. It was a cheap knockoff of the good stuff. I tried it some years later. It didn't do a thing."

"And that's how Sage died, as a slave?" Yusef stiffened at the admission. He could feel her pain, but he couldn't keep from asking. He might never get another opportunity to have her open up like this.

"No," she murmured, half awake, half asleep. "The man with the needle threw her into the wall because the other children were crying."

"Did anything happen to the man with the needle?" he asked.

She shuddered under his palm and he stroked her hair. She froze, keeping her fingers on his hair, before gently moving her hand to feel his heartbeat.

"He was the first man I ever killed." Olena sighed, feeling comfort in his nearness. A soft moan escaped her. He massaged her lower back, causing her words to tumble forth without thought. "I was ten. Jack had taken me in and showed me how."

*Ten? By all that was sacred!* Not even their warriors in training learned to kill at the age of ten.

"Jack bought you as a slave?"

"No, he was a pirate. He raided the ship of the man who bought me. He was trying to sleep with me when Jack found us. He killed the man and took me in. He was my new father before he died. He said he liked my spirit 'cause I didn't even cry when he stabbed that man and got blood all over my body. He said I would be a great space pirate and he was right. I'm one of the best. Jack left me his crew."

*A pirate!* That was almost harder to believe than the story of her killing a man at the age of ten. He thought of the gun and the ID's. Suddenly, all her rambling nightmares made sense. There was no other possible explanation for it. His wife was a pirate. With her nestled so trustingly in his arms, her voice a soft murmur against his chest, he knew she couldn't have thought to lie. She'd probably never remember any of this.

"I won't let any of them hurt you." His grip on her tightened. "I won't let them take you away. You're safe here."

Olena snuggled against him. "You'll have no choice, Yusef. If the demons come for me, you'll not be given a choice."

Yusef would have denied the claim a million times over if he thought it would do any good. He was never given the chance. The servant his mother had sent was knocking at the front door. Reaching behind his head, he pushed the intercom button to tell the man to come in. He had a whole cleaning crew with him and they set to work tidying his house.

By the time he finished intercoming instructions, Olena was fast asleep in the tub. The simple conversation had worn her out completely.

Yusef sat for a long time, holding her and contemplating what she had said. Her words only brought him more questions he couldn't answer on his own. If she was a pirate, then why was she here? Why did she come to be a bride? Was she trying to escape her former life? Was she running?

Somehow, he managed to get them both out of the water and dried off. Dressing was another slow-going affair as was combing their hair. Then, lifting her back in his arms, he pulled her close to his chest and pretended to ignore the servants who watched the couple cross back over to the freshly made bed.

Yusef, aware of their eyes on him and mindful of what his father had said about the Var spies, propped her arm over his shoulder. She smiled and made a noise of contentment. Lightly, he kissed her lips and she moaned. She stirred, holding the back of his head. The servants chuckled quietly to see the loving interplay between the Prince and Princess.

Closing the door behind him, Yusef set Olena on the bed. She blinked and her hand reached for him when he pulled back. Her expression was soft as he took her hand in his.

"Stay with me, knight." She yawned, as she barely woke up enough to make the request. "Just stay."

Urging him beside her, Olena rolled over and snuggled her back into his chest. She held his arm around her waist, her fingers interlocking with his.

Yusef sighed, content to hold her while she slept. Her wet hair tickled his face. His stomach growled as he smelled the food being prepared in the kitchen. He ignored his own discomfort, choosing instead to stay by her side.

Olena slept contentedly, oblivious to everything he did for her.

## Chapter Nine

"What do you think you are doing?"

Yusef blinked. Olena was wide awake, her eyes clear as she stared at him accusingly. Her tone had been deadly hard in its anger. She fought his hold on her waist and he lifted his arm to let her go. She scooted away from him, trying to get away by crossing to the far end of the bed.

She tried to sit up and flinched when she used her bad arm. Cradling it to her chest, her glare darkened. "What did you do to me?"

Yusef had heard the servants leave earlier and so he knew they were alone in the house. Her flaming red hair had curled around her temples in little ringlets, waving beautifully down her back. The soft cotton of her tight black shirt was crumpled from lying down. Her cheeks were a wonderful sleep-warmed hue of pink. Her lips pressed together as she eyed him and then herself.

Olena blinked, trying to figure out what was real and what was dream. She remembered running away from him. She remembered hiding. She remembered falling. The rest was vague, part dream world, part reality--part nightmare, part sweet agony.

"Don't look at me like that," Yusef said, growing a little hard at the accusations in her eyes. "I've been taking care of you."

"I don't need anyone taking care of me! I can take care of myself."

His brow rose in disbelief, as if to say, *Can you now?*

"I've done fine so far," Olena said, angling to stand from the bed. She clutched her arm more firmly.

"You'd have been dead three times already if not for me and we have not been together even a week," Yusef yelled, frustrated with her. All hope he'd felt at her drug induced softness was ripped away, leaving him bitter and very much alone. He'd wanted her from the first moment, had given part of his life to her, and she wanted nothing to do with him. She made that abundantly clear at every turn.

Then why did she choose him? She didn't even think, just ripped off his mask and chose to be his wife--no hesitation. Was this just a game to her? Did she not understand that his whole life was now wrapped up into her? He couldn't take it back, even if he wanted to. There would never be another woman for him. It was their way. When she broke the crystal, she broke any chance of him loving anyone but her. Even without the crystal sealing his fate, Yusef knew he would never have found anyone else.

Olena eyed him warily. What he said was true. He'd saved her life. But Jack had never taught her to apologize. Had never once said those simple words to her and she wasn't sure how to do it.

"I," she began. Pressing her lips together, she merely nodded her thanks to him. She didn't look pleased, or grateful, or angry. She just looked at him, studying his face. The words wouldn't come, so she simply asked, "Why?"

"You are my wife," Yusef answered just as simply, as if that one sentence would explain everything.

"You don't owe me anything. I never asked you for anything," Olena said carefully, almost defensively.

"I know, Olena," he murmured. Standing, Yusef scratched the back of his head. He was tired of this game of theirs. He wanted peace between them.

"And I don't owe you," Olena insisted, trying to convince herself more than him. Jack would be so disappointed in her. The thought caused her to stifle any tenderness she felt for Yusef. Jack had saved her. Jack had avenged her. And when he left her the crew, he had told her he loved her without ever having to say the words. It might not be perfect, but it was all she had.

Yusef nodded, turning away from her.

"So I can go?" she asked, wondering why the thought of freedom didn't sound so appealing.

Yusef turned to look at her. His eyes hardened. "No, you still have your chastisement to deal with. Law is law and I won't break it. Whether you like it or not, wife, you chose to be with me and we are forever linked because of it. If you don't like it, you have only yourself to blame. I am through trying to save you. It's like you said. I don't owe you a thing."

Yusef shut the door, closing her away from his sight. He

didn't want to see her right now. The pain was unbearable. He was at a loss. He didn't know what else to do. He didn't know how to please her, how to make her happy.

Olean's lips parted with a gasp and her eyes threatened to fill with tears. His words stung. She was still tired and lay back down on the bed. It was late and she was in no shape to continue fighting with him. Her gut ached in a way she couldn't comprehend. It was a feeling of loss, so intense that it rivaled the pain of her past with the pain of the present. Even when Yusef was unhappy with her, she wanted him. But it didn't appear as if he wanted her anymore. He was wiping his hands of her. Hadn't Jack always told her that a man's attentions would wane, but a loyal crew would always remain constant?

"Take what you want, Olena, take it with both hands...," Jack had said to her more times than she could remember. He squinted in quiet pondering, wrinkling out at the edges in lines so familiar to her even now. He'd give a gruff sigh, before adding, "...because no one is ever going to hand you a damned thing--including me."

Waking up in Yusef's arms had been the first real feeling of contentment in her life and it had scared the hell out of her. That's why she reacted in outrage. She didn't know how else to respond. For the first time in her life, she couldn't readily see what was in it for the other guy.

* * * *

"You have to be hungry," Yusef said from the door to the bedroom. It was morning and neither of them had slept all that well. Olena eyed him, cautiously.

He gave her no lenience. His face hardened. Her eyes danced with their usual mischief. He knew the mischief was a disguise, but he couldn't pry it apart again--not yet. He didn't have the energy to try.

Reacting on instinct, she spat, "What? Do you need your slave to cook for you?"

"You're not a slave," Yusef stated. "You are a wife."

"Same difference," Olena grumbled, starving.

"Think what you wish," he answered. "Your chastisement begins now. Everything you need to make breakfast is in the kitchen. Then I need you to clean the bathroom. The mud you covered yourself in is staining the tub."

"When exactly does this chastisement end?" she asked,

not liking the idea of cleaning. When she was little, she had made her way cleaning Jack's ship. She had sworn she would never have to clean another thing again. It looked as if she had been wrong.

"That depends on you," Yusef said. By the look on her face, he thought it would be a long, long time coming.

"What is the aim of this chastisement? To get me to say I'm sorry for injuring your manly pride?" A fake pout came to her lips. "To get me to part my legs for you, dragon, so that you may have your way?"

"An apology for drawing your husband's blood would be a beginning," he allowed, not falling for her baited contempt. "But the purpose is for you to realize what we have and what you will lose if you were to actually do me harm. The purpose, firebird, is to repent for doing it, to admit that you were wrong and that you were scared, and that you want me as I want you."

"I didn't want you. That was the whole point!"

"You did want me, Olena." Yusef's eyes took her in, glinting with golden slivers. Even like this, she was so ravishing it made him hurt. He took a step closer, stalking around the bed to get to her. Towering before her, he couldn't help saying, his tone low as it rolled over her in its thick burring accent, "I smelled it on you. I felt it on my hand when I touched you. I heard it in your voice as you moaned my name, begging me to take you."

Olena shivered at the bold words. Combined with the heated fire of his dark gray eyes, her desire for him aroused itself anew. He made a show of leaning forward to sniff at her. Olena reddened in mortification and turned her eyes icily away to stare at the wall, knowing he was sensing her body's treachery.

Not daring to touch her at the risk of losing his hard won control, he let his eyes flash golden. Whispering with a growl, he said, "Your body wants me even now."

There was no use trying to deny it so she said nothing. Her words were stuck in her tight, dry throat anyway.

"Today you cook and clean." Yusef pulled back as if nothing had happened between them. As he made his way around the bed, he said, "I keep your work light in respect to your injury. But do not think for a moment that I won't get more demanding should you slack in your duties."

Her eyes narrowed in resentment.

"Hate me if you wish, firebird." He reached the door. "But remember, you did this to yourself."

"Don't do me any favors, dragon!" she yelled at his departing back. He didn't answer her as he went to the patio door and slipped outside.

* * * *

Over the next several days, Olena cleaned things that didn't need cleaning, she cooked every meal, and she did it all in silence. She also discovered that chastisement also meant she couldn't leave the house or receive guests. Cordele stopped by once. Yusef told her that his wife was sick and sent her away. For Olena, who enjoyed an immense amount of freedom and loved the open air, the stifling prison walls of the house closed in on her until she wanted to scream.

During that time Yusef was a silent warden, all but ignoring her. The only time he spoke was to give her the morning's list of chores. Then, for the rest of the day, he pretended she wasn't there. She wished she could dismiss him as easily. But, everywhere she looked, she saw him.

Once he received documents from a courier. They looked very official. She dusted around him trying to get peek at what they said. All she saw was his emblem of a dragon on the top, before he stood without comment. He took his work to the bedroom and shut the door. Her curiosity nearly drove her insane and she cleaned with a fury, doing more than she was told to.

It was like that every day.

More often than not, she'd stare at him, wanting him to touch her, aching for one of his tender smiles or gentle caresses. As time went on, she remembered him bathing her with tender hands and taking care of her. She recalled telling him about her past, but couldn't be sure if she had done so. It was all so muddled it could have been a dream. He never once mentioned that he knew she was a pirate. Olena couldn't really ask him if he knew, without giving herself away.

Pride and pride alone made her obey his terms of chastisement. She refused to let him get the better of her. It became a mission to see who would break first and Olena swore on Jack's memory that it wouldn't be her.

The only time she almost wavered was when Yusef had sat out on the patio, practicing his *gittern*. He'd left the patio door open. The sad music drifted softly to her on the breeze. Even though he played for himself, she pretended that it was for her. The melody made her ache in a way only music could. She didn't go to him, instead testing out the rocking chair as she watched the door for movements of him. The curtain drifted slightly on the breeze and she would catch glimpses of the back of his head.

At night, he slept on the couch, leaving her to the bed. It was a sweet gesture--one Olena did not allow herself to read too much into. Nighttime was the hardest, when her body would fall into the warm comfort of the bed and sleep eluded her.

She imagined all the times Yusef had ever touched her in passion. His kisses, the feel of his body, it was all so very real. When she closed her eyes it was like he was right there, smiling at her in his devilishly handsome way, his eyes glistening like liquid gold. She'd wake up the next morning, drenched in sweat and aching from head to toe. The sweetness of those dreams was worse than the nightmares.

\* \* \* \*

Yusef watched his wife from the corner of his eye, poking a spoon into some soup she was preparing. She really wasn't a great cook, but he never complained. She sighed, her head tilting to the side in boredom.

With a hidden smile he thought that her restless nature might actually cave in before her stubborn determination did. He almost felt bad for her as she lifted a handful of diced vegetables and tossed them apathetically into the boiling contents of the pot.

Before he could stop himself, Yusef stood and walked to the kitchen. He sat on a stool to watch her, almost laughing to hear her singing to herself. She sighed in between notes, tossing another vegetable piece into her creation. Her voice wasn't bad, but her song was a brazen ballad praising the high skies, drunkenness, and debauchery. Undoubtedly, the tune was something she had learned from her pirate father. What was his name? Jack?

"...And we sail the high skies..." *plunk* "...looking for gold..." *plunk, plunk* "...looking for treasures that never..."

*plunk* "…grow old. The wind in our sails, lads, the stars at our feet…" *plunk* "…as we plunder for women, thick brown, and good mead." *ker-plunk, plunk, plunk.*

Olena dusted her hands on her apron, as she watched the churning water. How she longed for her crew! For a wide-open sea of stars with not a planet in sight! For a good starship chase through and past the horizon! For the feeling of freedom and trails of stardust! Her eyes welled with tears. She was homesick.

"What's thick brown?" Yusef asked quietly, when she just stared at the food, frozen. A wave of her sadness washed over him.

Olena forced the moisture from her eyes. She was amazed to hear his voice--any voice but her own--and it took her a moment to realize what he asked. With great effort, she managed to put the mischief back into her eyes.

"You shouldn't eavesdrop," she said into the boiling water, keeping her tone even so as not to give anything away. "It isn't polite."

Yusef felt her pain as if it was his own. She didn't have to say it. If she would only open up to him completely, she would be able to feel him the same way and the loneliness would leave her. Oh, but she was just too stubborn!

"I know. So what's thick brown?"

Olena smiled, laughing softly to herself. "Beer."

"Ah." He'd heard her use some interesting terms since he first met her. "Did Jack teach you that song?"

Olena stiffened. Her eyes narrowed and she forced a confused look to her face, trying to pretend she didn't know what he was talking about, as she turned to him. "Who?"

Yusef had hoped that if he gave her an opening to talk about her past she would. He could see that wasn't going to be the case. Quietly, he said, "My mistake. I thought you had said your father's name was Jack."

"Oh, Jack." She carelessly shrugged her shoulder. With a straight face, she lied, "He was more like an uncle. We weren't very close. I barely knew him."

"I see." Yusef knew better. If he had to venture a guess, he would say that this Jack person had been her whole world before he died. Yusef felt cold on the inside. He was jealous of a dead pirate named Jack, because the man owned so much of his wife's heart and loyalty. Yusef doubted he had any of it.

"You're speaking to me again." Olena turned and grabbed two bowls, carelessly ladling the soup into them. She put one in front of him and leaned on the counter to eat. "Does this mean you give up and I am out of chastisement?"

*She always does that,* Yusef thought. *Whenever the topic gets too serious, she tries to bait me into a fight. Not this time.*

Realizing she'd forgotten spoons, she turned around and grabbed a couple from a drawer.

"No," Yusef said at last, taking a hesitant bite. The meal was bland but edible. Hadn't his wife ever learned of spices? Getting up, he went to the cabinet and grabbed several little containers. Olena watched him with suspicion.

He took the bowls, emptied them back in the pot and began seasoning.

Olena came over, curiously studying what he was doing. "If you don't like my cooking, don't eat it, but you don't have to be rude."

Yusef smiled again and lifted the spoon. "Here, try this."

She furrowed her brows but leaned forward to sip. It did taste better than hers had. "Fine, it's better your way. But I never said I was a chef."

"Why are you always so defensive? Did I say anything?" He became aware of how close their bodies were. He'd almost gone insane the past several days, watching her bend over as she … ugh. It was agony. He didn't dare think of it now, not with her so close.

"Why are *you* so stubborn?" she asked.

"Me?" He laughed, amazed. "You're the one who won't admit that you were wrong and that you might actually like me just a little. That you're attracted to me and can't keep your hands off me no matter how hard you try."

"That's because I don't like you and I'm not attracted to you. I … I think you're ugly," she lied, blinking her way through it. "And … and you smell like … sweat."

*All right,* Olena thought. *So I am attracted to you, you don't smell like sweat, you are the most handsome creature I have ever laid eyes on and…ugh, curse you anyway, dragon.*

Yusef was smiling at her.

*No,* Olena thought in horror. He was laughing at her.

"You are absolutely, positively the most unappealing man I have ever had the displeasure of meeting." Olena drew closer to his mouth with each enunciated word. Suddenly, she frowned and pulled back. Was she flirting with him? She stiffened, waiting to see how he would respond.

"Is that so?"

"Yeah, that's so. And I know you are a dragon, but that doesn't mean you have to have the breath of one."

"So I have bad breath, too, do I?" Taking a step closer, he leaned into her face.

*All right, so his breath smells like mint,* she thought, trembling. *Think, Olena, think. This tactic's not working! Whatever you do, don't let him kiss you.*

"Are there any other complaints you would like to voice?" The words were low and sultry, giving her chills.

Olena thought about it, but it was hard to concentrate with him so close, especially when his dark eyes were studying her so intently. He was so close and he smelled so good, she wanted to run her hands through his hair and….

"No," she said weakly, breathless. "That's it."

"So I take it you are not ready to apologize?"

Lifting her chin with a bravado she did not feel, she said, "No. I have to stand by my convictions. I am not in the least attracted to you and no matter what you do, I'll never feel anything. When you touch me, it's like … like, oh, I don't know, having the dentist pull a perfectly good tooth without the numbing--unpleasant, irritating, and leaves you with a big hollow spot."

"I think it's time to go to the second stage of your chastisement."

Olena wasn't sure she liked the sound of that. "Second? Can't we just forget about it?"

"I'm sorry." He slowly drew closer and turned the burner on the stove off, never taking his eyes off of her. "The law is the law and no matter how distasteful you may find it…" Yusef shrugged, not finishing his words.

Olena's eyes widened in apprehension. "What's the second punishment, knight?"

"Tsk, tsk." His eyes flashed in darkening pleasure, as his steps forced her to back up. "It isn't punishment, firebird. It's chastisement."

## Chapter Ten

Olena tried to run from him. She took off across the floor, her bare feet pattering as she tried to reach the patio door. She almost made it too, before a strong arm wrapped around her waist and lifted her into the air.

"Oh!" she screamed. Yusef drew her back into his chest and held her tight. She struggled against him, trying to elbow him in the stomach. "Let me go, you stupid dragon!"

Yusef just laughed, as he hauled her kicking and screaming into the bedroom.

"I thought your kind didn't rape," She was outraged to be overpowered. Her arms flailed wildly to punch him, missing each time at her disadvantaged angle.

Yusef threw her on the bed with a growl. She bounced on the mattress and stared up at him in awe. His strength excited her even as it terrified. Blood rushed through her veins, only to be sped by his dark, piercing eyes as they shot into hers.

"Careful, wife, your words carry you too far."

"What will you do?" She was too week to move as she searched his face, her expression full of passion. She took a deep breath, thrilling in the sense of adventure she felt within him. Her life certainly hadn't been boring since he crashed into it.

"I'm going to make you face your passion," he proclaimed with a low growl. His gaze bore into her.

"No, I --" she tried, vehemently shaking her head.

"Quiet! I only need to know one thing from you right now. Do you take off your clothes or do I take them off for you?"

"I don --"

"I said quiet!" Yusef roared. Her mouth snapped shut, her green eyes wide in surprise. "The only things you are allowed to say to me are that you are sorry for what you did and that you want me. Do you understand?"

Her lips tightened and she glared.

"Do you understand?" He came to the edge of the bed.

Olena growled in response. There was so much promise in him, as if he knew she would easily succumb to his whims. And why wouldn't he think that? In the past it had only taken a kiss and she was tearing off his clothes. Well, not this time!

"I'm assuming that's a yes." He gave her a very dominant grin.

Olena's chest heaved in excitement, anticipating the challenge he so boldly issued. Yusef crawled forward on the bed, his eyes holding hers. Her lips parted, sucking in her ragged, panting breaths. He crawled over her, holding himself above her on all fours.

Olena's lips pressed and she tried to knee his groin. His leg twisted to hold her down.

"I will kick back," he warned. Olena let her leg drop.

Slowly, he reached forward. A sharpened talon grew from his finger as he reached for her. Olena's mouth opened wide as she watched his hand. The dangerous claw touched at the base of her throat, lightly circling around the hollow he found there. Her eyes closed. She held perfectly still, panting.

Yusef inhaled her mounting passion. He knew she liked to be reminded of the force within him. She liked the danger he presented when his eyes flashed and his body shifted. Her heart leapt in her chest, beating erratically as he drew his finger down. Snagging the cotton shirt, he pulled up, ripping the material in a long, slow tear. When he was finished, the material fell completely to the side. Her breasts were bare.

Olena weakly opened her eyes. He was licking his lips as he watched her chest rise and fall rapidly. She tried to reach for her shirt.

"No." Yusef took her wrists and pinned them together above her head. With his free hand, he made quick work of her shirt, tearing strips from it to tie her hands above her head to the bed. When he finished, he eyed his handiwork in satisfaction, saying, "There."

"I hate you."

"Last chance, firebird." He ignored her low words, as he brought his mouth down to her ear. "Tell me you want me."

Her jaw lifted in defiance. Her lips pressed tightly shut.

"I was hoping you'd say that," he chuckled, reaching to

nip at her ear.

Olena closed her eyes, trying to concentrate on despising him. It didn't work. As soon as his lips touched her throat, she quivered.

Yusef kissed his way down her neck. His touch was light and airy against her flesh. He let his breath do most of the caressing. His mouth began a haphazard trek along her collarbone, over her shoulder to nip at her inner arm. She shivered in pleasure at the little surprise. Next, he moved down her sensitive side, taking his time. He journeyed across her flat stomach, touching her in ways she'd never known. Her body tensed and jerked beneath him.

It was agonizing torture and he had barely even begun to touch her. Olena gasped, arching her back to him as he made his way from her navel to the center of her breasts.

Breathing hotly against an erect nipple, he asked, "Do you want me?"

She shook her head, denying him. She didn't want him to ever stop.

Yusef drew back from her breast, leaving it untouched and wanting. His kisses continued, steaming against her flesh. He leaned back, reaching her hips. His hands were warm as he drew them along her waistband. Meeting in the middle, he untied the laces.

Olena watched him. He drew his hands down her pants. They were followed by his lips as he kissed one hipbone and then the other. Qurilixen garments did not use underwear and so he met with little resistance. Kissing and licking a hot, wet path, he crawled his way down her legs and drew the pants off her ankles.

"Tell me you want me." His chest heaved. His eyes devoured her.

She stubbornly refused, shaking her head violently against the pillow. She couldn't speak. Her breath rasped out in heavy pants. Her throat worked as she tried to swallow.

This time when he touched her, his hand pressed more firmly to her skin. He ran his hand up her inner legs to her stiffening thighs. A slight moan came from her throat and she bit her lips to keep from screaming as his caress ran up her body. He moved around the curves of her breasts, ignoring the straining nipples.

Yusef's worked his legs in between hers. His erection

strained to be free of his clothing. Sweat glistened on her body as she tried to deny them both. Her knees bent to weakly rub along his waist.

His mouth near her breast, he said, "Tell me."

"No. I don't want you."

Yusef took her nipple in his mouth, biting the tender nub and then licking it. Her back arched. Spasms of pleasure jolted through her body at his every touch. Her muscles tensed. He moved his hand to her thighs, stroking boldly up to her center heat.

"Tell me," Yusef growled, insistent.

"No." Olena's hips bucked into his hand and he let her rub against his palm. She was ready for him--wet and hot. He kissed her other breast, giving it the same bittersweet torment. This time she did cry out.

His eyes flashing, he rose up on his arms. It would be so easy to take her like this. Their breaths mingled. Their eyes locked in battle. His erection begged for freedom, pulsing and reaching to her.

"Why won't you say you want me?" Yusef asked in manly frustration. He thought that this torture was surely harder on him than her. "I can see that you do."

Her body worked restlessly beneath him. Her arms pulled, the muscles bunching as they wrenched against the ties.

"Because I'll never want you!" Olena screamed.

"Damn it, but you are a stubborn woman!" Yusef pulled away from her, his eyes tormented. His arms tensed as if he wanted to strike her, but he knew he never could. He couldn't touch her like that, could never harm her, and he wouldn't force her body if her mind still refused.

Yusef turned, angrily digging through his dresser drawers. He pulled out a formal black tunic jacket and matching breeches. Next, he grabbed a silver belt. Keeping his back to her, he threw off his shirt and put an undertunic on in its place. He changed his pants. Olena watched his glorious body as it was unveiled and then veiled once more. Slipping a jacket over his shoulders, he tied the cloth belt around his waist.

"Where are you going?" she asked, breathless.

"I was going to take you to a celebration tonight at the palace. But seeing as you have no desire to be my wife, I'll have to leave you right where you are."

"What?" This time the ties were too short and she wouldn't be able to chew her way loose. When she looked at him, she saw that he knew it too. She wasn't going anywhere. "You can't leave me like this, Yusef."

"Then admit that you want to be with me," Yusef said. Unable to keep looking at her body, he grabbed her pants and jerked them back over her hips. Grabbing the covers, he threw them over her naked chest. He sat next to her and tenderly touched her cheek. "Come with me tonight as my wife."

"I can't. Why can't you understand that? I can't want anyone."

"Then why did you marry me?" The question was hard and loud, as he tore his hand away from her soft skin. He stood, glaring down at her in frustration.

There was a deafening silence. Olena's eyes narrowed as she looked at him. Her lips twisted cruelly.

"Because I had to! Because I need to disappear for awhile. I need to find a ship and my crew. Don't worry, as soon as they come for me I'll be out of your life forever. I never intended on staying here with you, Yusef. You're just some superstitious fool I'm biding my time with on this godforsaken planet until I can hitch a ride out of here."

Yusef looked as if she'd ripped out his heart and stomped on it. There was so much agony in his dark gaze that she instantly wanted to take the confession back. Slowly, he nodded at her--a stiff, regal nod. Without saying a word, he left her tied to the bed.

Olena held deathly still, listening for a sound. She got one. It was the front door closing as he left her.

"That should just about do it, Olena." She closed her eyes. A bitter laugh escaped her lips. "He won't want you after this."

Where she should have felt joy, she only felt excruciating pain. It was a loss much deeper than she'd expected. For the first time in her life since being sold into slavery, she began to cry. It was a wretched, awful sound that poured out of her heart. "I hope you're happy with your little pirate, Jack. I hope you're dancing in your grave."

\* \* \* \*

Yusef stormed out of his house as if chased by evil spirits. A hollow pain dug itself a comfortable home in his heart, eating away at him. He hoped it killed him. Anything would be better than the centuries he now faced alone. Without Olena, the organ was useless to him.

Keeping a mask over his dark features, he did not give anything away. He delivered curt nods and stiff smiles to passing villagers. Seeing Agro, the giant man fell into step next to him. Agro instantly sensed his sour mood, despite the drawn expression on the Prince's face. "The Var?"

Yusef nodded. "Olek says they are to be here tonight. He wanted them to witness our happy unions."

"And the firebird?" Agro noticed how Yusef's eyes narrowed into slits at the word 'happy'. He nodded grimly, sad for his friend.

"Burning in hell for all I care," Yusef said bitterly, storming ahead to the castle gate.

* * * *

The main common hall of the Draig mountain palace had steep, arched ceilings with the center dome for light. The red stone floor was swept clean. Banners of the family crest decorated the walls, one for each color of the family lines-- purple for the King and Queen, black for Yusef, green for Olek, red for Zoran, and blue-gray for Ualan. Each banner had the silver symbol of the dragon boldly woven into it.

Lines of tables reached across the floor for dining, filled with villagers and attended to by servants who carted out endless pitchers of various drinks and set them out on the tables. Their murmuring voices could be heard all around the hall as they excitedly awaited the start of the festivities. All of them striving to get a good look at the Princesses sitting at the head table.

Yusef sat alone at the royal table, much to the onlooker's contemplation. The Queen's maids were eager to inform that Yusef's bride was sick, as they were told 'in secret' by the distressed Queen. Yusef had to bow to the cunning of his parents.

He sat next to his brother, Zoran. Zoran was a fearsome man, decked in a red oriental style tunic. He was the Capitan of the Guards, in charge of training the soldiers and leading them in battle. His face was grim, a normal expression for the man, as he was a serious, hard-working person. Next to him was his wife, who Yusef had learned was named Pia. She was a quiet woman, who merely nodded at him upon introduction.

In the center were his parents, both regal as they spoke to each other. Beside the King was Nadja, Olek's wife. She was reserved and by the looks of her perfectly positioned hair, she was high maintenance. His younger brother Olek was the Draig ambassador. He had an easy way about him, a quick smile and ready laugh. Any peace they had with the Var was of his doing.

Next to Olek was the oldest brother, Ualan. Ualan was the future King. He had a heavy responsibility on his shoulders but he wore it with ease. His wife, Morrigan, had proclaimed herself a slave to purge her honor. It was suspected she also did it to keep her husband's sexual advances away from her. Though, when she looked at Ualan, Yusef saw that she didn't entirely dislike his brother.

Seeing Morrigan glare absently at him as she spoke to Ualan, he returned her dark frown. Then, glancing to his side, he sighed. From what his father said, all Princes were cursed with angry women and unhappy marriages. Yusef knew that none were as cursed as he. At least his brothers could bring their brides with them tonight, proclaiming them as their wives for all to see. He had to leave his frustrating wench tied up at home. It was the only way he could assure she wouldn't run away from him.

The Princes, the King, and the Queen all wore silver crowns of simplistic design atop their heads as a symbol of their sovereignty. The three attending Princesses had just received their crowns. He had been given Olena's for her. It sat on the table in her absence. He would have it delivered to his wing in the palace.

Yusef turned his dark eyes ahead, ignoring the plate of food set before him. He had picked at it absently, but found he had no appetite. Focusing on the real reason he was there in an effort to occupy his time, and to keep his thoughts from the fiery Olena, he turned his attention to a distant table in the back.

A group of silent, blond Var sat solemnly, ignored by most of the hall. Only one servant approached them, hesitatingly filling their goblets. The visiting noblemen held still as the timid man worked.

The largest at their table, King Attor, turned to stare at the royal table. He ruled the Var Kingdom to the south. The King's gaze lingered on the three Princesses as he studied them. Yusef picked up his drink, taking a sip of the wine. The Var King snarled in anger, though the man reigned in his emotion well. Yusef's nostrils flared, not liking the man's treacherous presence in his family's home.

He knew that this night was a necessity. It was a show of power to their people to prove the Princes were happily married and thus would produce many royal heirs to secure their lineage. It also showed they had no fear of the Var, daring to invite them into their keep on such a joyful occasion.

A shout of laughter sounded, drawing Yusef from his thoughts. He glanced down and saw the young boy, Hienrich, limping over the floor. He had been born with a bad foot that turned in as he walked. The deformity would keep him from ever being a soldier, so naturally it was what the boy wanted more than anything in the world. Hienrich should have known better, as he bravely approached a table of drunken Draig soldiers. Yusef shook his head, knowing what was going to happen before the boy even spoke.

The men laughed, bidding the boy to do some trick to prove himself. The eager boy hopped on his bad leg, falling over, much to the amusement of the men who only chuckled louder. The boy climbed to his feet to do it again. Suddenly, he felt Pia brushing past his back. Yusef blinked in surprise to see her rush to the boy's aide.

Turning, he glanced at Zoran. His brother silently watched his wife.

Hienrich blinked to see a Princess before him and instantly bowed. His position was precarious and he stumbled before righting himself.

"Leave him be!" Pia demanded to the table of stunned warriors. Yusef sat back, crossing his arms over his chest as he watched in silent curiosity.

"What do you want with Hienrich, my lady?" a burly soldier with a beard asked. "Does he offend you? I'll have him removed."

Yusef watched Pia's body shake. "He does not offend me! You, however…"

Leaning towards Zoran, Yusef said, "I don't think your wife understands that Hienrich is being put through his paces to prove his worth as a soldier. Perhaps you should stop her and explain before she makes a scene."

Yusef saw a grin come to the side of Zoran's mouth, though he hid it well. "Perhaps you're right, brother."

"My lady," the confused warrior defended, not understanding what he'd done wrong. "He knows we mean no harm. Don't you, lad?"

Heinrich nodded his head. He understood perfectly well. He too was confused as he looked at the Princess.

"See," the man said.

"Yeah," another added, drunker warrior with a pock marked face. "He thinks to become a warrior, don't you, boy?"

The men laughed good-naturedly.

"Well, I am a Princess," Pia announced. Zoran had stood, stepping leisurely around the table to fetch his wife. "And he will be my personal warrior."

The hall was stunned. Hienrich's mouth almost fell to the floor at her declaration. Yusef took a drink, trying not to laugh. Now here was a woman he wanted nowhere near Olena. With Olena's creative mind and Pia's temperament, the entire kingdom would be in trouble. Thinking of his wife tied to the bed, his laughter died in his chest and the grin left his dark features.

"If my lady wishes for a warrior," the bearded man said. "Let us battle for the position. Do not insult us by naming a boy."

A shout of agreement came from the men eager to do battle for such a coveted position.

"Do you dare to question a Princess?" Zoran called with authority over the hall. The onlookers instantly fell silent in respect.

"He is my warrior too!"

Yusef flinched. It was Olek's wife Nadja.

"And mine as well!" Morrigan said.

Yusef sighed. He was suddenly very thankful Olena wasn't there. He wasn't sure he wanted her around any of these crazy females. She was already crazy enough without company or encouragement.

Zoran glanced at his father and shrugged. "There you have it. You cannot deny the wishes of three Princesses. Hienrich is now under royal protection and will be treated accordingly to his new station."

The warriors growled and looked darkly at the boy whose chest was puffing up with his new authority over them. Yusef shook his head. Zoran was going to be in for a lot of trouble after this incident. Seeing the men's faces, he hid a smile. There might even be a small rebellion later that night.

Zoran lifted his hand and motioned the musicians to start playing. Pia told Hienrich to come to the table. She looked at Yusef expectantly and then to the empty seat beside him. Yusef glanced at Zoran, shrugged and moved over so the boy could sit beside Zoran. Pia waved a servant to bring the boy a plate.

The boy beamed up at Yusef. Yusef nodded wearily at him, moving to stand. Now that the commotion was over, he planned on joining the musicians so he could get closer to the Var. He looked at the blond warriors and noticed they were getting restless.

Smiling good-naturedly, Yusef motioned for a *gittern*. The man willingly handed it over, knowing the Prince well. He began playing, pretending to pay more attention to the livening crowd than to his task.

Chapter Eleven

"When I get my hands on you, knight, I'm going to tear out your liver and eat it for breakfast!"

Olena lay on the bed, straining her hands against her bonds. She was pretty sure that was one of her best threats yet. Too bad no one was around to hear any of them.

"I'm going to gouge out your eyes and feed them to a *givre!*"

Hearing a noise in the living room, she tensed.

*Yusef?* Olena froze, listening.

Keeping quiet, the skin on her neck crawled in warning. She heard a soft rumble and what sounded like light footsteps. Whatever was making that noise, it wasn't Yusef, unless he was playing some sort of a sick joke on her. Even as she thought it, she somehow knew he would never do that to her.

Olena's eyes darted around the dim room, looking for a weapon. She pulled at her wrists, rubbing them raw in an effort to yank them free. It did no good. She was completely helpless.

Seeing the door slowly creaking open, she tensed, burying herself into the bed. The rumbling grew louder. The door opened wider. Olena held her breath. Her head raced as she readied for the fight. It wasn't a man who entered, but a wild animal. From what she could tell, it sounded like a sort of mountain lion or a tiger.

Her legs tensed, her toes working to silently get the blanket off her body. Her chest was bared as she drew the blanket down lower. She didn't have time to care. Her legs were her only defense against the wild animal.

The door swung completely open, but Olena didn't see anything standing in the doorway. Her skin prickled. Every nerve was on edge. She felt someone – something--in the room with her. A flash of fur appeared over the edge of the bed. The footfall continued.

Suddenly, a roar sounded and the cat pounced onto the bed. This was no ordinary mountain lion. This cat was as big as a man. It had long arms and legs like a human, though fur covered its body. Eyeing the tunic shirt, she realized that this creature was another shifter. Olena gasped, kicking desperately to finish pulling her legs free. By the way the creature's deadly green eyes studied her body she could tell he wasn't a friend of the family.

The man-cat roared. His head cocked to the side as his face and body shifted to human form. Long blond hair covered his head, pulled back from his face. His nose hooked at the end, seeming to point at her. He had an ugly face that stared at her as a cruel smile curved onto his mouth. Soon three other men, similar in build, came into the room and stood above her.

"Ah," the one at the door said. His voice was low as he laughed. His eyes appeared blue beneath his thick brows, but it was too dim to be sure. "Look what the Draig has left us. A yummy little morsel all tied up."

The others laughed. Olena's jaw rose in defiance.

"Where's your little Prince, love?" the one with the hooked nose at her feet asked. He crawled towards her, watching her naked breasts in excitement as the jerking of his movements caused them to bounce.

"He'll be back any minute." Her eyes shot fire.

"I like this one," the shortest of them said. "Let's keep her, Brouse. I want to play with her."

"Oh, I intend to," the blue-eyed Brouse said. He narrowed in on Olena. The others stayed at his back as he came for her. He reached out his hand, growing deadly sharp claws that could slice her throat with one sweep. "Attor wants this one brought to him whole."

\* \* \* \*

Yusef forced a smile as he kept pace with the musicians. He nodded his head at some of the passing couples to acknowledge them. Someone stood nearby and sang along. Others danced merrily across an open section of the floor, joined by Zoran and Pia.

Yusef watched the Var out of the corner of his eyes. King Attor stood, drawing his full attention. The man spoke in low tones to his men and they all followed him as he went to the royal table to speak to the Draig King. Yusef couldn't hear what was said, but by the look on his father's face, he knew the Kings were merely laying voice to a formality.

The Var turned to leave, trailing silently out a side door. King Attor glanced at him. Yusef kept playing his song, never missing a beat as he returned the heated stare. The man had the audacity to smile and nod, but the dark, knowing look made Yusef nervous. The man was up to something.

When the men reached the door, Yusef looked up at Olek, receiving a nod of silent agreement. He ended his part of the song early and passed his instrument back to its owner who took up immediately where the Prince had left off. No one noticed the change as the dancing continued. Yusef followed the Var out of the common hall.

Seeing Agro in the passageway waiting for him, he motioned the warrior to move ahead. The Var silently made their way out of the mountain fortress. Though the man-cats never turned, Yusef knew they were well aware of being followed.

They made it through the castle without incident. Yusef motioned for Agro to follow the Var as they left Draig land. He stopped by the castle door, scanning over the valley from the advantage of the cliff's height. His eyes shifted with gold, taking in the detail of the trees to make sure no attack was planned on the village while the House of Draig celebrated within.

He squinted, trying to see to the Outpost where his wife was tied to the bed. His senses pricked in warning, silently urging him to go to her, telling him that she was in trouble and needed him.

Sensing movement behind him, he did not readily move his gaze from where Agro still followed King Attor and his men. Whoever it was behind him, he smelled the unmistakable scent of the Draig. He turned, expecting to see one of their soldiers coming to aid him.

Suddenly, a sharp fire pieced into his unsuspecting back and he howled. Yusef arched violently as he was stabbed several times in quick succession. He fell to his knees, never getting a look at his assailant. His head spun from the pain. His attacker kicked him hard, pushing him violently from the blade as he took off running down the hall inside the Draig keep.

Yusef moaned in agony, sure he was dying. The vision of

Olena, beautiful and defiant, worked its way into his head. The sick feeling that he would never see her again overwhelmed him.

He fought the darkness that threatened. Agro's feet were suddenly before him and the man was calling for help from passing guards. The guards shifted to Draig, jumping down from their high post above the castle gate. They landed unharmed.

At Agro's command, the Draig warriors helped to haul the fallen Prince to the medical ward. Yusef howled in pain, automatically fighting the soldier's hands. Agro ran ahead to warn a doctor. The doctor jumped to instant attention, sending his wife to fetch him more help. Agro took off down the hall to inform the King and his sons of what had happened, leaving Yusef in the doctor's care.

Yusef struggled, mindless as he fought the hands that would subdue him. He vaguely heard the doctor's words as he tried to seal his wounds with a laser. Agro came back followed by his brothers. Yusef fought them all, desperate to get up, desperate to get his wife to safety.

His eyes opened wide, seeing Ualan and Olek holding him down. His body was losing its fight. Ualan murmured something to him, but he couldn't hear him.

Taking up the last of his strength, Yusef called desperately, "My wife."

Ualan and Olek nodded in instant understanding of the plea. Yusef barely saw them as his world went completely black.

* * * *

A diffused light fell over the dense forest in a soft green haze that blended eerily with the fog from the nearby marshes. The air was damp in this part of the woods. Moss hung from treetops, unmoving in their windless isolation. There was a strange smell in the air and even the insects had deserted the area.

Olena glanced around through her lowered eyelids. Her captors, who she was silently referring to as 'the fur ball gang', were camped around a nearby fire. The soft orange glow reflected light off her hanging body, but unfortunately provided little heat. The fur balls thought it amusing to leave her topless. The chill was getting to her tender skin.

As they gathered around her on Yusef's bed, she knew

they weren't going to kill her right away. The way they constantly dropped the name King Attor made her suspect it was supposed to mean something to her. It didn't. He was more than likely the local ruffian who controlled these hairy annoyances.

Before cutting her loose with their sharp claws, they'd said Attor wanted her for himself. So until Attor got her, she assumed she had nothing to worry about. She'd been right so far. Aside from a few awkward pawings meant to intimidate her, they'd not tried anything.

Attor, whoever he was, was a foolish, foolish man if he thought four hairy minions were going to subdue her for long. Olena knew that she just had to play the meek, trembling female for so long before these men would lower their guard and make a mistake. So far they'd not given her an opening, but she stayed confident they would slip up.

Olena didn't know how long she'd been with the furry foursome, only that they had traveled through most of what looked like night. But, as the hours stretched, she guessed the shadowy marshes always looked like it was nighttime.

Olena's hands were bound above her head, tied to a tree branch, which she decided was rather uninventive of them. Her feet stayed firmly planted on the ground, giving her knees little room to bend. She refused to let fear overcome her. Jack had taught her that fear was never an option. Those who felt it were instantly defeated. Those who were brave and had a plan got away.

Olena always had a plan.

\* \* \* \*

Yusef's eyes jerked open from his never-ending nightmares, a frown marring his brow in confusion. His body ached with a liquid fire. The light was dim, or was it his eyes? Blinking, he felt a poke on his arm, a slight sting. He tried to focus on the brown-haired woman sitting beside him. Her lips were moving but he couldn't hear what she was saying.

Whatever she was giving him was working. His back was beginning to feel better. His eyes closed and he thought instantly of Olena. Hopelessness and despair surrounded her beautiful face. He knew she was hurt and he couldn't get up to save her.

\* \* \* \*

*Yusef!* Olena jerked awake. She trembled, her back throbbing with untold agony. It felt like someone had stabbed her. As she took a deep breath, the pain subsided. She looked around, feeling a chill that had nothing to do with the crisp marsh air.

*Yusef.* She didn't know how but she got the overwhelming feeling that he needed her. Before she was fully awake, a new, faster plan formed in her brain. "Hey, fur ball!"

Brouse awoke with a start. He instantly shifted into full cougar form, falling down on all fours. He crouched, sniffing the air. Olena smiled prettily at the hairy creature, pouting her lips and batting her eyelashes.

"Hey, you, come here," she purred softly. The man-cat's blue eyes blinked in question. Olena shyly bit her lip. "Please. I want to talk to you."

Brouse shifted back into human form. A lazy smile curled on his lips.

"I won't bite." She beckoned him with a come-hither fire to her eyes that could scorch any man. "Please, I just want to talk. I'm ready to be a good girl--a *very* good girl."

* * * *

Zoran lifted his hand and motioned Ualan, Olek, and the King to stop their progress. He sniffed the air. Then, pointing with two fingers, he motioned for his father to follow him and for his brothers to go around the far side of the Var camp. The men nodded in understanding, gripping their swords to their sides.

They all shifted to Draig, their skin hardening to prepare for battle. They looked macabre with their glowing yellow eyes. Their vision penetrated the darkness to see the Var campsite. It had been hard, but they'd found Yusef's wife and her Var kidnappers.

The Var hid in the shadowed marshes. The rotting smell of molding plant life and animal carcasses masked even the barest traces of scent from most of their kind--from all but the trackers, an elite bunch of Draig who were chosen for their highly developed sense of smell.

Zoran suddenly stopped, seeing a woman with flaming red hair tied to a tree. Her back was to them, her upper torso completely naked. King Llyr made a movement as if to say, *that's her.* To their surprise, she spoke.

"I won't bite." Her tone was husky with a thick promise

any male would pick up.

The King's jaw tensed. Zoran put a hand on his arm. He wouldn't move until he could assure his brothers were ready.

"Please, I just want to talk," the woman said. Her leg lifted in the air, falling open to the side. "I'm ready to be a good girl--a *very* good girl."

\* \* \* \*

Olena looked at the man in front of her, seeing his gaze drift down over her body, which moved in restless offering. He licked his lips, focusing on her naked breasts.

*This is too easy,* she thought. *Typical though, considering I may be one of the first women this kitty-cat has ever seen.*

"Oh," she pouted, with the 'save me big strong man' look. She bit her bottom lip, sucking it lightly before letting it go into a full pout. "My arms hurt so badly."

The man's eyes shot up to her, narrowing in suspicion.

She head cocked to the side. "I know you can't let me down, but do you think I could wrap my legs around your waist and let you hold me up for awhile? I just want to give my shoulders a rest."

The man licked his lips, glancing back to his sleeping comrades.

"Oh, they don't have to know. I promise to be good. I can be very, very quiet. Please." Olena gave him a wanton look. "I'm so cold. Can't you come warm me up? I'd bet a big man like you would be real strong and real hot."

She looked at his obvious arousal. The man-cat smiled. It was a dark and lecherous expression, as he decided to take her invitation.

"You keep quiet." His tone filled with the sound of rolling gravel.

Olena pretend to shiver, letting an excited smile come to her. With feigned excitement, she said, "Oh, yes, master."

A low growl sounded in the man's throat. Olena pretended to shiver in delight. Her eyes rounded as the man's hairy fingers reached for her breast. Pulling with all her strength, she jumped off the ground. Just as she wrapped her legs around the unsuspecting man's head, she saw a movement in the corner of her eyes.

Zoran darted forward, prompting the others to do the same. He watched Yusef's bride wrap her long legs around the Var's neck and twist her body around with a violent jerk. A loud *snap* resounded as his neck broke.

Before he died, the man growled in surprise waking the others. His fanged mouth opened and his tooth dug into Olena's thigh as he fell. She screeched in surprise at the pain. The other three lunged to their feet, partially shifted into upright cats, their stances ready for battle.

Olena trembled as three dragons met the three cats. There was a slashing of swords and claws, a gruesome melody of roars and growls. Ignoring her bloody leg, Olena tried to swing up to grab the branch. If she could just get her feet over the edge, she might be able to crawl off the end. The branch was angled up and she couldn't get enough leverage. That was why she'd needed Brouse. If the Draig hadn't of interrupted her, she would've used the dead man's shoulders, pushing up as he fell. She kicked viciously at the truck of the tree, swinging high only to crash her back into the trunk with a bruising thud.

After Olena's body crashed a third time, she was too dazed to try again. Looking over, she saw one of the Draig standing by her side, watching her in curiosity. She would have sworn he smiled at her with his rough, dragon face. Olena glared back. "Are you done staring? Get me down already, dragon!"

Instantly, his sword sung through the air, slashing through her binds. The breeze of the blade flew past her hands. If his aim had been off, she'd have lost her fingers. Without flinching, she nodded her thanks and shook her wrists free.

Olena lifted her hand out to him. "Your sword."

The Draig only smiled at her, lifting the tip of the weapon to the ending battle. The Draigs had conquered the Var, slaughtering them in a most honorable display of fury. Barely out of breath, the victorious dragons turned to her. They were covered with blood.

To their amazement, she placed her hands firmly on her hips. "What do you think you are doing? I had this under control."

The Draigs looked at each other and then back at the outraged woman standing half-naked before them. Her emerald eyes sparkled with a fire that did her red locks proud.

"Why isn't Yusef with you?" Olena demanded, studying

their shifted faces. Though the words were hard, they all sensed the vulnerable light in her eyes when she said their brother's name. Her bravery wavered. "Where is Yusef? He's hurt, isn't he?"

One by one the brothers shifted to their human form. Olena didn't recognize them. Hands on hips, she stared each one of them down, unafraid. The three brothers had never seen such a fiery display--or such an ungrateful woman.

"Do you think one of you could at least give me a shirt?" she asked, dryly. "Maybe then you could stop staring at my breasts long enough to answer me."

Zoran took off his overtunic and tossed it to her. She slipped it over her head, not caring that it was splattered with the blood of battle.

"Who are you?" she asked, as her head poked out of the top. It was still warm from Zoran's body. The sleeves fell past her hands.

"I am Zoran," Zoran answered shortly, prompting each brother to answer in turn.

"Olek."

"Ualan."

"You knew we were not Yusef?" Zoran questioned in admiration.

"Of course I knew. I know what my husband looks like. I only have one of them, you know." Olena shook her head, eyeing him as if he were daft.

The brothers grinned, seeing that their new sister definitely had fire. It amazed them that she could tell them apart in Draig. Many wives complained that their husbands all looked alike when they shifted--at least for the first seventy five years until they grew used to it. They could instantly see how Yusef had his hands full these past weeks. With her cutting tone, it was a wonder the woman only got chastisement.

"Where is Yusef?" Olena was unmoved by their smiles of admiration. She didn't think she would feel completely safe until she saw him again. Not that she cared, she told herself. He'd saved her life and she owed him one was all. She would never admit it, but her heart was stuck in her throat, refusing to beat until she heard that Yusef was safe. "Who are you to him?"

"We are his brothers," Olek answered.

"Brothers," she repeated, vaguely remembering someone saying he had them. She eyed them, not readily seeing her dark husband's looks in their lighter features.

"And I am his father," the Draig behind her said. He had been so quiet Olena had forgotten he was there. Spinning around, she looked Yusef's father over.

"Wait." She paled. "Is this some kind of a joke?"

The men looked at each other confused.

Olena pointed at Ualan. She wobbled slightly on her feet, her leg throbbing where Brouse's fang had cut her. "You're a Prince. You punched Agro at the Breeding Festival. He told me."

Ualan narrowed his eyes and curtly nodded.

"And you," she said turning an accusatory eye to Yusef's father, "are the King."

The man nodded to confirm. He too dared to smile at her.

"I married a Prince?" Olena swayed.

The sheer look of horror on her face was priceless. She had shown great bravery in fighting the Var and hadn't even flinched at their shifting. But now, as she found out she was a Princess, she suddenly looked like she was going to be violently ill.

Feeling lightheaded, Olena looked down and lifted her borrowed tunic to see her bleeding leg. Her eyes rolling in her head, she grumbled, "Oh, great. Not again."

Olena collapsed the ground, unconscious. Zoran grinned, chuckling as he hit Olek in the chest with the back of his hand. Olek flinched. Walking away, Zoran ordered the youngest brother over his shoulder, "You get her, Olek. I don't want to be the one holding her when she wakes up."

Ualan and Llyr laughed, moving to follow Zoran. Olek grimaced, looking at the red-headed wood sprite lying on the ground. Cursing under his breath, he went to pick her up.

## Chapter Twelve

*"Hold, woman!"*

Zoran and Ualan broke into laughter. King Llyr watched, amused. Olek was holding his side where Olena had tried to elbow him off his *ceffyl*. Gripping the center horn of his mount, Olek pulled himself back up behind the beast's bare shoulders, only this time he was careful not to touch the fiery woman in front of him.

Olena flinched, blinking herself awake ready for a fight. It took her a moment to realize she was on the back of a mount, riding before Prince Olek. She relaxed her tense arm, much to the relief of the other rider.

"Don't call me woman," Olena said under her breath, shooting all of them a dark glare. "My name is Olena."

The *ceffyl's* wide back shifted low at the weight of their movement, used to the rough handling. Its fanged mouth darted open with a hiss of its long tongue.

"Where are we going?" she asked, as if nothing happened.

"Good morning to you too, Princess Olena." Olek rubbed his stomach. How he missed his gentle Nadja at that moment. He was more than ready to rid himself of Yusef's hellion of a bride.

Olena grimaced at the name and Olek felt somewhat vindicated.

"Home," Ualan stated in answer to her question.

"But?" Olena saw the large mountain palace looming before them. Twisting around, she pointed behind them. "I live down there."

"Not anymore," the King decreed in a royal tone. "The Var smashed all the windows. Besides, the Outpost is no place for a lady right now. It's not safe. You will be better off in the protection of the castle."

"First of all, I'm not a lady and I can protect myself," Olena said.

Llyr gaped in surprise that she would dare to question a royal decree. Not even his outspoken sons did that--well, at least not often. The woman's lips pressed harshly, as if she was the one in control of all of them.

"Second," she continued. "I've slept in worse places and a little broken glass is nothing. And third, by Var do you mean the fur ball gang back there?"

Olek chuckled. She ignored him, expectantly watching the King.

"They are the Var," Llyr conceded.

"I'm not scared of them. If Yusef hadn't left me tied to the bed..." she didn't even pause when the King coughed uncomfortably,"...I never would have been taken."

The men exchanged looks. The Var who'd been sent after her were hardly a true showing of their enemy's best warriors.

"I've had time to study them. They would be easy to defeat," Olena announced, with a confident nod. "So, take me back to the Outpost. I'll take my chances there with Yusef."

Olena didn't want to go to the castle, despite her pirate instincts telling her it would give her thieving nature rich rewards. As a Princess, they would be watching her very closely. They would expect her to act a certain, civilized way. She couldn't do it. The idea of trying petrified her, though she didn't readily admit it to herself.

Besides, how exactly would the crew find her if she were locked away in a castle, being protected? She didn't want them to go up against the Draig army to rescue her. They would possibly be slaughtered if they came unprepared for it. Never in a million years would the crew think she'd married a Prince.

"Yusef is at the palace," Zoran said.

Olena turned to the large warrior in disbelief. "What? That knight is lounging at the palace while I ... *ooooh!*"

Olena shook her head in anger and moved away. Her dark look said more than her growling tone ever could. The brothers shared a frown.

The traveling party made it to the small village, riding through the center street. Olena lifted her head proudly and none of them spoke. People came out of their houses and shops to watch them. Young boys waved at the passing Princes, some cheered and shouted. They all pointed in excitement to see their blood stained clothing. The Princes waved back solemnly, acknowledging them.

A courtyard was before the hidden fortress. From the ground, because of the angle, she couldn't see the windows or balconies within the mountain's sides. Once they had passed the villagers and were making the climb up the side of the mountain base the front of the castle, the King stated, "Yusef was stabbed."

Olena spun around in surprise to stare at him. Olek stopped the *ceffyl* near the front gate. Her face paled. Olek swung down, lifting a hand to her to help her from the mount. Olena ignored him, jumping off the other side on her own. Her sore leg wobbled. She looked down at it, having forgotten completely that she'd been injured. The wound was roughly bandaged and didn't bleed.

"What do you mean he was stabbed?" She gave the men a hard loom. "He was in Draig, wasn't he? So he's fine. He was protected by that thick skin of his."

The brothers exchanged looks. The wound in her leg tingled now that she put pressure on it. Her hands shook and she clenched them into fists to hide the weakness.

"He was attacked from behind and stabbed in the back," Zoran stated. He tossed his mount's reins to Ualan and Olek took his father's. The two Princes walked the *ceffyls* to the stables, leaving the other two men to explain. "He didn't have time to shift."

Olena's heart nearly stopped beating. The anguish she felt was worse than any injury she'd ever known. Her eyes teared. She felt as if her whole body was being sucked into an abyss. "He is dead?"

"No," the King said, he took a step forward, ready to catch the swaying woman. Olena took a deep breath, glaring at his hand and stepping away from his touch. Her face turned to them, hardening as she waited for the rest of his answer. "He's in the medical ward. He's alive, but he is in bad condition and unconscious. The doctors say they are hopeful, but his life is still in danger."

"Take me to him." Olena's limbs stopped quivering by mere force of her will. She might not want to stay as Yusef's Princess, but she definitely couldn't stand to see him dead. He had saved her life. It was time to repay the favor. Whatever it took, she would make sure he lived.

\* \* \* \*

Olena stood frozen in the entryway to the medical ward.

There was a row of large empty beds along one wall and a reception desk by the other along with rows of glass cases. In the back were two private rooms and an operating room. To her distress, lying on one of the beds was Yusef. He was as still as a corpse, his naturally dark complexion nearly as pale as one. His eyes were closed, purpling around the sides of his lids. His handsome lips were edged with an eerie blue.

Her heart sank. Pressing her lips tightly together, she refused to cry.

As Zoran and the King led her to the medical wing, Olena didn't take in her surroundings. Her mind worked furiously with the lingering fear that Yusef might not be alive, that he might have died while they came for her. Damn her stubborn pride. If she would've just relented and said she was his wife, he would've taken her with him to the palace and she would've been able to protect him from whoever did this. Seeing his chest rise in a shallow breath, Olena could relax enough to breathe. She gave nothing away, as she studied her fallen husband.

Queen Mede was by her son's side, her face drawn. If she had any lingering doubts about who he was, they were squelched the moment she saw Mede. Olena stiffly nodded to the woman, before taking a step towards Yusef.

With so many eyes on her, she grew anxious, knowing they watched to see how she would react. How was she supposed to react? Did they expect her to cry and scream? Did they expect her throw herself into a womanly frenzy? She wasn't that type of woman. She didn't show weakness to anyone.

Their eyes alone kept her from crying out and rushing to him. She stared coolly at Yusef's unmoving features and went to his side. She wanted to touch him, but held back. "Has he woken up?"

"No, dear." The Queen eyed the emotionless woman. Seeing the bloodied front of Olena's borrowed tunic, the Queen frowned, unable to read her.

"Ah, Princess Olena?" The King pointed at Olena's leg. Olena blinked, hearing the title. "Perhaps you should get that looked at."

The Queen glanced to where her husband motioned. The bandage on Olena's thigh was seeping. Mede motioned to the doctor. Olena dutifully followed the doctor's command, hopping up onto a bed next to Yusef. The Queen ushered the men from the room to give the woman privacy as the doctor ripped through her pants. Before leaving, Mede told Olena she would be back in a while to take her to Yusef's home within the castle.

Olena ignored them all, letting the doctor work. Lying down, she stared at Yusef. He didn't move, save for the rise and fall of his chest. Inside, she felt as if she was falling through empty air with no landing in sight.

* * * *

Olena refused to go to Yusef's wing of the palace, saying she was tired and content to spend the night in the medical ward. Late that evening, Tal came in carrying a mug of steaming blue liquid. The man looked at her in surprise, but then slowly shook his head and continued back to one of the offices without saying a word. Moments later, he passed back by, nodding to her as he left.

Once they were alone, Olena sat up and hopped off her cot to go to Yusef. Looking around to make sure no one saw her, she touched his forehead. He was warm, not anything like the deathly cold she imagined. She trailed her hand down his neck, feeling for a pulse. It beat steadily against her fingers. She sighed in hesitant relief. Next, she moved to his naked chest to feel the rise and fall of his lungs. His breath was shallow, but it was there.

Olena frowned. She didn't know what she was doing. She wasn't a nursemaid. She was a pirate. Taking the pirate approach, she leaned over next to his ear. Goading him, she ordered darkly, "Get up off that bed now, you lazy good-for-nothing knight."

She pulled back and studied him for a reaction. He didn't move. She leaned over again.

"Did you hear me, knight? If you don't get up right now I'm going to rob your family blind and burn down your precious mountain fortress."

She pulled back, swallowing. Not even a twitch.

Olena frowned, standing tall. She didn't touch him again. Not knowing what else she could say to convince him to wake up, she crawled back into her bed and pulled the blankets over her body.

"If you survive this, Yusef," Olena said softly, turning her

back on him. "I'll kill you for scaring me."
* * * *

The next morning, Olena was awakened by Queen Mede. The Queen smiled at her when she noticed her opened eyes. Brushing back a strand of Yusef's hair with a tender, motherly hand, the Queen stepped around to look at her son's wife.

"Did you get some rest?" Mede asked, her voice gentle and kind.

Olena nodded. She had indeed slept, though her dreams were as troubled as always. Only this time, instead of Sage dying, it had been Yusef. She stretched her arms above her head.

"If you like I can take you to your home here in the palace," Mede said. Olena started to refuse, but the Queen added, "He won't be going anywhere for awhile and you look as if you could use a change of clothes and a shower. I had some of the soldiers go to the Outpost and get both of your belongings."

Olena tensed, thinking of the floral bags. She had hid them in the closet and had put her ID's up in a crevice. Her gun was still missing, but she didn't have time to ponder it.

Olena allowed the Queen to lead her through the red passageway halls. She made sure to pay attentions so she could find her way back to the medical ward. Tapestries, statues, and paintings decorated it. Olena saw that both depictions of human and Draig were on the tapestries. The paintings were mostly landscapes and portraits.

The Queen only stayed long enough to program Olena's voice to the command-activated front door so she would be able to get out of the house. She told Olena to make herself comfortable--that it was her home as much as her son's. Olena nodded, not really speaking to the woman as she left.

Yusef's palace home was nothing like the beautiful Outpost. There were hardly any windows, except a large ceiling dome in the front room to let in light and smaller domes in the bathroom and bedroom. The floors were wide and made of marble. Everything was pristine and white, and to Olena it looked to be extremely sterile. She much preferred the earthy, comfortable feel of the lodge.

A large black banner hung over one wall, a white dragon embroidered on it. The fireplace was an overbearingly large construction of light block marble. A white couch, which looked as if it had never been sat upon, was before the fireplace. Between the fireplace and the couch was a white fur rug.

The kitchen was clean, the cabinet and refrigerator empty. Yusef's bedroom was a little better. The bed had a black coverlet with red pillows. She found her clothes already put away in the dresser. The closet was nearly bare except for some formal, princely looking, tunics. She found a large silver crown next to a smaller one, some weaponry, boots, and house slippers.

Taking her clothes, she went to the bathroom. A shower was fitted in one corner, long and wide with many showerheads and spouts. There was an immaculately clean sink and countertop. The cabinets were stocked with the barest of essentials. This house wasn't exactly lived in.

Seeing a natural hot spring growing up from the floor with the red sides of the mountain, Olena sighed. She tested the hot, bubbling water before climbing in. With a groan, she sat down on one of the carved seats and let the bubbles massage against her feet.

Washing at leisure, she got out and dressed. She found a brush and made quick work of her wet hair. She hated to admit it, but she did feel a little better. Thinking of Yusef lying in the hospital made her feel a lot worse. Not bothering to pick up her old clothes, she left the house without a backwards glance. Her boots hit upon the stone passageway as she walked. The halls were empty as she made her way back to the medical ward. Not saying a word, she went to sit on her bed from the night before. Yusef hadn't moved since she'd left.

* * * *

"Olena?"

Olena had been staring at Yusef's chest for so long that she'd become hypnotized by its movement. It took a moment for her name to register. Turning, she saw Nadja from Galaxy Brides.

"Nadja?" Olena tried to give the woman a smile. Nadja's hair was pulled back at the nape of her neck. Her eyes were kind as they shone from her porcelain skin. "What are you doing here?"

"I married Prince Olek." Nadja's smile faded slightly.

"The youngest brother."

"I'm sorry," Olena said before she could stop herself. Nadja laughed.

"I am too most of the time," Nadja admitted. "Morrigan Blake married the oldest son, Ualan. He's moody from what I can gather. And I don't know if you remember Pia?"

Olena nodded.

"She married Prince Zoran. He's a frightful creature." Nadja shivered.

"I met him and the other Princes." Olena thought of her kidnapping.

"Oh," Nadja said, as if she suddenly realized her comments were foolish. "I forgot, you would have, wouldn't you?"

Olena glanced back at Yusef.

"I only came to see how you were," Nadja said. "And Prince Yusef, obviously."

"The doctors say he is making a quick recovery. But, I don't see a change in him."

"And you?" Nadja asked.

"I'm fine," Olena answered, not caring to get into it. She liked Nadja, found her to be a likable woman, but she wasn't about to start playing nice and making friends.

"Oh." Nadja smiled shyly, not looking at all offended by Olena's short tone.

"Has anyone heard anything about who did this?"

"No," Nadja said. "I don't know anything. Morrigan was poisoned the same night. She's recovered now and I believe the Princes are pretty sure King Attor is behind it. He is ruler of the Var, the kingdom to the south. The men spend a lot of time together and one can only assume they are working on finding out what they can. Everyone has been really concerned about the both of you."

Olena didn't say anything. She was sure Nadja was just being polite. The family was most likely only concerned about its reputation and the life of their Prince. They didn't know her so couldn't possibly be concerned about a stranger.

"Well, they're about to serve dinner. You're welcome to come to the common hall with me if you like. The family usually dines together there." Nadja turned when Olena shook her head, saying a quick goodbye.

When Nadja was gone, Olena frowned at Yusef. She wasn't sure what she should do. She didn't want to leave him, but she didn't want to be in the palace either.

Olena waited as a doctor came and took some reading from his patient. He gave Yusef an injection. The doctor's wife brought Olena a tray of food. She tried to eat, but in the end pushed the tray aside.

Finally, everyone left for the evening and she was alone with her husband. Gulping, she felt a tear slide silently down her cheek. It was easy to be mad at first, but as the day turned into evening and he still showed no signs of waking up, she could hardly take the suspense of waiting.

Going over to him, she sat by his side. Taking her hand to his heartbeat, she felt an overwhelming fear that he would never wake up.

"Damn you, Yusef," she said. "It's not like this is going to make me stay here with you. I don't even care about you. As soon as my crew comes I'm leaving you behind."

Yusef's chest rose and fell. Other than that, he didn't move.

## Chapter Thirteen

Another day passed with Olena looking at Yusef, more than looking after him. The doctors attended most of his needs. She was pretty much in their way, but they never complained and she refused to leave. His parents and brothers came and went. They had few words for her and she had even less to say to them. Olek watched her cautiously, careful to keep a distance. This amused Olena, though she doubted she could take Olek in a fair fight.

Olena told herself she was just going to make sure Yusef was fine and then she would concentrate on leaving him. He wasn't a bad man. He'd been nice to her, taken care of her when she was sick. The least she could do was return the favor.

Olena was lying to herself. She knew it. She refused to acknowledge it.

Olena eyed the King and Queen looking over their son. They appeared so pitiful with their worried faces and tenderly murmured words. No one she ever knew was helped by such things.

Finally, she couldn't take it anymore--all the half-gestures and whispered words of distress. Dwelling wasn't doing anyone any good. It was time to light a fire under Yusef's very immobile backside.

"Give me a moment alone with him," Olena said. It wasn't a request. Her voice was hoarse from little use and the royal parents seemed surprised to hear her speak after so long being silent. When they didn't jump to obey, she said harshly, "Please."

The King glanced at his wife. Mede nodded him towards the door, saying, "We'll be just outside if you need us."

Olena waited for the door to close. Oh, but Yusef was handsome, even lying there so sick and helpless. His color had improved ever so slightly, though not enough to please his wife. As far as Olena could come up with--and she'd had many hours to contemplate how to rouse him out of his coma--there was only one way left to try. Slowly, she kicked off her boots. Eyeing him, she said, "I'll get you up, knight. If this doesn't work, we might as well tag your toe and put you six feet under. Hell, I'll even dig the hole myself."

Licking her lips, she pulled the covers off his naked chest. The hard muscles hadn't softened from his days in the hospital bed. He wore a pair of light cotton pants on his legs. His feet were bare.

Climbing up on top of him, she straddled his hips and let her body press intimately into his relaxed member. She leaned back to look at the door and swallowed nervously. All was well. They were alone.

She watched Yusef's features for any sign of a reaction. Taking her fingernails, she ran them over his chest, scratching his skin lightly from thick neck to strong stomach. His body was so firm. There was no fat deposited on his muscular frame. His warm flesh felt so fine against her palms that she stroked him a few more times.

Olena could easily remember how expertly his body would move against hers. Despite herself and her mission to rouse him, she grew excited by what she was doing.

She became more caressing, pressing her hands firmly to the flesh she explored. She rubbed his small nipples, raising them to her touch. For a moment, she thought she felt his breath catch. But she had been so wrapped up in her own exploration, that she wasn't sure. Pausing, she watched him. There was no change.

Phase one of her plan wasn't working. Olena decided to go to stage two.

Keeping quiet, she pulled her shirt off and set it behind her by Yusef's feet. She supported her weight as she leaned over. Letting her nipples graze his chest, she lightly rubbed her breasts over him. Olena bit her lips, closing her eyes as the sensations spread like wildfire through her.

Olena lifted on all fours, getting slightly carried away as she moved her erect nipples up towards his face. Naughtily, she parted his lips with the tight bud, shivering to feel his hot breath against it. She wanted nothing more than for him to open his mouth and suck it deeply between his lips.

When she pulled back to once more settle her hips on his, she felt as if he had aroused some beneath her. Without thinking, she said fervently, "Stage three."

Olena climbed off the bed, only to strip completely out of her clothes. Once naked, she got back on top of him. Sitting astride his thick, manly thighs, she drew the drawstring apart at his waist. With a tug, she drew the waistband down, over his hips to expose his member nestled in dark hair. Even prone, his manhood was daunting in its size.

Olena didn't stop. She ran her hands to his thighs, running up his hip bones and stomach as she tried to get the nerve to touch his member. She rubbed her breasts over his hips next, pressing more fully when she discovered the shocking pleasure of his hair roughened thighs on her sensitive nipples.

Yusef's member twitched between her breasts. Olena was hot for him. She could feel the moistness his nearness stirred between her thighs. Without thought, she crawled up his taut body, administering her kisses like medicine to his skin. Beginning at the flat navel carved into his stomach, she licked her way up his chest, flicking her tongue over his nipples, before continuing to his neck. His pulse had sped up since she last checked it. Or was that her heart she felt beating so hard and fast?

Her hips settled next to his groin, heating it to grow with her moist fire. It stirred and twitched against her, driving her mad with a powerful lust. Pleasure shot through her to feel him. His arousal became thick and she let it press intimately into her. Slowly, her hips rubbed along him, rocking, building tension and need.

Going to his ear, she bit the lobe and said, "Damn it, Yusef, if you wake up right now I'll give you the wildest night of sex you've ever had."

\* \* \* \*

Yusef felt himself coming out of a black hole into a whole new kind of dream. This dream was hot and moist and was doing wicked things to his prone body. His lips were parted. He tried to move, but he was too weak to do anything about the erotically charged tracing of his mouth.

Was that a tongue that slipped into him? No, it wasn't wet like a tongue.

"Stage three," he heard a whisper and the heat was gone from his body. His entire being lurched in protest. He wanted the heat to come back before the black hole consumed him once more.

His wish was answered. The heat came to him, only this time it was on his hips. He felt a brush to his naked manhood, awakening as it had his mouth. Whatever it was that was doing it, he didn't want it to stop.

*Oh,* he thought in dazed pleasure, *now that is a tongue.*

The ruthlessly delightful caress moved over his stomach and chest, detouring at his nipples, only to continue to his neck and ear. His loins lurched at the sensation. Then, he felt the press of womanly offering. His erection filled with painful urgency, ready to probe the damp and torturous heat.

The tongue met his ear, swirling around the rim, and teeth were soon behind it to bite his lobe. Hearing words he would never forget, in a voice that called to him like a siren's song, Olena said to him, "Damn it, Yusef, if you wake up right now I'll give you the wildest night of sex you've ever had."

His hand twitched, fighting against all odds to move.

"If you get out of this hospital tomorrow, I'll even give you a second night as your love slave," Olena swore, more for her own naughty pleasure than a real promise. It wasn't like he could hear her anyway. She moved her kisses to his mouth.

Yusef heard. Yusef memorized. Yusef planned to collect.

She'd been so worried about him. Feeling his arousal, she needed him more than anything to wake up and finish the ache he'd put in her the first night in the tent. Her tongue dipped in short thrusts to tempt his mouth to moving. Hotly, she said against his lips, "I'll do any sordid thing you want, in any position, in any place. Just come out of this blasted coma."

Breaking free, Yusef moaned. He lifted his hands to her hips, running over her smooth waist. His mouth parted and he pressed her teasing lips more fully to his, deepening with an instantly passionate kiss.

Olena jolted in surprise, but as his expert lips parted to taste her, she forgot her plan to stop as soon as he awoke. He edged his finger up to her breasts, tweaking the hard nipples. Olena moaned into him.

"Oh, firebird," Yusef moaned into her. His voice was husky from his passionate awakening. She felt like a soft, warm dream. Her hips worked along his manhood, not taking him in, but not pulling away as she rocked herself against his hardened length.

He pulled his hands from her breasts, knowing what her body wanted from him. He wanted it too. With a strength he shouldn't have been capable of, he firmly grabbed her hips and lifted her up. Olena gasped in surprise, pulling up and away from his lips. It was too late to stop his intent.

Yusef positioned himself with blind ease. Her fire called to him. He didn't stop to think. A woman as bold and passionate at this would know what she asked for. With a jerk of his strong hands, he impaled his arousal deeply into her warm, tight body.

Olena froze in horror as he broke through the seal of her virginity. A cry left her lips in a soft whimper of burning, agonizing pain. Her mouth trembled, but nothing more than a light plea came out. His enormous size hurt so badly. The pleasure faded from her body at the searing claim of him. He gripped her so firmly that she was too scared to move away. She waited for the pain to stop. It didn't.

Yusef felt her passion draining to be replaced by fear. Suddenly, the uncomfortable tightness of her body sunk into his dazed brain. His eyes blinked open, already shifted to yellow in his passion. He saw her clearly, the stunned horror of her expression.

"What was that, firebird?" His mind might have been subdued, but his thick arousal was still ready to complete its task.

"Oh," she said instead of answering, catching her breath. She struck out the only why she could think to answer. "I should have known you were faking sick, knight!"

Yusef blinked, completely confused.

Olena sprung into action. She pulled herself off of him, flinching once the hardness was gone. Without stopping, she hopped down to the floor, her legs wobbling as she landed. Digging through the sheets at his feet, she tossed it over his naked body to hide him from view. She refused to look at him, as she found her shirt and tugged it over her head. Anger was easier to handle than fear and pain.

Yusef tried to sit up, but it was too hard to move. His back shot in agony. Olena bent over and he saw the telltale sign of blood on her creamy inner thigh. It hit him like bricks to the gut. She had been pure.

Only when she was completely covered, did she turn back to look at him. She had regained some of her fiery composure, but her eyes were not so mischievous when she looked at him. Her lips opened, looking as if they were ready to scream. Her jaw snapped closed and she did the most dignified thing she could think of. She ran away.

Yusef watched her leave, desperate to go after her. Her confusion and torment washed over him and he wanted nothing more than to pull her back into his arms and show her that coupling didn't have to be like this--that if she had told him she was innocent, he would never had embedded himself into her so roughly or deeply. He would have broken her body in slowly. If she would have told him right off, he would have taken a different approach to her passions.

How was he supposed to know the brazen beauty he had married wasn't as brazen as she seemed? The woman kissed like an expert. She walked around, seemingly free with her nudity as if it were the most natural thing for her to do, as if many had seen her body and she knew how to use it.

Olena didn't turn back. Hitting the button on the wall, she watched as the door slid open. To her mortification, she realized Yusef's parents were waiting literally right outside the door. Seeing her pale face, they shot forward in worry.

"Your son's awake," she croaked to stop their questions. With that she took off down the corridor, leaving the confused King and Queen to stare after her before rushing to their son.

\* \* \* \*

Yusef was surprised to see his parents. He had been doing his best to work his pants back over his hips and was glad they were mostly righted before they walked in. Seeing the concern in his mother's eyes, he shot her a crooked smile. Instantly, she relaxed.

"Yusef," She didn't touch him now that he was awake, but the motherly instinct was strong in her and he read it well in her face without her having to say a word.

"Where did Olena go?" he asked, trying to sit up.

"She took off down the hall," the King said. "Don't worry. All the guards have orders not to let the Princesses out of the castle.

Seeing Yusef's concern, Mede added, "She'd been by your side since she got here. I'm sure her running off is just because she's embarrassed."

Yusef frowned. Did his parents know what just happened between him and his wife?

"Olena was kidnapped by the Var," the King said. Mede frowned, but sat back to let the men talk. Father and son had their own ways. The King quickly filled him in on the whole story, finishing with, "She handled herself well."

Yusef nodded, his heart racing to think what could have happened if his family hadn't been there.

"You see," the Queen added, breaking in with her soft wisdom. "She wouldn't let us check her in the medic for internal injury. When your father and brothers found her, she was tied to a tree, naked from the waist up. It's our fear that she's…"

Yusef thought of what just happened. He knew it wasn't possible she'd been raped.

"Well, that could be why she ran out of here so fast," the Queen said. "She might be shamed by what happened. She has a proud, fighting spirit."

Yusef nodded. "I will speak to her."

Mede sighed, knowing her son wouldn't judge her for it. Rape was never the victim's fault.

Glancing at Mede, the King said, "Go get the doctor."

Mede nodded and stood.

"Now, about your attack," the King began when they were alone, looking Yusef over. "What exactly happened?"

\* \* \* \*

Olena didn't stop as she hurried past the front entrance to the castle. The guard nodded at her as she passed but did not block her way. By the look on his face, he didn't know who she was.

Seeing the village before her in the valley, she ran for the forest path that would lead down to it. It was dusk, but the three suns merely tamed themselves, giving a dark blue haze to the ground that she could easily see by. All she had to do was get to the Outpost to grab her Galactic ID's and some clothes. Then she would be out of Yusef's life for good.

Even if she had to go before King Attor of the Var and make a deal, she would never go back to the Draig palace!

And nothing and no one could make her!

"Captain Olena."

Olena froze as the dark, deep words came calmly from the forest. It was as if their speaker had been waiting for her. Her jaw lifted. The voice was not of her crew.

"I didn't realize you were pirating these parts," the man's words continued. "It seems a little beneath your skills."

Olena looked around the colossal forest, seeing the red earthen path before her surrounded by yellow ferns that looked green in the twilight. She didn't move until she detected movement at her side. It was the flick of a match and a light of an old fashioned cigar. Only one person she knew smoked cigars.

"Doc?" Olena asked, blinking in surprise. She never imagined she would find the head of the Medical Alliance here. Taken aback, she couldn't speak through her confusion. Doc Aleksander was someone she had crossed paths with a few times on minor jobs. He stayed out of her way and she stayed out of his, after paying a small fee of rights of course. It was robbery on his part, but Olena just smiled. It was usually robbery on hers. Finding her voice, as the orange glow illuminated the man's dark face, she said, "I didn't know the Alliance was doing missionary work on this forsaken planet. What brings you?"

Aleksander stepped out from the trees, pushing off the rough bark, as if he were in the finest of gentleman's clubs. His movements were graceful and refined. When he waved his cigar around, it was with an air of elegance. He wore a dark suit, expensive and handsomely cut. His hair was slicked back, the locks matching the black of his thick mustache, which twitched when he spoke or took a long draw as he was doing now. He smiled as the smoke curled out of his lips.

"A minor detour," he dismissed with a wave.

Olena didn't dare move. She didn't dare show fear. Men like Doc Aleksander never traveled alone. She could just imagine the goons he had hidden in the trees. Pretending as if she had all the time in the world, she said, "Me too."

"So you don't have something going, Captain?" His eyes roamed over her tousled hair and pale cheeks. Taking in her lithe body, he let an interested smile form on his lips.

"Sorry, Doc," Olena said.

She held her ground as he stepped daringly closer. Nerves jumped all over her skin. This man was bad news. She'd heard horror stories about what he'd done to people who merely looked at him wrong. He'd surgically remove their eyes without putting them under.

"You know I've always been straight with you," Olena said. "I lost my ship and had to hitch a fast ride. The ride landed me here. If I had a scam, I'd let you in on it. But you know me. I always end up where the money is. I'll find something to pay my insurance policy with. I just need a little time first to get the angle. For a primitive race, these shifters aren't too bad off."

"Shifters?" the Doc asked. Olena thought he would have known, he usually was rumored to know everything. His brows narrowed slightly in displeasure. He was also rumored to be a purist. He put up with alien races out of necessity, but he didn't think they were good enough to wipe a human's ... well... "Tell me Olena, do you know your way around here pretty well?"

"Well enough," she answered, forcing herself to shrug. "There's not much to know. This place is dreadfully barbaric."

The man's arm came forward to leisurely drape over her shoulders, as he strolled down the path with her, leading her deeper into the forest, away from the palace. Suddenly, her stomach lurched and she thought of Yusef. Doc's cigar dipped dangerously close to her cheek, warming her skin. She smiled slightly, ignoring it. She didn't for a moment think it was an accident.

"How would you like for you and your crew to never pay another insurance premium again?" he asked.

Olena's ears perked up, intrigued by his offer. Such an opportunity never came up lightly. "I'm listening."

"Do you think you could steal me a prize?" he asked smoothly, stopping to turn to her. His arm slid across the back of her shoulders as his free hand rose to touch the base of her throat. "It would be worth your while."

"How worth?" she asked like a true pirate. Doc grinned in appreciation of her, as his hand trailed leisurely over her neck to rest lightly above her breasts. She didn't flinch as he touched her, but she wanted to. His embrace was nothing like Yusef's--even if her body still ached from where he'd skewered her.

"Name your price." Doc moved his hand to flick the cigar before puffing. He dropped his hands from her chest. "Ah, damn, it's too bad I'm a married man."

Olena ignored the confession as his gaze moved over her like he wanted nothing more than to press her into the earthen floor. Feeling the twinge Yusef put in her body, she said, "Passage off this rock."

"Done." Doc nodded.

"Fifty thousand," she continued to barter, as was expected.

"Done."

"My own spacecraft?" she questioned, letting an impish smile cross her features.

"I appreciate your greed," he chuckled heartily. "Don't push it."

Knowing he wouldn't be trying anything, she shrugged. Pursing her lips together she affected a sultry pout. "Can't blame a girl for trying."

"Especially one as devious as you, my dear Captain," the Doc said. There was only pleasure in his tone, no disapproval.

Passage and fifty thousand? Not to mention immunity from the Medical Alliance for her and her crew. This deal was too good to pass up. The only drawback was that she had the feeling she would be going back inside the palace. If what he wanted was outside the fortress, he would have just taken it himself. She did not relish facing Yusef again. She was too mortified. But, if she refused Doc Aleksander's direct request, she'd end up dead.

*Better humiliation than torture,* she thought.

"So, boss, what you looking to get?" she asked with a vivid smile and a sparkle to her mischievous eyes. "If it can be lifted off the ground, Captain Olena can rightly steal it."

The Doc's smile wavered from his features, as his face lost all its delightful charm. Cruelly, he said, "My daughter."

## Chapter Fourteen

The palace keep was a dazzling place. For a palace designed and decorated by a race of antiquated, warrior men, it was fantastic. There was five wings built into, up, and around the tallest mountain on the planet. Olena was told that each Prince had designed his own section. Too her amazement, and judging by their homes, she discovered that the brothers were anything but carbon copies of each other. Whereas Morrigan's home with Ualan was all fire, marble, and fur, Zoran and Pia's wing was constructed with a wood finish, giving the place a real oriental lodge feeling to it. Yusef's home was too plain, though she had a feeling the Outpost is where he spent most of his time.

Prince Olek and Princess Nadja's home teemed with lush plant life. It grew out from a sunroom to vine around a door and part of the trellised ceiling. Giant fish tanks took up an entire two walls. One was clear with an oversized pink sucker fish adhered to the glass and blue fish with big, blinking eyes. The second had dark murky waters that Olena couldn't see into except for hints of life that fluttered past the glass.

In the center of the hall was a natural water fountain, relaxing and calm in its resplendent beauty. It too had plant life growing in its stone crevices. It did nothing to soothe the sour temperaments of the four gathered Princesses.

Olena didn't go back to Yusef in the medical ward, choosing to do the cowardly thing and hide out. He was trapped in the hospital and so couldn't go to his palace home. She took advantage of that fact and quarantined herself from the rest of the family. Only by the grace of Queen Mede was she fed when a servant brought her a tray of food. The Queen had come to the home once to give her a tour of the palace and to introduce her to her new 'sisters'. It had been extremely awkward.

She was surprised to get Nadja's invitation to join her and the other Princesses at her house for a visit. But, thinking of Doc, she knew she had no choice. She had to go, if only to judge his daughter for herself. She didn't see a way around it. If she didn't retrieve the woman for him, he would find a way to get to his daughter himself and Olena's body would never be found.

Looking around at the other high-backed chairs, Olena noticed the others looked as dismal as she felt, especially Morrigan whose unusually pale face and red eyes screamed that she was hung-over. Stretching her arms over her head, Morrigan yawned. It was the most movement she had made in awhile.

"So, have any of your husbands lied to you about who they were?" Olena tried to encourage conversation. Her hair was pulled back into a bun and her eyes flashed with purposeful mischief to hide what she was really feeling. Maybe the Doc's daughter would want to be rescued and returned to him. Maybe she'd be doing the woman a favor by taking her back.

"I thought mine was a prison guard," Pia chuckled darkly. Olena glanced at her. Okay, there was one unhappy Princess.

"I used to call mine a gardener," Morrigan said, tucking her hand beneath her head on the high-backed chair. Mumbling softly, she said so as not to disturb her delicate head, "And a caveman."

The women chuckled. Olena frowned slightly. Morrigan didn't appear to be too unhappy, though she was obviously miserable. Olena couldn't tell if it was because she didn't like Prince Ualan or because she'd drunk to excess the night before.

Nadja just blushed shyly. "I call mine a dragon."

*Hum,* Olena thought, *that answer was vague.*

"They're all dragons, if you ask me." Morrigan winked at Nadja.

Nadja halfheartedly laughed as she rose to answer a summons from the door. It was the Queen.

Mede stepped into the intimate circle of women and nodded. "I heard you all were hiding out here."

Olena didn't move. She kept her expression veiled as she watched the three women. Nadja smiled in genuine kindness. Morrigan miserably refused to move. Pia looked guarded, as if she didn't know how to take the Queen.

"How's Yusef?" Olena asked, before she could stop to

think. She suddenly blushed at the outburst and refused to glance at the other women.

"Still awake," the Queen answered. "And still with his brothers. They speak of fighting and fighting always makes warriors happy, for it is something they know how to do."

Olena nodded, leaning back in her chair and trying to pretend she didn't care either way. No one was fooled.

Mede glanced at the hung-over Morrigan and raised her delicate brow slightly. Morrigan had to turn away. To her credit, the Queen said nothing.

Nadja suddenly asked if anyone wanted something to drink. Morrigan balked and instantly declined, turning a shade paler. They all laughed, despite their mood.

"No, dear, we're fine," the Queen answered. Silence followed. Mede was disappointed that the women weren't going to continue to talk freely. She had heard their soft laughter and had been anxious to be a part of it. But, she also knew the women were troubled in their own ways. She couldn't blame them. Her sons were great men, but were sometimes too stubborn for their own good. "Daughters."

The Princesses looked at Mede expectantly. The Queen came forward and took a seat amongst them, looking them over in turn.

Olena saw the woman's cunning and wondered what she was up to. When she had given the palace tour, Mede had tried probing her. Olena had given the woman nothing, artfully avoiding all her veiled questions.

"Enough of this. This planet is in desperate need of more women and I intend to see that each one of you explore the power you possess," the Queen said. "Your husbands are warriors. I expect now each of you has a clear idea now of what that means. But just because they made the rules, doesn't mean you can't use them. You have more power than you think. So, tell me your problems with my sons and I'll give you the Qurilixen solution. I think it's time that the royal woman had the upper hand for once."

Slowly, one by one, the women smiled, growing more and more trusting of the earnest Queen--all but Olena who only smiled because it was expected of her. The Queen nodded, happy. Yes, Mede thought to herself, that was how it was supposed to be with daughters. She had waited too many years to let her sons ruin her plans for a giant family.

"Pia." Mede looked pointedly at the woman. In that moment, Pia was well aware the Queen knew her hesitance for her, but was being patient. "Why don't you go first?"

Before Pia could answer, Olena slowly stood, drawing all eyes to her. Quietly, she said, "I should go check on Yusef."

The Queen nodded. The Princesses were silent, all except for Nadja who ordered the door open. Olena silently trailed out of the home.

"Has she said anything about her kidnapping?" the Queen asked when she was gone and the door was shut.

The others shook their heads in denial.

"Poor, poor woman." The Queen turned her sad eyes back to her daughters. "I can't imagine the horror she went through."

\* \* \* \*

Yusef was surrounded by his brothers. He grinned and laughed with them, as they made jokes about the blow his manhood had received from his wife. Yusef was still sore about having to put her in chastisement. However, discovering that she was a virgin at the time lessened his irritation with it enough that he could receive his brother's jests in good humor.

"On the way back to the palace," Zoran stated, "she almost unseated our little brother from his *ceffyl*."

Olek frowned. "I don't envy you a bit, brother. I almost did you the favor of dropping her back off at the Var doorstep."

Yusef chuckled, knowing Olek jested.

"I owe you all a great debt in retrieving my little firebird." Yusef turned serious. "Her medicine is just what I needed to come around."

"Oh," Ualan laughed wryly. "I don't want to hear any of that!"

Yusef just grinned, proud and unashamed.

"So how are your wives?" Yusef asked. Instantly, the Princes' expressions faded. Yusef sighed. They didn't say a word. Then, to lighten the mood, he said, "Well, at least they didn't try to dismember you."

The brothers laughed anew.

\* \* \* \*

Olena came quietly to the medical ward door, her heart

hammering in her chest at the sound of male laughter. She paused, not understanding what they said as they spoke in their own tongue.

She had left Nadja's about an hour ago, only now getting the nerve to face Yusef. She only came now because the doctor had seen her out wandering the halls and told her to retrieve him. He was free to go home, but the doctor wanted him supervised for the walk and thought his wife the best one for the job. He then rattled off a bunch of care instructions, which Olena was sure she would never remember.

Suddenly, a servant rushed past her into the medical ward and the laughter stopped. He came back, followed by Prince Zoran. Olena lifted her jaw at the Prince. He nodded distractedly back in return.

Olena stepped forward to face her husband. It didn't take but a moment for his eyes to find her. He looked almost completely recovered, except for the sling around his arm. It lay against his delectably naked chest. Olek and Ualan looked at each other and quickly stood to leave. Olena glanced at them both, returning Olek's slight frown with one of her own.

When they were alone, she asked softly, "Are you ready? They said for me to come and get you."

Yusef threw his legs over the side of the bed. She looked lovely. He devoured her every curve of her with his eyes, itching to touch her, hold her, kiss her. He lurched with a curious possessiveness to know he was the only man to have ever had her.

"Olena," he began.

Olena scowled. His tone was too tender for her. Turning her back on him, she said, "Mention it and I'll do more than earn chastisement."

Yusef had to grin at her fighting spirit and at the view he was given of her very firm backside when she walked away from. He limped slightly to keep up with her and his back spasmed and strained. Olena hastened ahead of him into the passageway leading to his palace home.

"Hey," he called, needing to stop from the furiously growing pace. Olena turned to him at the grunt of his voice. He leaned against a wall, resting. To his husbandly pleasure, her face fell as she forgot everything else to rush to his side.

Olena looked over his grimacing face. She lightly moved her hands to the folds of his bared chest in concern. All embarrassment at seeing him again left her as she ran her fingers over his sides in an effort to see his back.

What she found when she looked made her blood run cold. Over a dozen long, angry gashes slashed over his skin. They were healed shut, but Olena knew that they must hurt him terribly. Blinking, she looked up at him.

"What happened to you?" Her voice was hoarse, weak.

Yusef was taken aback by her tormented whisper, as the arm that wasn't in a sling reached up to touch her face. He met her cheek with his fingers, stroking her gently.

"Didn't they tell you?" he asked.

Olena nodded. "But you really didn't see who did it?"

"No. But, we will find them." Yusef's thumb moved to trace her lip and to his delight he felt her shiver. Suddenly, his eyes turned sad.

"What? Are you hurting?"

Yusef merely smiled and she wrinkled her nose at the obviousness of her question. Instead of answering, he asked a question of his own. "Did you mean it when you said you meant to leave me?"

Olena had almost forgotten who she was until those words. She drew herself up, straightening away from him. Her eyes clouded once more, the delicate bond between them severed by her will.

"I'm not Princess material, knight." She slipped an arm around his lower back to help him walk. He leaned slightly on her as they took a slower pace. "How about we leave it at that for now?"

Once back in Yusef's palace home, Olena let him go. They had walked in silence. Yusef was tormented by her words. Olena, hating herself for what she would do to him and his family, couldn't bring herself to look at him.

Eyeing him, she said, "I was told to see if you needed help bathing."

No, he didn't need help, but he wouldn't admit to as much. A small plan forming in his mind, Yusef decided that maybe there were ways to convince his stubborn wife that she belonged with him. Anything was worth a try.

"You wouldn't mind?" He affected a small groan of pain.

It wasn't too much of a stretch. His back did hurt.

"No," she rushed, "of course not."

It was the least she could do, seeing how she was going to run out on him and steal one of his sisters-by-marriage.

Yusef's brow rose at her ready answer.

Olena hid her flush, as she said, "Well, you did bathe me when I was sick. It's the least I can do for you. And the doctors did leave you to my care. Though, I have to tell you, I am no nursemaid."

"I'm sure you'll do fine." Yusef's eyes lit as he thought of how she'd brought him out of his coma. A little more of that medicine and he would be doing back flips like the best of them.

"Maybe you should shift." She bit her lip thoughtfully. Although, she meant it as a way to help him, she had to admit she was curious to see what he looked like-- *completely shifted.* She wondered if everything turned hard with armor, like if his ... well…. Olena turned her back to him before he could see the look on her face.

Yusef felt the rush of her desire hitting him and was relieved. It would seem their little encounter in the medical ward hadn't turned her off to him completely. He would just have to show her that a soft, gentler approach to her body could melt her to him. The greater, straining, rougher passions would come later. He wondered how hard it would be to convince her to let him soothe the ache he delved into her. She had softened to his will so easily in the past.

A long, awkward silence passed for Olena. Her body heated with familiar longing for him.

Finally, Yusef said, "I can't. It would stress the wounds."

"Oh," she mumbled.

Yusef grinned. Was that disappointment he heard? Damned, but if his wife wasn't an intoxicating vixen! If she was that eager to play with his Draig form, he would gladly let her. Not that he could feel her so well behind the hard armor of his skin. Smiling, he knew there were other games they could play that would include the Draig form before he shifted to take her. Captive and Captor came instantly to mind, as did Hunter and the Hunted.

His eyes flashed with golden hues of passion, which he quickly subdued before she could see the full force of his desire.

"Well, come on." She glanced at him. "I think you should probably use the hot spring so you can sit down."

The hot spring was all right with Yusef. Thinking of her administering hands on his body, he groaned. When she glanced back at the sound, he turned his lustful gaze to an instant grimace of pain.

"Maybe they let you go too early," she said, more to herself.

"No, I made them let me out." Before he could stop himself, he teased, "I was promised a love slave if I left. I believe the exact words were, I'll do any sordid thing you want, in any position, in any place."

Olena balked. "I only said that to get you to wake up."

"It worked."

Olena hid her red face from him. Just thinking of it was waking him up, though not in the manner she meant.

"Oh, stop!" She glared at him, her hands on her hips. "Let's just get it all out now. So I was technically a virgin. It doesn't make you some kind of conquering hero or anything. You just happened to be the first man opportunity arose with. I mean everyone else I had been with up until you I was trying to steal from and they got stuck with the firefly pin before anything could come of it. And there was my crew, but they are even more alien and stranger than you are. So, get your back pats over with and let's drop it. Okay? Great."

Yusef merely grinned, unfazed.

"Oh, you're impossible." She grimaced, rolling her eyes. "Come on."

Yusef followed her into the bathroom. When he didn't undress, she looked at him expectantly. He let a sheepish frown come to his features, as he said, "Would you mind? I can't bend over yet."

Olena gulped slightly, automatically looking down to his groin. Shaking herself, she cleared her throat. "No, of course you can't."

Olena kept her eyes averted as she stripped off his pants, refusing to look at him. It's not like she hadn't seen many men before him. But now, remembering how overpowering he had been inside her, it made her nervous. Yusef tried not to laugh as she bit her lips and tried to take his pants down by pinching the sides with the tips of her fingers. It took her awhile to realize his pants were caught on his erection. Whatever happened to his bold little wood sprite?

"Would you mind getting my sling?" Yusef's voice dipped. Her eyes darted to him, vivid in their green loveliness. He saw her composure waver. "Is something wrong?"

"Ah. No, no, nothing."

Olena went to him. The sling was tied at his shoulder and she had to press close to his side to untie it. Yusef let his naked thigh brush against her pants. He felt her tense and shiver. Her hands fumbled longer than they should of, but when she pulled back he was freed.

Yusef smiled at her, stepping into the hot bath. He slowly sank down onto the seat. The hot water did wonders for him.

"Why don't you take your clothes off and come in?" Yusef's eyes lit with challenge, seeming to say, *you're not embarrassed, are you?* "You'll be better able to help me."

Olena eyed him, but in the end thought he was too injured to do her much damage. Feeling very aware of her body for the first time in her life, she pulled off her shirt. When his eyes lit with satisfaction, she had a new sense of gratification in his interest. She wasn't so quick to take off her pants and reveal the opening of her womanhood to him. That significant part lit with its own memory of him. To Olena's surprise, it wasn't at all angry with him for what had happened to it. In fact, it was treacherously eager to have him try it again. She felt its pull, growing slightly hot at the mere look of him in the bubbling water. It took her longer to step into the bath than it should have.

Yusef was gentleman enough not to comment. His gaze dipped down over her throat and chest as she lowered herself into the warm water. Her breasts floated on the surface, the water lapping against her nipples to make them hard. His hands twitched as if they would disobey him and touch her.

Olena took some soap and handed it over to him. Again, he said, "Would you mind terribly?"

Olena's mouth went dry, but she pushed forward. She parted her lips slightly as her finger found the flesh of his hard chest. She lathered him in circles, running all over his upper body. She touched his back lightly, mindful of his wounds.

Olena pulled back. She looked at the water. "Can you lift your foot?"

Yusef flinched, but managed. As her breast brushed against him, he didn't care about his injuries. She cleaned one foot and hair roughened calf, then the other. When he was again seated, she eyed him.

"Maybe you should stand." Olena licked her lips. The texture of his skin was doing something very alluring to her senses.

Yusef, thinking of his risen member beneath the water, only hesitated for a moment. Was it just him or was her words a little too husky?

As he stood proudly before her, cradling his arm slightly to his chest, Olena gasped. He was at full arousal.

Yusef shrugged. "I can't help it. Can you work around it?"

Olena nodded. She moved her hands from where the water hit his lower thighs, working up over his legs to his hips. She rose as she cleaned him. His member came temptingly close to her mouth. She'd never taken one between her lips, but she had heard some of the men speaking of such things and how it brought them endless pleasure. Would it bring Yusef pleasure?

Yusef saw her mouth part as she passed by his shaft. It took all his control not to thrust forward between her sweet lips. Olena's fingers skimmed over to his buttocks. She lathered him, standing so close to his chest she could feel the heat of his body next to hers.

Yusef's eyes darkened when her fingers stayed too long on his backside, her fingers turning from washing to caressing, to all out fondling as she gravitated naturally closer to him. Touching her face, he asked, "Do you still hurt?"

Olena's shy gaze turned down at the bold question. When she didn't answer, Yusef slid his hand down her side.

"Turn around," he urged.

Olena pulled her hands away.

"Trust me. I want to show you something."

Olena couldn't refuse the soft entreaty of his eyes or the firmly moving lines of his lips. Yusef grabbed her about the flat of her stomach and drew her back against him. Their bodies angled so that his erection pressed into the softness of her backside, parting her slightly against his length. Not moving to penetrate, he glided his good hand over her flesh.

Yusef drew his fingers over her nipples, circling and pinching them with agonizing attention, before moving them down over her flat stomach to rest briefly above her opening. Olena tensed, her head falling back on Yusef's shoulder. She shook in ragged anticipation.

His lips were at her ear, nipping and soothing. "I'm going to give you the pleasure you should have felt the first time."

Olena shivered, awakening enough from her haze at his words to try and pull away. Yusef's strong arm tensed around her. He pulled her once more into his hardness. He delved his fingers forth to part her body ever so slightly.

Olena couldn't stop her hips from responding as he rubbed at her sensitive center. Her back arched into him and a whimper of pleasure escaped her lips. His kisses pressed her neck as his hand pressed her mound. Her hips jerked, naturally seeking to ease their tension as they thrust up and down in light movements. Olena's body was fevered from washing his flesh and now, to feel him touching her, she moaned.

Yusef bent lower, pushing his fingers along her slick heat. He felt the beginnings of a tremor beneath his hand and he hadn't even entered his fingers into her moist body. To his surprise, her hips bucked and she shook with a sudden force. Hot moisture pooled on his hand as she racked against it in pleasure. Her body must have been on the brink for her to react so suddenly and with little probing.

Yusef growled, her cry echoing around him. She fell limp, leaning into his arm for support. Her ragged breath fell onto his arm as her lips turned naturally to nudge him.

"Yusef," she said, awed by what she felt. Yusef's arm slipped around to hold her up. She turned, her head lying against his chest as she tried to slow her heart.

His body still ached to be fulfilled. His back hurt from leaning over in such a way. But it was worth it as he felt the openness of her pleasure flowing through him as if they were connected as one and he did not protest his own discomfort.

## Chapter Fifteen

"You shouldn't be left in such a state." Olena looked down at his arousal, still tense and pulsing with need.

Yusef body lurched. He couldn't believe his ears.

Olena's body became moist once more with the potent smell of his clean flesh and the look of his rock hard body. Still quaking in the wake of her pleasure, she forgot who she was. Being with him was all she wanted. She leaned into the support of his chest.

"Tell me how to ease you." Her eyes didn't meet his, as her hand fluttered forward to touch his arousal. She curled her fingers around him. She'd never taken things this far and was in new territory. But, what better partner to teach her than her husband who already showed generous desire for her?

Something in the back of her brain warned against such things, telling her it would be harder to go if she let him continue. Another, stronger voice, told her it would be harder for her if she didn't. She couldn't keep resisting him and still manage to think straight at the same time. To deny him was to deny herself. If she just let him complete what they'd started, maybe he'd be out of her system and she could again get focused on returning to her old life.

When Yusef didn't move, Olena glanced shyly up at him. His lids were lowered in pleasure at her willing touch. Why did her old life of adventure suddenly seem so dull and uninteresting? Why was this ugly, white house suddenly holding more appeal than the luxurious comforts of her Captain's quarters? Why was being bound to this dragon-man more tempting than precious freedom?

Her lips parted. The ache inside her became unbearable, making her want to run. The pain had nothing to do with the desires festering inside her stomach. Tears made her eyes moisten into big sparkling emeralds. She would never allow them to fall even as they radiated her agony to him.

"Yusef?" She thought of Doc Aleksander and what she had to do for him. It's not like the man had given her a choice. And when the Medical Mafia wanted something from you, you didn't naysay them. To do so would mean certain pain, death if you were lucky, and, most assuredly the destruction of everything and one you held dear before both.

"What is it?"

Olena's hand left his arousal to skim up his chest.

*I need to tell you something,* her mind whispered.

"It's nothing," she said, breathless. "Could you just kiss me?"

Yusef gave her a quizzical smile, but couldn't resist the sweet, almost innocent request of her soft lips. He lowered his head, onslaughting her senses with a tender force of passion that left her mind numb and her limbs liquid. As he pulled back, her body shook and Olena was sure she was going to just disappear into nothingness.

Yusef looked at her face. She was leaning into him, holding his heart beneath her gentle palm. Her eyes were still closed, her lips still pursed as if he were even now against them. He smiled a devilishly handsome grin that she missed. Her lashes fluttered. He dipped down once more to keep her bewitched in the spell he wove so naturally over her senses.

Olena panted softly, a moan coming from deep within her. Giving herself over to him, she was too far gone to think or calculate. She wound her hand up his broad neck, shaking somewhat as she ran her fingers through the soft silken texture of his dark hair.

When he pulled back to let her breathe, she whispered without thinking, "I was so afraid that you were going to die."

Yusef felt a dam break within him at her admission. It was not a sentiment of love, but it was the closest she'd ever come to admitting she cared for him. Her hands moved and he felt her lightly touching the scars on his back.

"They will heal, won't they?" Her wide eyes moved to capture his. "You're going to be fine, right?"

Yusef nodded. He wanted her so badly that the need was becoming painful. Leaning over, he pressed his mouth to hers, deepening the kiss as he passionately ground his mouth forward, diving into her to suck at her tongue and possess her lips. This time her body did evaporate. Her legs fell from under her and she swayed against him as if she would swoon. Only by the power of her hands around his shoulders and the strength of his good arm around her back, did she stay upright.

When he pulled back this time, his eyes were flecked with golden promise and Olena knew she had her answer.

"I'm not going anywhere, firebird," he said tenderly, "except to take my wife to bed."

Olena trembled. The bedroom seemed so intimate, so permanent. She couldn't allow herself to fall deeper into his maddening spell. A smile coming to her parted lips, she let an unmistakable mischief come to her gaze.

"Why not here?" She smoothed her hands onto his body and pressed kisses on his chest and stomach. Yusef tensed, unable to deny her mouth as she trailed it lower.

He moaned. He tangled his fingers into her hair, urging her to continue her wayward descent. Her breath fell rapid and hot against his flesh, rippling over it like little pools of undulating desire.

Olena kissed the tip of his arousal and Yusef thought he would go mad from the sweet torture of her lips. She kissed him again before tracing feathery caresses along the shaft to the base. His body lurched.

Yusef's back spasmed. No matter how much his body wanted to stand rigid and take her torture, his wounds wouldn't let him for much longer. Having no wish to faint dead away at such a pleasurably rewarding moment, he sat down. Olena blinked in surprise.

"Come here," he said in a voice that was all syrupy with promise. "I'll show you how to ease us both."

Olena crossed over the bubbling water, seeing he intended for her to sit on his lap. The heat from the steam was making her hair stick to her creamy flesh like streaks of fire. A long wave curled around the bend of her breast and he nearly lost himself at the seductive sight. He lifted his hand to follow the wet trail of her locks, moving to brush them back as he unveiled the nipple puckered beneath. Olena shivered. Yusef caressed her with the backs of his fingers.

Slowly, his eyes burning into her, his hand moved down her stomach to grasp her hip. Pulling her forward, he urged her to sit astride him.

"I've burned for you, Olena, since the first moment I saw you, standing defiant and beautiful at the mouth of that spacecraft. I knew I would have you then, as I want you now."

He dipped his fingers into the water, reaching to feel her even as he cursed his useless arm for its limits. Olena's hands fell to his shoulders as he stroked a fire into her. As her hips responded in restless motion against him, he slid a finger inside of her to stroke more intimately.

Soon the hand wasn't enough. She need more--much more. She needed him. She needed to feel him inside of her. Olena leaned over, kissing his wet neck, drinking from his glorious skin. Her lips nipped at his ear, delighting in the shivering response she felt in his skin at the touch.

He took his fingers from her, urging her to move so he could enter. Olena stiffened slightly, remembering how full he'd felt the last time. Her thighs clenched, keeping him from easing her downward.

"Mmm." He felt her resistance. Nuzzling into her as she kissed his ear with dizzying effect, Yusef said, "You control the depth. Don't be afraid of me."

Olena couldn't resist the plea in his words as his hand once more pulled her to take him. Not looking up, she felt his hand against her leg as he guided himself to her opening. He rubbed the tip several times against her, letting her get used to his hardness. Then, ever so slowly, he pushed his arousal just into the slick entrance of her body.

Olena was rewarded with an overwhelming sense of pleasure and need. With a slowness that made sweat bead Yusef's brow, she loosened her legs and slid down to capture him. Her breath came out raggedly along his flesh.

Yusef wanted nothing more than to grab her and slam her down. Biting his lips, he resisted. He clenched his hands almost desperately against the soft flesh of her hips, letting her set the pace while at the same time praying she would soon set a faster, harder one.

Olena gradually fit him inside her, feeling the unyielding fullness of him as his length compelled her to fit around him, to accommodate his size. Olena pushed up from his shoulder by small degrees. He went deeper still and she gasped.

His voice harsh, catching as he spoke. "You must move Olena. Move me in you."

Olena pulled up a fraction and then lowered as her body wanted him back into its fold. The thrust was achingly shallow.

Yusef's hands gripped her tighter as he fought the beast within him that wanted nothing more than to begin mindlessly pumping and ramming into her moist softness.

"Again," he commanded.

Olena pulled up only to repeat the same aching torment. Her body burned for more, but she was reluctant to let him out of her just yet. She was still getting used to the feel of him, still discovering the sensations he was causing.

"Again." His voice ground out in a pain that had nothing to do with his back. In fact, he couldn't even feel his wounds, so exquisite was her soft to his hard.

This time when she moved, he lifted her up higher. Olena protested and forced her hips down against his hand. The water caused her to slide from his grip and, she came down forcefully upon him. Olena cried out in pleasant surprise. She was rewarded with a gratifying wave of pleasure.

Yusef's groan followed her.

"Just like that, Olena, oh … yeah … just like that, firebird." Yusef's hand was again on her hips as he lifted her. "Do it again."

Olena lifted up only to push down hard as her buttocks hit upon his legs. Yusef's hand kneaded along the curve of her back, moving to her breasts to circle and pinch her nipples.

"Do it faster," he urged, moaning. "Take me in faster."

Olena obliged and was richly rewarded. Her hips took over, mindlessly driving her body against him, building in unforeseen ecstasy. Yusef growled loudly in appreciation as she obeyed his plea. It was like nothing she had ever felt. His body was so strong and protective and gentle, yet commanding and sure at the same time.

Feeling her tense, Yusef pushed up from the seat and thrust up into her, going as deeply as her body would take him. Olena howled, arching back in the most beautiful display Yusef had ever seen. Her body quivered violently. His body answered her call to him, jerking roughly inside her as he released all the tension that had been building since the night they first met.

Olena dropped against his flesh, terrified that she could feel so much, unable to process the rush flowing between them--not only with their physical release, but their minds and bodies as he tried to connect to her. Shudders still wracked her thin frame. It was too much for her to handle, as she knew she would leave him soon, would deceive him so horribly that the affectionate expression on his face would never hold. After she delivered his brother's wife to Doc Aleksander, he wouldn't even be able to look at her.

Something had to give and since her body had a mind of its own, still encasing him inside her, it was her emotions that shut off to him, blocking the connection before it could take root.

Yusef felt the snap between them as sharp and real as a slap across the face. They'd been so close. Only a second more and he would have been able to read her completely, and she him. But she refused the intimacy of his mind and soul. The feeling left him cold and weary.

"Olena?" He wondered at her mental withdrawal.

"Hum?" Olena moaned into his neck, still suffering from the aftermath of their pleasure. She detected pain in his voice and mistook it for physical. She took herself off him, her wide eyes checking him over for injury. "Oh, Yusef, I'm sorry, your back!"

Yusef let her think what she wanted, not wanting to put unreturned feelings at her feet. He did have some measure of pride left, even if this vixen he called a wife had taken everything else from him--including his heart.

Her flushed features filling with concern, she said, "Why didn't you stop me? Oh, you didn't break anything open, did you? Can you move? Are you paralyzed?"

Yusef chuckled despite himself as she tried to move around to see his back. If ever he was to be injured, let it be with her thrusting like a flaming tree-witch on top of him.

His member grew with alarming speed at the thought. His mouth twitched, as he wickedly replied, "Feel me and see if you think me paralyzed."

Olena blushed furiously, all the way to the roots of her hair. She looked down. Indeed, she could see the tip of him in the water. Gulping, she asked, unsure if she could handle another round of such pleasure, "Again?"

Yusef grinned and shrugged. "It seems I like your

medicine better than that of the doctors."

Even as she wondered if she could take him into her again, Olena felt a stirring inside her womb, answering his lurid call.

"Should we get out of the bath?" she asked, hot from their lovemaking and the steam from the tub.

"Where would you have us go?" He captured her lips. His back did indeed feel loosened from the hot water, ready to try something more vigorous.

"I," Olena turned as red as her hair and couldn't think of a single thing to say. Every sarcastic comment she'd ever had left her in the face of his sultry dark, animalistic gaze. The gray burned with golden hues of promise. "Where do you want me?"

Standing, he pulled her with him. Her breast slid over his body, hardening into him. Boldly he kissed the breath from her lungs, only to release her when her knees were bending and her hands were clutching at his shoulders. Growling against her mouth, he said dirtily, "I would have you deeply impaled on my shaft."

\* \* \* \*

Olena sat curled on a chair, fully clothed, chewing absently on her thumbnail as she watched Yusef. Her body ached in a hundred different ways, all of them a testament to how much he had recovered. Only after the third time coming together on the white fur rug before the fireplace, did Olena climb off of him and demand he go to bed.

When he lay down, his body worn and past all imaginable limits, he had reached for her to join him. To Yusef's obvious dismay, she refused, using the excuse of his injuries not to lie intimately beside him while they slept, lest she hurt him when she tossed in sleep. Making herself a bed on the white couch before the roaring fire, she had inevitably drifted off into the nightmarish world of her dreams.

Now that it was morning, she felt the weight of her world bearing in on her. Doc Aleksander wouldn't wait long for her compliance. Comforting herself with the fact that Doc was a family man--so much so he wouldn't cheat on his wife no matter how hot his desire was--Olena tried not to feel guilty. Surely the man would welcome his daughter with opened arms, taking her back into the protective fold of his world. Besides, the reasons why the woman left him in the first place was a family matter, best resolved between them as a family.

Yusef stirred, drawing her thoughts. He'd grimaced a few times in his sleep, but his body was stretched out and his arm didn't appear so locked against his chest in pain. He blinked, automatically sensing her presence in the still room. Turning to look at her, a soft smile curled his features, until he was reminded of her rejection to lay with him throughout the night.

"I was about to wake you," Olena said quietly. "It's still early, but you have to meet with the war council."

Yusef had said as much to her the night before--in between orgasms. King Attor was being given the right of defense, as per a truce set before the Draig and Var nobility yeas ago. If it was the King who was responsible for Morrigan's poisoning and Yusef's attack, then there would be justice and possible war.

Olena could do nothing about the war. And the bloodthirsty, vengeful side of her nature would gladly see justice done on Yusef's behalf. But this was a matter for the royal Draig family. Even though she was technically a part of their family, she knew she could take no real stand with them. She wouldn't be staying to see any of her hotheaded declarations through and she wouldn't be the cause of a battle she couldn't fight herself.

Olena also knew she wasn't to leave the house this day. Yusef had told her that spies were most likely afoot in the palace. Whoever had stabbed him knew the back passages well enough to escape through them without being caught. Attor himself had been far enough away to shield him from direct responsibility for the attack. Unless, the Var King confessed, many nobles would be hesitant to face another war without solid proof. Yusef admitted that they remembered all too well the losses the last war had brought them. Many had died and no one had won.

"Come here." Yusef wondered if he was a glutton for punishment. But he had been looking at her sad, contemplative face and couldn't resist the urge to hold her.

Olena unfolded her body and climbed off the chair. He was naked beneath the coverlet, his bare chest more than doing its share of tempting. She went beside him, studying his handsome face as he didn't move to sit up.

"Come lay with me," he urged.

Olena wanted to. Oh, how desperately she wanted to. "No. You should get up and ready. I imagine with your wounds it will be slow going as it is. I can walk you to the war council --"

"No." He forced himself to sit.

The coverlet was thrown from his body and Olena instantly looked to see the condition of his manhood. It was half erect, just at the edge of filling. If she were to touch it, it would rise eagerly in her fingers ready to pleasure her with mindless enchantment.

His body ached, but Yusef could well deal with it. Her touch had sent him fast on the road to recovery. "It isn't safe. You must stay inside."

Olena nodded her head and Yusef was surprised when she did not protest the order.

"I mean it, firebird," he insisted.

"Fine," she stated aloud with a stare that mildly hardened her face for a moment. Then, sighing, she went to the closet. "Which tunic do you want?"

"The council tunic is black with a silver dragon embroidered within a shield." Yusef stretched his arms slowly to unclamp the muscles in his lower back.

Olena flipped through his clothes. Something flashed before her eyes. It was a gold encrusted bracelet, fitted with rubies and emeralds. It was big enough to fit Yusef's bicep. She licked her lips. Now that was a prize worth stealing.

"Did you find it?"

Olena shook to her senses, and lied, "I'm just looking for boots ... ah, got them."

She came out carrying his war tunic and shoes. Olena helped him don the tunic. It fit snug over his chest. If he even dared to look at her with his bedroom eyes she would have pushed him over and climbed on top of him. She turned quickly to retrieve his pants.

Yusef couldn't help the manly satisfaction at her interest in his body. He'd felt her fingers quiver. What had ever happened to his bold wench? Who was this fluttering, blushing maid now set before him?

Olena knelt before him, looking up as he made a sound. It was a mistake. His eyes had lowered as his member had risen. Her breath caught, as he said, "I don't have to leave right away."

Olena swallowed, reading his intent well. Would this man never get enough? He was insatiable. As her body stirred to desire, pooling her midsection with hot wetness, she wanted to groan. Would she ever be sated?

"Come," he said. "Climb on my lap."

Olena hesitated. She had worked one foot into his pant leg.

"I promise you won't regret it."

Olena's gaze again went to his arousal, engorged to the point that she saw the distinct trailing of veins.

Yusef reached a hand to her, lifting her up. Her will was weak and she let him guide her. When she was standing, he latched his fingers into her waistband and jerked her pants off. Olena kicked the material from her feet.

Then, turning her so her lush backside was before his face, he growled. Olena shivered, wondering what he was up to.

Yusef leaned forward and nipped a cheek. Olena jerked. He wanted to lean her over to taste her wet center, but knew his body wasn't recovered enough for such stunts. So, instead, he pulled her firmly onto his lap. His legs nudged hers apart as she sat facing away from him.

"Lean forward," he commanded with a growl forming in the base of his throat. "That's right, just like that."

Yusef's hand explored her back, feverishly igniting her skin as it memorized every curve. When he felt her body tighten with desire, he backed up so that his calves were pressed firmly to the bed's side.

"Bring your knees to the bed," Yusef told her, relishing the view he was going to be privy to with her kneeling over him. Olena obeyed, using his knees for support as she leaned forward over the bed. The unsecured position made her heart race, knowing she could plunge helplessly to the floor if he released his hold on her hips.

Olena looked up, noticing how the mirror reflected her sordid reflection back to her. She watched her body squirm. Yusef's hand curved around her shoulder to pull her back onto his awaiting arousal.

"Oh, you look so good like this." His eyes lit with fire as he watched their bodies join. "You're so wild. I want to tame you."

Olena loved it when he talked dirty to her. It thrilled her, made her feel naughty. And there was nothing more pleasurable to a pirate than the feeling that you were getting away with something. At his urging, she lifted in repeated thrusts against him, driving him deep inside her body.

"Yes," she howled as he moved her with his controlling hand. A passionate rhythm was struck up between them. "Talk to me, Yusef, let me hear your words."

Yusef nearly lost himself at the request. "You're so hot, wrapped tight around my shaft."

Olena instantly trembled before he could get another sinful phrase out--though he had plenty more he could say to her. She worked her body faster until she was too overcome with pleasure to move. She yelled violently until his body jerked in instantaneous response.

Weakly she climbed off him, keeping her eyes down as she pulled on her pants. She hid her face from him behind her hair. When she finished, she helped him to dress. Then, running her hands over her face to secretly wipe the tears that fell, she swiped the moisture across her face and buried it into her hair as she pulled the heavy locks back.

"Olena," Yusef began part in demand, part in question.

"You're going to be late." She affected a bright smile. "Go see to your justice."

Yusef nodded, knowing she was right. "I need my crown."

Olena nodded, retrieving it from the closet and setting it gingerly atop his head. She brushed his hair back from his face, combing the dark strands with her fingers.

Wearily he stood, his body sated by hers. Leaning over, he kissed her cheek. Then, grabbing his sling from the dresser, he wrapped his arm and strapped it along his neck as he walked to the front door. Turning for one last look, he eyed her thin frame in the doorway to the bedroom.

"Don't wait up. These things can take all day," he said. "A servant will come round with food. Have him drop it off at the door. Don't let anyone in."

Olena obediently nodded.

Yusef turned from her, the memory of her beauty burning into him. With a stiff command to the door, he strode from the house to do his duty.

## Chapter Sixteen

King Attor denied all charges with a sardonic grin. He knew as long as he was under the protection of the convened council, he wouldn't be touched. Nothing was accomplished during the seven hours of talks. But, then again, nothing had been accomplished in the centuries of fighting that had occurred between the two kingdoms. Death attempts on both sides were nothing new, though none had occurred for over a hundred years.

Zoran was in charge of military matters, representing the Draig with a Var warrior of equal ranking opposite him. Olek presided over the whole affair, doing his best as ambassador to keep the peace, though all the brothers knew he would like nothing more than to spill King Attor's blood for his insults to the royal Draig family.

Yusef sat in silence through most of the affair, as did Ualan. They did not see the point in speaking with the Var leader when all they would receive in turn was more of his lies. They smelled his falsehoods on him as easily as they breathed in the hall's air.

After the meeting, it took another four and a half hours to make certain Attor and his men were gone. A thorough search of the castle revealed nothing and the high alert was taken off the village so that the villagers could again leave their homes using caution.

Yusef's back pained him, but he did not let the discomfort show. The night of passion was beginning to catch up with him and by the time he went home, he was too exhausted to see straight. Olena was asleep on the couch, her hair spilling over the side in beautiful contrast to the white. He left her there, her parted lips in his memory as he went to bed alone.

\* \* \* \*

The warriors cheered good-naturedly as the four Princesses, wearing dark breeches and tunic shirts, aimed knives at the practice post. Pia had received a gift of knives from her husband and, eager to try them out, invited the women to join her for a little sport.

Olena thought a day out of the house was the perfect remedy from the melancholy of being trapped within it for a day. Yusef was agreeable to the event and escorted her to the field to watch. Olek and Zoran were there to give their support. Prince Ualan was still abed, according to Morrigan, who merely blushed at the confession.

Olena was the first to throw. She was not a novice when it came to the blade. Although her targeting wasn't dead center, she knew she could strike her mark enough to subdue or even kill.

She did fairly well, as each knife made it into the post, near the center. The gathered soldiers clapped and stomped. She glanced at Yusef, trying to act like she didn't seek his approval. A white bandage slashed across his arm but he looked so much better. He smiled widely for her, dark and handsome in his approval, and nodded his head. Olena refused to blush, but she knew what that look in his eyes meant.

Nadja was hopeless, missing the target completely on all five tries. She glanced at Olek in embarrassment. The men applauded anyway. Morrigan managed to hit the post on her turn, though they weren't centered. She curtsied as she received her cheers.

"Maybe you ladies should let a man show you how it's done," called a voice from the crowd.

Morrigan rolled her eyes at the others, retrieving the silver blades for Pia's turn.

"Ach," Agro cried. "You're hardly a man, Hume!"

Pia flashed a grin at Hume, who immediately crushed his hand over his heart. Olena watched the antics with a stifled chuckle. She saw Zoran's face cloud ever so slightly in jealousy. She was glad Pia Korbin wasn't Doc Aleksander's daughter. She would hate to see that possessive warrior on her trail.

Pia took up her new set of knives, weighing them carefully in her hand as she tested them. Getting to the third one, she lifted it and studied the blade. Frowning, she went to her husband and handed it to him. Zoran uncrossed his arms and took it from her hand before she grabbed a replacement blade from his waist.

At his curious glance at the replacement, she announced

loudly for all the men to hear, "You need to check the balance on that one. It will pull a fraction to the right."

With hardly moving a muscle, Zoran threw the blade over her shoulder. It stuck just to the right of the target. The men laughed heartily in approval.

Olena was too busy pretending to listen as she watched Yusef from the corner of her lash veiled eyes. He was laughing light-heartedly at his brother. His look of pleasure twinged her heart. Her mouth went dry.

Not turning around, Pia said, "Told you."

Going before the target, Pia took a deep breath. She tossed the first of the blades at the post. Not waiting to see it land, she rapidly dropped to the ground to throw two more in a roll. Then, coming to kneel, she threw the last two. The fourth blade struck against Zoran's to knock it free, before sticking in its place. On the fifth, she turned her arm and it missed the post completely. The warriors watched in stunned silence, their gazes following the path of her last throw. It was a foot before Hume, sticking hilt up and tipped towards the man.

"You missed," Hume said, to break the silence. The men went wild cheering. Pia took a graceful bow. The woman jumped in excitement, basking in Pia's victory.

Morrigan turned to see her husband storming onto the field. The women, hearing her gasp, followed her eyes. Pia and Olena exchanged looks of amusement.

"Careful," Olena teased Morrigan, moving close to the woman. "Or else we might think you actually like the barbarian."

Morrigan blushed, turning her eyes away. Pia handed Olena the blades for her next turn.

Olena glanced at Yusef, he nodded his head. Pia, seeing the woman's look, quietly said, "It would seem Rigan isn't the only one enamored by her warrior husband."

"We've got a bet going. All I have to do is hit this post with these five blades and I win." Olena let a mischievous smile light her eyes. It had been her roguish husband's idea. He seemed to think that since she was so confident she'd hit near her mark that she should put her blades where her mouth was, so to speak. His terms were simple. If she won, she got to request one thing from him. If he won, he got to do the same from her--no complaining.

"Come," they heard Prince Ualan say.

Pia and Olena turned around to watch Ualan leading Morrigan off to the forest. They shared a look.

"Zoran tried to lead me around like that." Pia shook her head in disapproval. "He had to carry me off kicking and screaming. I nearly got away, too. I did get a few good punches in."

Olena laughed, "I hid in the forest for a night, but broke my arm. Yusef had to come rescue me."

"We're waiting!" came a cry from the crowd.

Pia turned to glare good-humoredly at Hume. Wryly, she called, "Don't make me aim higher, Sir Hume."

Pia meant his chest, but the rowdy warriors were only too ready to guess something much bawdier.

Zoran gulped. Pia looked in confusion at the men's snickering. Olena laughed, understanding the men all too well. As a slightly worried Pia went to consult her husband, Olena threw. The first four landed fairly well. But, then, in an unexplainable effort to gloat, she looked at Yusef. He winked his dark eyes at her and blew her a kiss. She faltered mid throw. The knife hit, but went too far to the side and instantly fell back out with the weight of the hilt.

Yusef grinned. Olena gulped to the sound of cheering. She forced herself to retrieve the blades for Pia.

"We need a blindfold," Zoran called. Miraculously, the call was quickly answered as one was passed over the front to Zoran. Zoran crossed over to Pia and tied it around her head. He then smacked her hard on her backside and the men laughed.

During the commotion, Olena sidled near Yusef.

"I believe I won," he gloated.

Olena blushed furiously. "I hit the mark. You said nothing about the blade sticking."

"Make your throw!" Zoran called.

Pia lifted her arm, taking aim. She threw.

Hearing the blade land on wood, Olena glanced at the post before turning back to Yusef.

"Do you try to renege?" Yusef's brows rose in mock surprise. "Where is your honor?"

Pia threw the second and third time. Each blade landed in the post. Suddenly, a loud cheering came up over the crowd. Zoran grinned as she stiffened. He had motioned the men to make noise.

Yusef and Olena ignored it, concentrating only on each other, while pretending not to.

Yusef meant his words as a joke, but Olena took the bait. "I have never backed out of a bet! A deal's a deal. I will honor it!"

Pia lifted another knife. The fourth hit, though it was not as deep as the others.

"Oooo," shouted the men in unison.

"I'm glad to hear it," Yusef murmured with a meaningful growl, "for I'll enjoy collecting my prize."

"Zoran!" came a panicked shout. "Olek! Yusef!"

Olena was too lost in Yusef's arduous eyes to hear the shout. The hair on Yusef's neck stood on end when he felt more than heard Ualan calling to him. His brother was in trouble.

Zoran motioned to Agro to keep the men at the field. He ran towards Prince Ualan's voice, drawing the sword from his waist. Yusef broke away from the wide emerald of his wife's eyes. Instinctually, he nodded to one of the men, who tossed his good hand a blade. He, too, took off running, his body blurring slightly at his speed. Olek was right behind them.

Olena blinked as he left her, not understanding why he suddenly ran away. Then, seeing Pia as she tore the blindfold from her head, Olena was spurred into action. The warriors began to murmur amongst themselves, but followed Agro's command not to give chase. They didn't move. Nadja glanced at Olena and they were both soon behind the others.

Twelve light blond Var warriors pursued Prince Ualan from the trees, over the forest path. Their bodies grew with fur as they shifted with the vicious, snarling features of wild cats. Ualan dragged Morrigan with one arm. She was unconscious, a dart sticking out from her throat.

Ualan had been forced to shift to Draig, using his natural armor to deflect the enemy's blows as he fought them off with his free arm. He tried to protect Morrigan, her feet trailing in the dirt. Soon the Princes were by his side, shifting into the Draig form as they fought against the Var. The one armed Yusef bravely hacked forward with his sword, giving Ualan time to get Morrigan to safety.

Olena glanced away from the spectacular show of her husband at battle, as Ualan dropped an unconscious Morrigan on the ground. Ualan turned back to join the fight against the attackers. Pia didn't hesitate as she ran swiftly to join the men, throwing her blade into one of the creature's throat. As Zoran swung his arm, she ducked beneath him to grab the knife from his belt.

Olena heard Nadja's feet ground to a halt. She turned to the woman. Olena was used to fighting and death, and had been afforded more than enough views of both shifting species to not be alarmed. But, as she saw Nadja pale in horror, she knew the woman had no clue what she had married.

Nadja's lips trembled as she watched Olek and his brothers in battle. For a moment, the woman blinked, before stiffening in fear to see that the fighting creatures-- human dragons and human tiger-like beasts--were very real.

"Nadja," Olena yelled to get the woman's attention. Seeing Morrigan, she knew she had to help drag her to safety. Besides, she had to get the pallid Nadja away from the battle before she too fell unconscious to the ground. She couldn't drag them both. With command in her voice, she ordered, "Help me!"

Shaking herself, Nadja darted forward to the fallen Princess. She trembled to see a dart sticking from Morrigan's throat.

Olena lifted one of Morrigan's arms. She watched Nadja shivered anew, as her eyes darted around to look into the trees.

"Help me." Olena tried to pull Morrigan away from the approaching fray.

Nadja and Olena dragged Morrigan down the path to safety. Olena's eyes kept glancing at Yusef's back in worry until she could no longer see him. The sound of battle rang out all around them. When they were far enough away, Nadja stopped. She dropped down to her knees.

"Should we pull it out?" Olena asked. Surely Doc Aleksander's daughter would know what to do--more so than a pirate.

"No," Nadja answered. Again she trembled as she looked at the trees. Her eyes searched them for movement but saw nothing. Olena wondered how someone with such a devious father could be so squeamish. Maybe, after seeing her reaction to Olek's Draig form, she would really be doing the refined woman a favor in taking her off this planet. Anyone as sheltered as she apparently must have been, was more than likely doted on and protected as a child. "Don't touch it."

Back at the battle, the Vars retreated into the forest. Ualan turned, smelling Morrigan's trail as he took off down the path, Yusef and Olek were behind him. Zoran hung back with Pia to make sure the men weren't followed.

Olek froze, instantly detecting Nadja's pale face. She was by Morrigan's side, her narrow eyes examining the wound. The dart was still embedded in Morrigan's neck and the woman wasn't moving.

Nadja jolted to see Ualan's Draig face as he came beside her. He immediately shifted back to how she knew him. Looking around, she suspiciously eyed Olek's human features. Olek watched her mouth tremble before she turned away from him. Olena noticed it too, her resolve stiffening in her course as she convinced herself Nadja would be grateful for what Olena was going do.

Ualan reached forward.

"Don't." Nadja's voice was raw with fear. Olena saw her jump away from Ualan's hand. Ualan drew back in surprise, but Nadja only nodded at his arm where red blisters were forming on his skin. "She is poison to you."

Ualan's jaw tensed, but he held back. Hearing her calm, eerie tone, Olena had no doubt Nadja was the seed of Aleksander.

"You can't move her yet." Nadja obviously tried to remain calm.

"But, the poison..." Ualan began, desperate to help his wife.

"Quiet," Nadja ordered. Zoran and Pia approached from the battle. They hung back, quiet. Nadja refused to look any of them in the eye. Her hands shook as she tried to focus. Inside her heart pumped furiously. Olena could see the pulse jumping beneath Nadja's skin. "Let me think, I need to concentrate."

Ualan looked at Olek. Olek shrugged. He was worried about his own wife. Nadja quivered.

"Give me your knife," Nadja said to Pia, holding out her hand in determination. The woman instantly handed it over. Taking a deep breath, Nadja cut into Morrigan's throat where the dart was embedded in the skin. Instantly, green liquid began to drip and ooze from the wound, mixed with red blood. Soon, she had dug out the star tipped points of the dart.

Nadja dropped the blade and continued to bleed the poison out. When she had finished, she quietly told Ualan, "Try touching her."

Ualan did. He was left unharmed.

"It's as I thought," Nadja breathed. The knowledge brought her little pleasure as she again looked frantically to the trees. "I've seen this kind if poison before. Usually jealous old lovers do it for revenge. If you had torn the dart out of the skin, it would have released a poison into the blood stream. She would have lived but you never would have been able to touch her again. It's ironic really. That way it's the current lover that poisons the woman, sealing their fate."

Olena saw her looking at the forest, searching. She wondered if she considered running or if she was scared the Var warriors remained hidden within them. Or did she detect her father hidden there? Shaking her head, Olena knew there was no way Nadja felt her father's presence. She most likely considered running. Olena almost wished she would run away on her own. It would save her the trouble of a delivery.

"You should get her to a doctor," Nadja said, her tone lowering to a mere whisper. She stood, warily trying to edge away from the Draig shifters to go down the path they'd come. Olena watched her carefully.

"I would say that whoever poisoned her didn't want you to be with her," Nadja said to Ualan. Suddenly, she turned and ran from them, desperate to get away. Olek was right behind her.

Olena stood, watching the woman run until she was gone. Her eyes narrowed. Solemnly, she said, "She didn't know about the Draig."

Ualan picked up Morrigan. Yusef fell into step beside Olena, wondering at the direness of his wife's flat tone. He felt a cool resolve wash over her feelings, but didn't know what to make of it. Pia and Zoran were right behind them. As they followed Ualan, he carried Morrigan to the medical ward. No one said another word.

\* \* \* \*

"Why do they attack the Princesses?" Yusef frowned. Olena stood by his side, her face unmoving. Nadja and Olek hadn't joined them, but Zoran and Pia stood next to Ualan and Morrigan. Morrigan was in the hospital bed, having been checked by the doctors and given some medicine to help along her recovery.

Pia glanced sidelong at Zoran and said, "Because without us you will have no sons. Your line will end."

Zoran stiffened at her soft words. Olena's eyes drifted to Yusef. He looked tenderly at her with a strange light in his eyes. She quickly turned away.

Pia's lips stiffened. "It makes perfect sense. I've seen you all fight. Especially with all four of you banded together, you would be a formidable opponent. You expect the attack. We are new here and it would be assumed that we had no clear idea of the dangers. Plus, we are women. Men … ah, no offense to anyone here … men, especially those from warrior classes, often misjudge women as unworthy opponents."

The Princes listened closely to her words, giving away none of their thoughts.

Pia looked up at her husband. Her face was taut with concentration. "If you were to destroy an enemy, Zoran, would you attack their weakness or their strength?"

"Only a fool would choose to fight a strength if a weakness was to be had." Ualan nodded at the woman's insight.

"Only they have obviously underestimated the strength of our women," Zoran added.

"What better way to end this age old feud than to wipe out the leaders before they are born?" Yusef frowned, unconsciously drawing Olena under the protection of his good arm. Olena found herself melting eagerly into his warmth. He moved his hand up to cup her elbow. She closed her eyes, breathing in the scent of him. She wanted nothing more than to club him over the head, drag him back the house, and hold him there as her love slave.

Yusef felt her shiver. His nostrils flared slightly as he

smelled the faint trace of her mounting desire. His body lurched in response, but he tempered it back. Now was definitely not the time.

"For, if we were to die," Ualan said, "there would be an heir that could sometime rise against them. If they secure that our line is ended, when we die there will be no one to avenge us. With no King or protection, our people will be left without defense. Everything will be in chaos."

"It is imperative that we discover who is spying for the Var," Yusef said.

"Spy?" Pia blinked in surprise. She turned to frown at Zoran. "You said nothing of a spy!"

Zoran sighed.

"Olena," Pia said. "You remember that servant at the festival, don't you? The one who spilled his drink? It has to be him. He was no more fitted to be a servant than I am."

Olena shook her head, barely recalling anything but her husband from that night. Thinking of him wrapped in nothing but fur, she shivered anew. Yusef felt her sigh, smelling her need for him grow as her body reached out to unwittingly tempt him. His arm tightened on her waist and she shook out of her trance to look at him. He let a roguish smile play his mouth, as if to tell her he knew her wicked thoughts. Olena's eyes darted away from him, embarrassed.

"What are you talking about?" Zoran demanded, turning to grab Pia's arms.

"There are too many servants in the kingdom," Ualan contemplated. "For festivals many come to help. It would take forever to locate them all just to find this one."

"No," Pia said. "He was at the coronation. The spy would be here in the palace kitchens. I remember watching him fumble with some plates. He only carried two, unlike the other servants who carried four or more. It has to be him. He was graceless serving. Yet there was something different to his walk and his hand had a sword callous along the ridge. I would almost bet my life he was your man."

Morrigan, who was pale but alive, said through her hoarse voice, "I recorded that night on my camera."

Everyone turned to look at her.

Sheepishly, she admitted, "I'm an undercover reporter for an intergalactic newspaper chip."

Ualan stiffened but did not stop her from speaking.

"I was supposed to write a story about the royal weddings," she said softly, turning to Ualan. "My camera will have recorded part of that night. Maybe Pia's servant can be found on the relay."

"It's worth a shot." Yusef watched Ualan's features harden. Whatever his brother was thinking, it was best he saved it for another time.

"I'll go find it." Ualan left the hospital room, his arms stiff. It was silent until he got back. When he did, he handed a small eyepiece and an emerald to Morrigan.

"Can you make it work so we can all see?" Yusef asked.

Morrigan nodded. "I think so."

She requested some saline and wetted the lens before sticking it in her eye. Slipping the emerald on her finger so it could react with her nervous system, she turned the stone. A light shone from her eyes, darkening as she blinked. They watched in amazement as they saw a picture of the Breeding Festival floating on the air.

Coming around to stand across from Morrigan, they eyed the round picture.

"Can you see it?" she asked.

"Yes," Ualan said.

"All right, just let me leaf through these." Morrigan closed her eye and the picture disappeared. Olena saw her turn bright red and wondered about it.

"Morrigan," Ualan began.

Morrigan blinked in surprise and a flash of Ualan's naked backside came up bigger than life before his brothers.

"Oh," Morrigan panicked. Zoran and Yusef laughed heartily and Yusef felt his wife chuckling next to him. Morrigan's face turned red and she squeezed her eyes tight.

Wryly, Ualan said, "I had no idea I looked that good from behind."

He was rewarded with punches from his laughing brothers.

"Here." Morrigan got back to business, swallowing over her mortification. A screen of the festival came up. "I can't play sound, but you should see the picture moving like a silent movie."

They watched in silence. Then suddenly, Pia pointed. "There, stop, that's him."

Morrigan froze the picture.

"Yeah." Olena leaned forward to get a closer look at the corner. "I remember him. Now that you mention it, he was rather strange."

"He has the coloring of a Var," Yusef said.

"But not the scent of one," Zoran said. "Do you think he has found a way to mask his smell?"

"He wears the tunic of the kitchen staff," Yusef said. "We will find him and question him. If he is Draig, it will be easy for him to prove it. If he is Var, he will come up with an excuse not to shift."

Ualan nodded. Yusef and Zoran left with their women by their sides.

Once the couples were alone, Pia asked Olena, "Did you know Rigan was writing a story about us?"

Olena shook her head. "She said she 'was' not 'is'."

Zoran and Yusef exchanged looks. They didn't much care for their private lives to be made known to the entire galaxy. The Qurilixen, by tradition, were a race that kept to themselves. However, they also knew Ualan would feel the same way and would undoubtedly talk his wife out of such a thing.

\* \* \* \*

Pia's blond servant was apprehended almost immediately upon the Princes Yusef and Zoran entering the palace kitchens. They found him hiding behind one of the large brick ovens, ducking from his work. Zoran's nose picked up the Var smell beneath an all too potent scent of Draig.

The soldier must have known that he was found out, because he tried to run. It was no use. Yusef was standing in the doorway and with a swing of his good arm he punched the man square in the jaw, laying him out on the floor.

The Draig servants blinked in surprise at the sudden attack, but as they witnessed the lazy man sprawled on the ground, they cheered even without knowing his deception. As a fellow worker, the slothful Var spy was not well liked in the kitchen.

## Chapter Seventeen

Olena left Yusef to tend to the matter of the spy with his brother. After seeing Morrigan laid up in the hospital, knowing that Nadja had saved her life, she couldn't force herself to turn the woman over to Doc Aleksander. No matter the cost, for once in her life Captain Olena was going to make the right decision. She was going to do the right thing.

Thinking of Yusef, she knew she was making the right decision. He had shown her the true meaning of honor. It wasn't a simple, silly little code that you followed. It wasn't a set of rules and self-punishments, self-denials. He'd shown her that there could be a purpose in life higher than gold and fortunes, more rewarding than sailing the high skies. He'd shown her that belonging to one man, and a family, was so much sweeter than having all the freedom in the world.

Her decision made, Olena pulled back her hair into a serviceable bun. Then, stealing into Yusef's closet, she grabbed the valuable gold bracelet and slid it over her thigh, hiding it beneath her black pants. It pulled tight against her skin as she walked. Once she had to stop to press it higher so it wouldn't fall and give her away.

Then, strolling out the Palace's front gate, she was happy to discover that the guard did not stop her. Affecting an air of nonchalance, she strode into the evening light settling on the forest and didn't look back.

* * * *

Yusef came home to find his wife gone. He frowned, wondering where she could have gotten off to. He took the sling from his arm, stretching and bending the muscles. The limb felt much recovered, so he threw the sling aside and left it unbound.

A big relief overcame the royal family as news was spread of the spy's capture. Olek had escorted the man down to the lower dungeons and even now the Var was being questioned by Agro. Yusef had no doubt that the

beefy giant would discover much from the man. When
Agro chose to shift, he could be most persuasive.

Taking a bath, he waited for Olena to come home. It was
beginning to get late. He wondered if she was still with Pia.
She had been with the woman the last he saw her. Perhaps
she was checking on Morrigan or visiting with Nadja.
Nadja had been upset and no doubt needed to have some
kind of girl talk. Yusef grinned. Olena didn't seem the kind
for girl talk.

With a sigh, he dressed. He'd give her a little more time
before going out to search for her.

\* \* \* \*

Olena didn't have to walk the path long before hearing a
noise within the trees. Freezing, she cursed herself for a
fool. How could she know Doc Aleksander would be the
first to find her? There could still be Var hiding within the
forest, eager to kill a Princess.

"Captain."

Olena sighed, forcing her heart to slow at the sound of the
man's voice. At least the right enemy had found her. That
was something at least.

"I hope you have good news for me." This time he held
no cigar as he stepped from the shadows of the forest.
Olena felt the hairs on her neck curl at his hard look. He
definitely wasn't going to be happy with her.

"I can't get you what you want," she said, direct and to
the point. Direct was better. Men like Aleksander could
respect direct--somewhat.

"Really?" His eyes narrowed, contrasting the small smile
that curled on his lips. A little too mocking, he said, "I
thought you could steal anything."

"She's too well guarded. She doesn't trust me," Olena
said. "I've tried to get her outside the palace alone with me,
but she won't come."

"Try harder." Doc gritted teeth.

"I have." Olena looked him square in the face. "They
have all the Princesses under tight guard."

"Princess?" Aleksander mused. "My daughter married a
Prince that keeps her prisoner?"

Olena shivered. Oops. It would seem he didn't know that
bit of information. Or did he? Was he toying with her?

"I am truly sorry I couldn't bring you what you asked

for," Olena said as bravely as she could manage. Leaning over, she began working the bracelet from her leg. The Doc tensed, watching her closely, ready to defend himself. When she pulled the bracelet from her thigh and out her pant leg, she offered it to him. "As per the Pirate Code, what I couldn't obtain for you, I have replaced with something valuable."

To her hesitant relief, Aleksander smiled. He snapped his fingers and motioned to her. Olena tensed as a henchmen clone came from the trees. He took the bracelet from her and handed it over to Doc. The man studied it very carefully before nodding his head.

"Nice," he murmured in approval. "A very fitting replacement of the Pirate Code, Captain."

Olena nodded. "Again, I am sorry, Doc. I wish you well in your endeavor and give you my word as Captain of the high skies that I'll not impede your goal."

"That is very commendable." He passed the bracelet to the henchman at his side. Olena swallowed, preferring to see the man get angry. His silent calm was terrifying.

"Well, I should get back in before they start looking for me." Olena turned her back on him and walked away. Not making it more than two steps, his words stopped her.

"Oh, Captain?" Doc called, his words ringing with the oddest mix of sweetness and ease.

Olena froze. Fear overcame her in agonizing waves and she couldn't help but shiver at the coolness of his placid tone. Forcing a muted smile, she turned to look at him.

"I only see one problem, my dear Olena, with your pirate's offering." Doc's growing with a damnable smile. He picked a cigar out of his pocket, clipped the end, and lit it. Taking a deep puff, he pointed the tip at her. "You see, I'm not exactly a pirate."

Olena tried to run but the path filled with the Doc's goons. Hands clasped her. When she would have kicked her captors and gotten away, she felt a hard jab of a needle in her arm. Her vision blurred, her body swaying instantly. Right before the black pit of unconsciousness hit her, her eyes focused for the last time on Doc. He saluted her, a grin spreading over his features as he waved his goodbye.

* * * *

Yusef sighed, slipping into his clothes. Olena still hadn't

come home and he was tired of waiting around for her. Just because the spy had been caught did not mean she was safe to roam. There could be others lurking in the palace.

Slipping on his boots, he heard a pounding at the door. He frowned, standing. Yusef strode into the front hall, calling for the door to open.

"Where is your wife?" Olek demanded, storming inside. He looked around.

"She's gone." Yusef scowled at the rude intrusion.

"Then would you mind explaining the meaning of her letter to me?" Olek asked. He handed over a piece of paper.

Yusef glanced down, reading, *Your wife's father is coming for her. Ask her what that means. I go to put him off. You must keep her safe. He is an evil man.*

"I don't understand," Yusef stated, confused. But, seeing his brother's tightly drawn face, he swallowed.

"It was delivered from your wife," Olek said.

"Where is she?" Yusef demanded in panic. He took off out the door to sniff her out. Olek was running behind him.

"I was hoping you could tell me," Olek said. "My wife is missing too."

\* \* \* \*

Olena blinked, fighting to regain consciousness. Her head filled with wild images--images of the past, of nightmares, of death and blood, of her crew, of random men she had seduced and stabbed with her firefly pin, of the crash, of Yusef. They jumbled in her head, confusing her, making her feel like a helpless child, making her feel like a woman, making her feel like a prisoner.

No, that would be the ties on her hands that made her feel like she was a prisoner.

Olena flinched, blinking rapidly in the dim blue light. She moaned, but a gag stopped the sound from leaving her lips. Her mouth worked, trying to be free of it. It was clamped too tightly, stiffening her jaw with its pull.

Taking quick stock of her surroundings, she saw she was in a tent. The bold curve of the Medical Alliance Missionary symbol was on the outside wall, glowing dark in the blue artificial light of a camp light. She didn't know where she was, but she guessed she was still on Qurilixen. There had been no time for Doc to get Nadja back and leave the planet for another. Plus, she highly doubted Doc planned on taking her along as excess baggage.

No, by the feel of the gurney beneath her back and the restraints on her hands, she wasn't going to get much farther than this.

"Father, no!"

Olena froze. That was Nadja screaming. She twisted her head around, trying to get her bearings. The tent flap was over her head. She saw it flutter in the breeze, showing a little crack of what was happening outside. Nadja was strapped down to a chair, her eyes pleading with her father for mercy. Olena struggled to get free. The bonds were too tight, of unbreakable steel.

"There, there Nadja," she heard Doc answer. "If you're telling me the truth, you have nothing to worry about."

Olena couldn't see what was happening. She tried to force her hand to slide through the clamp at her wrist. She felt the raw sting of blood on her hands, but she couldn't get loose. Nadja's whimpering surrounded her. Olena froze. If this man was willing to torment his own daughter, then he wouldn't think twice of torturing her.

"Go make sure she wasn't followed," Doc ordered. Olena again tried to see out, but the flap wouldn't move. The breeze had died down. She shook, her mind yelling to Yusef to come for her.

\* \* \* \*

"Olena." Yusef stopped, his head cocking to the side. He looked around the red passageway of the palace. Panic overwhelmed him with a sense of urgency. Turning to Olek, he said, "Quickly, they're in trouble."

\* \* \* \*

"Who have you whored for?" Doc Aleksander yelled at his daughter. "Give me his name."

Olena froze, hearing footsteps coming around to the front. Quickly, she whipped her hair over her face and held completely still. The hair would allow her to peek without being detected. A presence entered the room. She saw a large, looming shadow pass her vision, moving behind her.

"Last chance," Aleksander warned. "I'll have a name."

Olena realized he was still outside the tent. She forced her body to stay motionless as Nadja whimpered in continued agony. She couldn't hear everything that was said, but she didn't need to.

"Unfortunately, I don't have all night," Aleksander said. His henchman didn't move from Olena's tent. "You see, daughter, I have made some friends of my own on this accursed planet. It seems your precious Draig aren't liked by my friends. And if I help them, they'll help me. So tell me, which Prince is yours?"

There was no answer.

Olena stiffened. The henchman was at her feet. The gurney was slowly rolled forward towards the flap. She wanted to scream, but knew that she had to be calm. Fear only defeated and she needed a plan.

"You are such a disappointment." Aleksander sniffed in disgust at his daughter. "Well, if hurting you won't get us anywhere, what if I hurt one of your little friends?"

Oh no, Olena was starting to panic.

To Olena's horror, the Doc yelled, "Bring out the pirate!"

Olena closed her eyes and didn't move. Her heart hammered wildly in her chest. Everything she had called to Yusef, begging him to save her, to come for her. Her face was pointed the wrong direction and she couldn't see anything but the passing of trees and tents.

"She had nothing to do with this," Nadja said.

"Olena," she heard the Doc to say gently. He hovered close, as his fingers moved to tap lightly at her face. "Time to wake up."

Olena blinked, automatically stiffening against her bonds at the feel of his hand. She thrashed back and forth on her shoulders to get him off her.

"What shall I do to her, Nadja?" Doc didn't take his eyes away from his newest victim. There was a perverse pleasure on his face as he looked at her, more perverse than his carnal attraction had been. He took a laser scalpel to Olena's face. Olena stopped moving, her wide eyes following as it moved down. "Carve out her eyes? Her nose? Take off her lips?"

The laser skimmed the bow of her upper lip, grazing lightly. Olena didn't dare move, braced for the worst.

"Don't." Nadja sounded weakened.

*Don't!* Olena's head screamed in unison.

"Then tell me what I want to know! Who is the father of that bastard you carry?" he bellowed, storming away from Olena to scream at his daughter. Olena relaxed slightly as the blade was drawn away. Her nose flared as she tried to gain control of her fear. She had to get out. She pulled desperately to be free. She had to get Nadja out. If she would have just told Yusef what was going on, they wouldn't be here now. "That bastard inside you will be dissolved."

Olena stopped to watch from the corner of her eye. To her surprise, the manacles were freed from Nadja's wrists and she was allowed to move. She couldn't see all that was happening, but Nadja was pulled to her feet.

"The time for being a child is over, Nadja," Doc whispered. "It's time for you to take your place amongst your peers."

Olena felt tears coming to her eyes. Her mind and body called out for Yusef. She needed him. She couldn't get out of this on her own. Not this time.

"Do you love me, Nadja?" Olena heard Doc ask. She didn't hear Nadja's answer, but his next words left her cold. "Then dissect her."

"What...?" Nadja breathed, her wide eyes turning wild as she looked at Olena strapped to the table.

Olena saw the large laser scalpel in Nadja's hand. Doc was pointing in her direction. Nadja's eyes were fearful as she looked at Olena and then her father. Olena could see she had been pushed to the edge. Blood trailed down one of the woman's arms from a narrow cut. Nadja didn't pay attention to the wound.

"She is a common thief, a pirate." Doc shoved his daughter toward the bound woman. "She broke her word to me."

"No." Nadja gasped. The scalpel fell from her fingers to the ground. Olena took a deep, gasping breath of relief. Nadja turned to run. Her father caught her easily.

"Cut out her eyes," he ordered with a cruel twist of his lips. "Or I'll burn your lying ones from your head."

To prove his point he motioned for a hot poker to be brought from the fire. Nadja watched the angry red metal smoke and curl with heat. Olena screamed against her gag for him to stop, the sound was muffled terribly by her gag.

"Hold her down." Doc motioned towards Nadja. Olena tried to get free, but her wrists only bled more.

"No!" Nadja screamed. Hands were all over her, gripping

her shoulders and her arms, lifting her legs into the air when she would kick. Her father took off his jacket and rolled up his sleeves. The hot poker waved dangerously.

"It's time you learn, Nadja. You don't lie to your father."

Nadja kicked, trying to get free. The poker loomed closer to her face.

"Will you do as you're told?" His voice mocked his daughter with its calm, soothing rendering.

To Olena's horror, Nadja nodded.

"Let her go." Doc handed the poker back to one of the men who threw it into the flames. Then, reaching to the ground, he retrieved the scalpel. Nadja took it at his insistence, her fingers shaking horribly as she pressed the button. A long laser shot out, nearly six inches long and sharper than the most deadly of blades.

Olena moaned, shaking her head as her eyes pleaded Nadja to stop.

Nadja sniffed, the wild calmness returning to her. Doc led her forward to Olena.

Nadja's fingers trembled as she lifted her hand to Olena's cheek. Olena's eyes pleaded with her. Nadja's fingers slipped in Olena's tears, her own falling to splash in droplets on Olena's shoulder.

Damn Jack and his theory on fear. She was terrified! She had no plan of action, no way out. Yusef was her only idea.

*Yusef!* her mind cried out. *Yusef, please!*

"I'm sorry." Nadja lifted the scalpel close to Olena's eyes. Olena closed her eyes to the woman, trying to turn her head away, knowing that her eyelids were no match for the scalpel. Nadja's fingers pressed deeper into her skin to hold her still. The laser dipped close to Olena's cheek. She heard it humming softly, felt its heat ready to sear her flesh. Olena glanced at Nadja, trying to plead with her. The woman didn't see her, was looking through her. Then, Nadja turned to her father and said, "I love you."

Doc Aleksander smiled. To Olena's utter disbelief, Nadja turned, thrusting the blade into her father's heart. The man blinked in surprise. Nadja stood completely frozen, unable to move as a fine mist of blood sprayed from Doc's chest over the two women. Doc fell to his knees.

Chaos erupted all around the campsite. Yusef and Olek burst from the trees, subduing Doc's men with slashes to the throat and rips through their gut. Olena's heart leapt in her chest. He had come for her!

Nadja didn't move throughout the whole fight. Olena moaned at her, trying to get her attention. Nadja didn't hear her. She was staring down at her father.

Soon Yusef was above his wife, his body shifted to Draig. Olena would recognize him anywhere. His hands were on her wrist, pulling at the steel with all his strength. He opened it enough to let her slip free.

Olena gasped, tears streaming down her shaken face. Her bloodied wrists reached up and Yusef gladly pulled him into her chest.

"You came!" She clung desperately to him, feeling him shifting to human form beneath her fingers. She didn't dare open her eyes. This was one dream she didn't want to end. "You came."

Yusef ran his fingers over her body, making sure she was unharmed. Aside from her raw and bloodied wrists, she was fine. Glancing at Olek, he saw him standing before his wife. Nadja was kneeling on the ground by her father, unmoving. The danger was gone. Olek motioned Yusef to get his wife to safety. Yusef nodded in ready agreement.

Yusef ran, sprinting to the safety of the palace with Olena in his arms, clinging to him. His Qurilixen voice rang as he called up commands to the guards, ordering them to Olek.

Olena shivered at the power in his tone. He didn't stop running until he reached the medical ward. The doctors came at his call as he set her on a bed.

Olena blinked. Looking at Tal, she said, "They injected me with something."

"Let's put her in the medical unit," Tal said to Yusef. "We'll do a complete set of tests to make sure she is unharmed."

Yusef picked up his wife, refusing to let her walk as he carried her to the back room. He set her down, standing her between two large metal plates.

Then, pressing a button on the unit's control panel, Tal said, "We have to go in the other room. The unit will X-ray her and test her to make sure she wasn't poisoned."

Yusef ran his fingers to tenderly brush back Olena's hair, as she whispered, "You came."

## Chapter Eighteen

Olena was in the medical unit for what seemed like hours. After it finished scanning her body, Tal came back in the room to start the next sequence of testing. Yusef was there, watching her from the doorway. Then, to her surprise, she saw Nadja standing beside him.

She whispered something to Yusef, who frowned but nodded his head. He motioned to Tal. Tal pushed a button and the two women were left alone.

"I'm sorry," Nadja said instantly. "I didn't mean to scare you."

Olena chuckled lightly. "Don't apologize. You saved my life."

"I couldn't let him kill again. You have nothing to worry about." Nadja swayed slightly on her feet and Olena could tell she was worn. "As Doc's heir, I dissolved the family. They won't be back."

Nadja moved over to the machine as it beeped. Absently, she moved to the panel and pushed a button for it to continue. She pulled up a chair, waited as it cycled, and then pressed another button.

"Nadja, I'm sorry. I know he was your father."

Nadja held up a hand to stop her. "I am one of the few who could have done it without backlash. No, it was time for his terror to end."

"Still," Olena began.

Tears came to Nadja's eyes and she sniffed. Shaking her head, she held her hand for silence. No more words were needed on the subject. A part of her was saddened, but she did not regret her actions. "Thank you."

The unit beeped again and Nadja glanced down to the screen.

"Are you in pain?" Nadja asked at the panel's prompting.

"No," Olena said.

Nadja pressed a button.

"How's your baby?" Olena asked.

Nadja read the panel and grinned. Laughing lightly, she

said, "Hopefully as healthy as yours."

\* \* \* \*

She was pregnant. Olena wasn't sure how she felt about that. Nadja had looked at her like she should have been ecstatic. She was numb. Should a pirate even have children? Should an ex-pirate? Surely there was some sort of cosmic law against it--or at least there should have been.

By the time the medic unit finished fixing her up, she was exhausted. Nadja had erased the information about her pregnancy for her, saying that men should find out from their wives, not medics. Olena also got the feeling that Nadja understood her hesitance and was giving her the precious gift of time to mull the news over.

Dawn was fast approaching. Yusef waited up all night by her side. Sometimes, when it was allowed, he sat beside her, not saying a word. Olena kept her eyes closed and her head back, resting against the machine. She pretended she was too tired to talk.

As she finally finished with the extensive checkup, it was determined that she had near perfect health. Tal determined she was good enough to leave, warning her to be more careful in the future--though it was clear he knew the warning was lost on Olena.

Yusef nodded his thanks to the man as he lifted his wife into his arms. Olena's head rested on his shoulder, snuggling into his warmth. By the time Yusef got her home, she was fast asleep. Not waking her to give her a choice, he laid her on his bed and slept by her side.

\* \* \* \*

During the late morning hours, Olena awoke to feel Yusef stroking her cheek. He was fully dressed. He rubbed his fingers over her hair. Tenderly, he said, "I have to go. Agro discovered that Pia was right about King Attor's motives. He seeks to kill Morrigan, Nadja, and Pia."

Olena blinked, looking almost hurt. "What about me?"

Yusef chuckled. "It seems that he's taken a liking to you, firebird. He saw me cart you away at the Breeding Festival and decided he wanted you for himself. That is why you were kidnapped and I was attacked."

"Well," she murmured, still sleepy. She yawned, covering her mouth. "Can you really blame him?"

Yusef laughed louder, just happy she was safe.

Everything else could be figured out in time. "The spy gave Agro directions to Attor's hidden camp. The trackers go there even now to confirm it. If he is there, then I'll go with my brothers to face him."

Olena lurched, sitting up and blinking herself awake. "No, you can't leave."

"Do you think I'll dishonor you in battle?" he asked, frowning.

"No," she dismissed with a frown. "I know you will beat him. I just want you to stay here with me today. Can't you go killing another time?"

"Ah, well." He leaned to kiss her. "Tempting as you are, wife, I would have this finished. I don't know about you, but I would like to get back to the Outpost. This house is too…"

"White?" she offered, with a grimace of distaste.

"Exactly. Now, go back to sleep. I'll send the Queen to check on you later."

Olena nodded, instantly closing her eyes and burrowing under the blankets. To Yusef's amazement, she was asleep before he even turned around.

* * * *

When Olena awoke later in the afternoon, she was still a little groggy. For about an hour, she laid in bed, not moving. Her dreams had been sweet and full of hope for the first time in her life. She barely remembered her conversation with Yusef until she heard the Queen calling to her from the front door.

Olena stumbled from the bedroom, still dressed in her clothes from the night before. Sleep wrinkles pressed into her cheeks from the blankets and her hair was tousled into mess.

"You didn't answer the door," Mede said. "I was worried."

Olena yawned through a smile, absently scratching her backside where her pirate's brand had been. The Queen chuckled at the disoriented woman.

"*Aaoow,*" Olena yawned loudly, stretching her arms over her head and twisting back and forth in a stretch. "Don't worry about it. It's fine. I needed to get up eventually. Where's Yusef?"

"He asked me to come and check on you and tell you that

they are off to battle the Var."

"Oh," Olena said, rubbing her eyes. "When will they be back?"

The Queen smiled, glad to see the confidence Olena had in her son.

"Agro discovered --" the Queen began.

Olena nodded, breaking in, "Yusef said something about it this morning--that is if I wasn't dreaming it."

Olena walked over to the couch and sat, leisurely motioning to Mede to join her.

Olena continued, "The trackers found the campsite I take it?"

"They did. It's a small encampment south of here next to the borders. They could be gone for the rest of the night."

Olena frowned at that. She wanted Yusef home now.

"Olena," Mede said. "I have to ask. Are you happy here with my son?"

Olena blinked, surprised by the forward question. She could only be happy with Yusef. There was nothing else for her but him. She had never known true happiness before meeting her dark warrior.

Seeing the look, Mede had her answer. "Does he know you're happy?"

"Why?" Olena sat up straight and looking very alert. Very insecure, she asked, "Did he say something?"

"As a mother, I have a bond with him. I know my son. He is troubled and, I do confess, I pressed the issue. He thinks you mean to leave him."

"He said that?" Olena was stunned. How could he not know how she felt? She was sure it was written all over her face.

"He did. He made me promise not to talk to you, but, ah, I am his mother and he can't boss me around."

Olena laughed. "Are all men blind or just mine? I figured everyone saw me as a besotted fool. I'm surprised I haven't been drooling and trailing after him."

"You hide yourself better than you think," Mede said. "When I first met you I couldn't tell a single thing you might be thinking. I could only hope you meant it when you took his life to yours."

"You mean because I married him?" Olena asked, questioning the Queen's dire tone of finality. "If it didn't work out, couldn't he have just found someone else? It's not like I would have ruined him."

"Ah, but you have ruined him for all others." Mede sighed. None of her daughters appeared to understand what was happening. Giving her the same speech she gave Morrigan earlier, she said, "Qurilixen men are given a crystal when they are born. It's their guiding light. When you were paired by the crystal, your lives became joined in such a way that can never be taken back. You exchanged part of your souls. By crushing the crystal, you assured that the exchange would never be reversed. In a way, you are now his guiding light."

Mede's gaze shifted to gold with her meaning. Olena listened silently.

"He has put his every chance at happiness in you, Olena. He gave his life to you," Mede said. "There will never be anyone else for him so long as he lives. That is a long time for our people, and for you. By giving you his life, he shortened his and extended yours so your fates could remain together. If you were to choose to leave him, he would be alone for the rest of his days. That is a long time of loneliness. When he took you to his tent, it was his choice. When you stayed, that was yours. There will be no other in his bed or his heart. There simply can't be."

"I am such an idiot. But if you say he can feel me then can't he feel that I was just scared? That I don't intend to go?"

"Ah, they may hide it well, for our warriors are men of extraordinary albeit sometimes frustrating pride. But inside they are still men and men have fears like all others," Mede said. "And I think that it might be worse for our husbands, because they will never permit themselves to show it."

"They're afraid?" Olena asked, suddenly breathless.

"Deep down at their core they are impossible romantics." The Queen moved to stand and smiled a secret smile. "They fall hopelessly and unreservedly in love at first sight and can never hope to fall out again."

\* \* \* \*

Olena's nerves jumped with nervous tension. Queen Mede's words fluttered in her head for the rest of the day, distracting her. She went to bed early, only to rise before dawn. She had no idea when Yusef would be back, but she wanted to be ready for him. Mede thought they should expect the men to return late morning.

Olena bathed and dressed in her most alluring of clothes--which unfortunately was plain cotton pants and a tight black shirt that showed only a hint more cleavage than the rest. She let her hair dry in soft waves over her shoulders.

"Olena?"

Her heart jumped. Yusef was finally back. Taking a deep breath, she fussed with her locks in the bathroom mirror.

"One second," she yelled. Then, to stall as she pinched her cheeks, she asked lightly, "How was the battle?"

"King Attor is dead," came the tired answer. She could hear him moving around in the front hall, putting down his sword and kicking off his boots. "We tried to arrest him but he called his troops to fight."

"Uh-huh!" Olena hardly heard a word, as she adjusted her breasts beneath her top to get the maximum affect. She wondered if she should just take it off altogether, but then thought better of it. It wouldn't do to distract him before she said everything she needed to.

"Attor's son will take the throne," Yusef said. "Olek is speaking to him now, negotiating a peace. It looks hopeful that our battles have ended."

Yusef sighed, ready to get back to his simple life at the Outpost with his wife. It would be slow going, but peace could be achieved. Some of the older nobles would protest on both sides. However, in the end, they would bow to the decision of their leaders.

"What are you doing in there?" His voice had drawn closer. Olena took a deep breath and rushed out to meet him. Her eyes lit at the sight of him. They roamed over his body. She could hardly even tell he'd been stabbed in the back. When he moved, he looked completely healed and his arm wasn't in the sling.

"I," she began. Her eyes found his gray ones flecked with a subtle gold and she forgot everything that she had spent all night rehearsing. "I need ... to talk."

Yusef's face darkened but he nodded.

"I'm a pirate," she admitted, weakly, captured by the smell and look at him. Oh, but he was a handsome man, so dark, so strong.

"I know." He nodded. There was a sadness to him as he

said the words and his body stiffened as if he braced himself.

"I mean ... I was a pirate. Jack was my pirate father. He took me under his wing and showed me how to protect myself, how to steal, how to convince people to believe whatever I wanted. It was his idea that I stay a virgin so when I went through security checks--anyway. He taught me how to seduce men to get what I wanted from them."

Olena frowned. Her words weren't coming out right at all.

"And you miss it," Yusef stated, as if he understood.

"Yusef, I," she hesitated. Her eyes teared. "Jack taught me everything I know. But, he didn't teach me how to love."

Yusef closed his eyes, a pain searing through him. She was incapable of loving him.

"I..." She felt his pain and all masks dropped from her features. No longer caring that her speech was all muddled up into a blob of incoherent half-thoughts, she said the most important truth, "I love you. I'm pregnant and I love you. And I'm scared that you don't feel the same way, because I can't ... tell ... what love would look like on you."

Yusef's heart stopped beating. He opened his eyes. She was trembling, beginning to cry. A flood of her emotions, so sweet and insecure, washed onto him. All walls were broken, all her defenses crumbled at her feet until she could no longer hide behind her mask of mischief.

Yusef rushed forward, sweeping her up into his arms. Before she could even blink in surprise, he kissed her deeply, letting her body fit into his, letting her feel his arousal, his unyielding, unending heart's desire for her.

"If you can't see that I love you, foolish woman," he said into her mouth, "then feel that I do."

Olena beamed happily, her whole world colliding into this one perfect moment. A stream of feeling rushed into her from him, warm and secure. She ran her hands over his body, eagerly dipping along his neck to find his naked back beneath his tunic. Lifting her swiftly into his arms, Yusef hugged her to his chest and broke his lips free. Her feet dangled above the ground.

"I believe I'm ready to collect on my bet now," he said. Slowly, he set her down on the floor. His hands were on her shirt, pulling it up over her head.

"What would you have?" she murmured in full invitation. Yusef pushed her drawstring pants off her hips. Her fingers were on his waist, trying to free his center to her. "You get one demand. I can't complain."

"I would have you stay with me always, as my wife."

"Done." Then, batting her eyelashes, she said, "Now take me to bed and make a few more demands."

Yusef grinned. Lifting her up, he pressed her back into the white wall. With a swift stroke, he was inside her willing body. Olena gasped in delight, never wanting him to stop. Yusef buried his face into her hair, and asked, "Who can wait for a bed, firebird?"

\* \* \* \*

*Four months later...*

Yusef frowned, following his wife at a distance as she made her way towards the east pond. It was late in the evening. Olena did not detect him as she searched the dimmed trees. His Draig eyes darkened to a bright gold, seeing her slightly rounded waist--a testament to his growing child in her womb.

Hearing a low whistle, foreign to Qurilixen, Olena grinned. The demons had finally come for her. Covering her mouth, she trilled softly in return. Soon the path was alive with beastly figures.

"Captain!" one of the men cried.

Olena yelped in excitement and Yusef watched as she jumped into a pair of hairy arms.

"MoPa!" Pulling back, she said, "Hedge, Lufa, Caz, I can't believe you're here!"

"Ah, Captain," Lufa's voice gurgled. He was a giant upright amphibian. "You could've picked a closer planet."

Olena grinned.

"So you ready to go?" Hedge, a prickle-headed being, asked. "We've got a transport waiting."

Olena's smile drifted. She had missed them so much.

"What happened here?" MoPa glanced down to her stomach where he'd felt a slight bulge.

"The nightmares are gone, MoPa. I'm not going with you," she whispered. The men's faces fell and they protested--all but MoPa who nodded, a gleam of happiness in his eyes for her.

"Quiet, now!" MoPa ordered darkly. "You don't dare question the Captain's orders."

"You all can stay with me, MoPa," she offered. "You will be protected here."

"There now, Captain," Hedge said. "You know we can't be doing that. The high skies call us. It's in our blood."

"I'm not your Captain anymore." Olena reached behind her back and pulled out her gun. Handing it over to MoPa, she said. "But I am your friend. MoPa, the crew is yours. Do your worst."

MoPa smiled, he solemnly nodded his head at her. She saw his look and knew he would be sorry to see her stay behind.

"Give this planet hell," he stated quietly. Olena nodded. With a flick of MoPa's hand, the crew disappeared into the trees as if they were never there.

She stood silent, watching where they had disappeared. There was no long last look, no goodbyes. It was the pirate way and she understood it all too well.

Startling slightly, Olena felt Yusef's strong hand on her shoulder. She smiled, turning around into his awaiting arms. Her cheek pressed into his chest to feel his heartbeat, before she pulled back to look at him.

"What was that?" Yusef asked, basking in her loving expression.

"Ah, just the demons coming to visit," she said. She felt a hard press against her back. Frowning, she reached behind her to pull a carving out from her husband's fingers. It was a figurine of her, her stomach slightly rounded. Chuckling, she said, "You really need to get a new model for these things."

"Why, firebird?" he asked, lifting her up into his arms. "When I have no desire to look at anything else?"

Olena laughed softly. And, as she kissed him, she murmured, "You could at least put clothes on me. Our son will think I walked naked the whole time I was pregnant."

"Ah," he murmured against her. Yusef swept his wife away with him to their home and into their bed. "I think such a thing can be arranged."

## THE END

Printed in the United States
53228LVS00001B/268-330